Spectral Lives

Dea anseo isteach agus bog libh a mhallachtaí

Mick O'Shaunghnessy

MindMyBunionPress

ISBN: 978-1739327347

CONTENTS

D.H.T

One

The alarm clock spoke,

'Seven o'clock, Matt.'

He woke with a start and sprang out of bed.

There was no time for a proper breakfast – a bite of toast and a gulp of instant coffee had to do. Then he was heading for the front door, where two letters protruding from the aluminium letter flap brought his breathless departure to a juddering halt.

Valentine's Day!

Yesterday, you idiot, said a voice in Matt's head. *Valentine's Day was yesterday.*

True, very true, but his letters often arrived a day or two late, so he could still hope, couldn't he? Especially as neither of these Valentine's cards could have possibly come from his girlfriend.

He had got hers already.

Oh God, could it really be?

Perhaps, just perhaps, a certain young lady cherished secret feelings for him, in the way he did for her…

Two letters. Two punts on the lottery of love!

The first was a gas bill. A red one too – even though he'd paid it off last week. He tossed this onto the small, self-assembly table that stood beside the front door. The second letter – well, the envelope itself was enough to flash-freeze his ardour, for a government-department insignia was embossed in one corner, with the motto— *The D H T (Serving You Right)*—underneath.

'Love from the D H T? Sweet.'

He had never heard of them, but he reckoned he knew what they were after – demanding money was all the Government did these days.

He tore the envelope open and scanned the contents for the amount being invoiced, but he couldn't seem to find any figures.

Frowning, he read this:

Dear Mr Gunovski

Your request for immortality has not been successful and I regret to inform you that your loan of hair and teeth is to be recovered over the next twenty-three years, beginning from the Seventeenth of February. If you wish to appeal against our decision, then please phone this office to make an appointment to see me as soon as possible.

Yours sincerely,

Philip Symmonds.
Secretary to the Minister.

Matt squinted, as if that would help.
Immortality?

He read the whole thing again. No, there was nothing about how he could pay by *Direct Debit*, by phone, over the internet, or at the bank.

But if they weren't after money, then what on earth did they want?

Immortality? I don't think I've heard of... But maybe I should phone...

Lost in thought, he absently hooked a forefinger under one of his frayed shirt sleeves and drew it back to reveal his wristwatch.

Fifteen – no, *sixteen* minutes past seven!

It can wait.

Matt dropped the letter beside the gas bill and resumed his precipitous journey to work.

Two

The traffic went all his way for once, from the curb outside his inner-city apartment all the way to the silvery complex of *Acerlo Synthetics Ltd*, which stood alone amongst the bare fields of the wintry countryside.

And because the traffic had gone all his way, he had arrived thirty-two minutes early.

But that didn't mean he had arrived in good time.

Oh no, indeed not, for his favourite parking place was already occupied by a ruby-red *Mercedes* sports car. And so, for the third time this month, he had to park his dented *Ford* next to the waste bins.

He happened to meet Melissa at the front-desk. She was collecting a package.

'You're early too.' He smiled.

She smiled back. 'Morning, Matt. I'm really glad I caught you.' As she spoke, he revelled in the alluring gaze of her chocolate-brown eyes. Even though she hadn't sent him a Valentine's Day card after all. 'Allen wants us to work on the *Upcycled-Nitrates-Production Presentation*.'

'A little light relief, then?'

She flicked back her long, luscious, chestnut hair – something she did when a trifle ruffled.

'Yeah. So, it's you, me and *PowerPoint*. Yeuch!'

'Yes, yeuch. When do you want to do it? Now?'

'I thought lunchtime. We could take a laptop to the *Cheshire Cat* and have a drink. I'll need one.' She exchanged a collaborative smile with the receptionist. 'I've been whisked off my feet this morning.'

'Oh yes? Well, lunchtime's fine for me. Great, rather. Shall I tell Allen?'

Allen was their line manager.

'Already have. He said, *Bugger off then, no one's going to miss you.*' She smiled affectionately at the recollection. 'Typical, eh?'

'Yeah, typical.'

'Twelve o'clock then. Here?'

'It's a date.'

Matt continued to his laboratory, where he brooded.

He really wished that Melissa, the person he most liked at *Acerlo*, wasn't so sweet about Allen, the person he most disliked at *Acerlo*.

However, he had to forgive her, didn't he? She was only giving as good as she got. You see, Allen nurtured an old guy's paternal soft spot for his gorgeous colleague. A great big soft spot actually. In fact, he'd probably have a heart attack if Melissa ever left *Acerlo*. And Matt wouldn't blame him. At the same time, however, Matt was conscious that Allen *wouldn't* have a heart attack if he (Matt) left. He might even say, *Bugger off then, no one's going to miss you.*

Only this time, he'd mean it.

Ironic, really, when you remembered that Matt had single-handedly developed, *CSt44* – *Acerlo*'s very latest fertilizer compound. This *CSt44* stuff was the sort of product that actually kept *Acerlo* in business, and Allen in paid employment. Without Matt, Allen wouldn't have a job. In fact, one might venture to say that, compared to Matt, Allen was an entirely superfluous human being. The sort to whom one should be able to say, *Bugger off then, no one's going to miss you.*

But that wasn't going to happen, was it?

You see, these superfluous human beings had a trick up their sleeves. They could get everyone to take them far more seriously than the non superfluous human beings.

It was only a trick, but it still meant Allen was Matt's line manager and not the other way round.

It's just not fair, is it?

At twelve sharp, he was back in the reception concourse.

Melissa was a trifle late, but her warm smile was worth waiting for.

They left the building together.

As he would be driving, Matt said, 'My car's around the back. Good old Gideon has parked himself in my space.'

'Is it your space, Matt?'

Her lack of sympathy took him by surprise.

'I've only used it for the past seven years. But that doesn't make it official, I suppose.' He gave her a quick glance and added, 'You know, Allen seems very taken by Gideon.'

'Jealous?'

'No, I'm not jealous. How could I be?' But Melissa's remark still stung. 'I have to say, though, Allen did annoy me a little at last week's meeting.'

'How's that?'

'When he asked for Gideon's view of the degradation issue in *F332.*'

'Did he?'

'He did, yes. What does he think he's up to asking Gideon? *I* developed *F332*. Not him.'

'That's right.'

'And he didn't seem to notice when Gideon couldn't give him a fully informed answer. He just waffled. But then, Allen wouldn't know that, would he? He's a manager, not a scientist. Truth be known, that's all Gideon is too. A manager.'

'He has a Ph D.'

'Oh, it's a very mediocre piece of work. Regurgitation rather than synthesis.'

'Weren't you on his interview panel when he was up for the job? Didn't you give Allen your opinion of Gideon then?'

They had reached his car and he stared at her over its unwaxed bonnet. 'Sure, I gave him my opinion. I told him Gideon wasn't up to the job. As a matter of fact, the rest of the panel were with me, but Allen overruled us.'

Melissa did not answer. Her eyes drifted away. Matt gazed at her heart-stopping profile for a moment before he realised she was waiting for him to unlock the car.

Okay then, I'll unlock the car. And while I'm at it, I'll drop the subject of Gideon.

The *Cheshire Cat* was a large restaurant/pub/hotel that stood on the edge of the nearest village. Its convivial atmosphere emphasised rather than alleviated the dreariness of working on the *Upcycled-Nitrates-Production Presentation*. Matt noted how the other guests glowed and bubbled.

Melissa did not glow. Nor did she bubble. She seemed bored and restless and this dispirited him. He felt shipwrecked on a little disenchanted island.

And yet, meeting her for the first time had been the most wonderful moment of his life. The attraction was instant – on his side. Still, Melissa had been far from unfriendly. She had shown much interest when he demonstrated the titration apparatus in the labs – just two short years ago.

Ah, but how discouraging it had been to learn, five minutes later, that she was in a relationship!

Ah, but how uplifting to learn, six months ago, that she and her partner had split!

And now, how very painful his indecision was!

For a time, he sensed they had grown closer. Well, the signs were subtle. A smiling glance. A question about what he would be doing over the weekend. Once even, she favoured him with something like a lingering touch, when that storage box nearly fell on his head and she reached out and held his arm and asked if he was all right.

'I'd like to get this over with as soon as possible,' she said now, without tenderness, 'but we have to be careful not to let it look like a rush job. Gideon might raise a fuss.'

'Gideon again. What does he have to do with it?'

'I didn't like to mention it, but Allen has put Gid in charge of the presentation review.'

'Oh? Fair enough. That's all he's good for. Presentation.'

Melissa sighed, not unkindly.

'But don't you see, Matt? That puts him on the management fast track.'

'Why? It's presentation – not real work. We don't sell flim-flam, we sell actual products.'

'Flim-flam?' Her smile was hard. 'I haven't heard that expression in years. Old fashioned, isn't it?'

'I mean it's all spin. Allen takes spin more seriously than technology.'

'Yes. Which is probably why Gideon shows an interest in the presentation side.'

'He's crawling to Allen then?'

She flushed.

'No. He's feeding the birds.'

'He's what?'

'Business is a game, Matt.' She spoke as if he were being obtuse, thus hurling yet another shaft into his sensitive heart. 'And it's no use complaining when other people play it.'

He looked at the laptop screen, which displayed a pastel-coloured flowchart. *It looks like something from a child's colouring book*, he thought. 'But then, I wonder, doesn't it have any meaning when I develop a new product, rather than just *talk* about it?'

Her expression softened. 'Of course it does.'

'And the world can't just run on bullshit, can it?'

To his perplexity, she bridled at this perfectly reasonable observation.

'But we can't *all* develop new things. Someone's got to *talk* about it. Sell it. You see…bullshit,' she couldn't help grinning, 'has its place too. Oh, you're right, I suppose. Gideon and Allen are kindred spirits. They chime, don't they?' She gave him a rueful smile. 'I know, I know. It just isn't fair, is it? *Sorry, Matt.*'

Three

Having updated the presentation, they returned to *Acerlo Synthetics*.

Matt went straight to his laboratory, found the technician and detailed the series of tests that he wished her to conduct that afternoon.

After that, he had nothing to keep him at work for the rest of the day. Dejected, he went home early.

The cramped streets looked more tired the closer he got to his apartment. He didn't live in a good part of the city. Those living around were mainly third-world immigrants and the poor and embittered. The neighbourhood was not friendly.

As he mounted the wooden steps to his flat, which stood above a betting shop, he noted an overweight young man, wearing nylon tracksuit bottoms and a sleeveless shirt, smoking a cigarette as he loafed on the balcony of a squalid block of flats across the way.

He told himself, *At least I actually own the crummy flat I live in*.

Once upon a time, this reflection might have brought him some comfort.

Not today.

Melissa had defended Allen, damn it.

But what had Allen ever done to deserve her favour? Wear an expensive suit? Sound plausible? Trick everyone into taking him at his own estimation? What was *so great* about that?

Except, of course, Allen's reward for not being *so great* was a five-bedroom country house.

And as for Gideon… Matt dreaded to think how much better his apartment was than this dump.

It just isn't fair, is it? Sorry Matt.

Whatever else she'd done, Melissa had certainly hit the nail on the head.

He took a shower.

Shaving in the mirror, he was disconcerted to see how weary and faded he looked. His face was entirely ordinary. Not good, not bad. The solid, dependable sort of face that required minimal maintenance. His appearance, including his haircut, hadn't changed significantly since he had left college.

Hence the dismal surprise he got today. The more he stared himself, the more appalled he became. All at once, it seemed, he had begun to look his age.

Thirty-six.

Thirty-six wasn't old.

Then how come he felt life was passing him by?

His reflection in the mirror answered without moving its lips, *Want to know what I think? Life wouldn't pass you by if you had Melissa.*

But he didn't have Melissa. What he had was Abigail, his girlfriend of ten years and a librarian who was simply itching for…retirement.

He was itching too. Itching to swap her for Melissa.

However, Melissa gave no sign that she would agree to swap places with Abigail. Indeed, she had been cooling towards him of late. He hadn't wanted to believe it, but after this morning, there was no longer room for doubt. She had actively sided with Allen.

Thwack!

And even with Gideon.

Thwack! Thwack! Thwack!

He only had himself to blame, didn't he? Melissa knew that he had been with Abigail for ten years. Married in everything but name and address. And Melissa wasn't the kind of woman to steal another woman's man, or so Matt pessimistically presumed.

So, as matters stood, he would be with Abigail for the rest of his life. And it would be for the rest of *his* life too – not hers. For although she had apparently aged more than him over the past ten years, Matt sensed Abigail would outlast him. The library where she worked was nice and warm, the job wasn't stressful and she was drying out nicely. Getting tougher and more fibrous by the day.

It just isn't fair is it, Matt? Sorry.

Sorry? That was no good. Didn't Melissa understand? With her at his side, he could see off Allen and Gideon and rise to the top of *Acerlo Synthetics Ltd.*

What was he saying? If Melissa belonged to him, he could start his own company. A company to rival *Acerlo.*

He would be unbeatable. Absolutely unstoppable.

If only…

Four

Matt woke up on the sofa, where he had stretched out to take a quick nap. Instead, he had fallen into a profound sleep.

The last flickering images of a long, troubling dream dissolved before his mind's eye. Something about an endless, desperate journey to keep an indefinite appointment – catching trains, hurrying through strange city streets to the next station (the name of which was always obscured by passing clouds) and pouring over inscrutable maps and timetables.

It was dark. The luminous panel on the HD recorder displayed the time as twelve.

He started upright. Never in his life had he put his head down during the day and woken in the middle of the night.

Perhaps he ought to make a habit of it though. He felt tiptop.

Soon he was bustling about, putting a meal together and tidying up to the sounds of light jazz. Despite his strange, anxious dream, his deep slumber had revived his confidence in full. He felt more self-possessed than he had in years. The day before, he'd been weighed down by problems and depression.

Why had he been so weak?

Why hadn't he seen the obvious answer?

If he didn't have prospects at *Acerlo Synthetics Ltd,* all he had to do is get a job someplace where he would be appreciated. He knew there were lots of openings in Germany. Wasn't it a *wunderbar* country? Sure it was! And where better to make a new start than in a *wunderbar* country? After all, what, or who was holding him back?

Abigail?

Melissa?

...Sorry, Matt.

'Yeah, yeah. So am I.'

He ate in a hurry, anxious to get surfing for a new position.

On the way to the spare bedroom, where he kept his computer, he spotted the letters he had received that morning still lying on the table by the front door.

Ha! Happy Valentine from the Gas Board!

But what about the other letter? Why hadn't that been quite so funny?

Matt picked it up.

'Hm,' he mused aloud, 'The Department of Hair and Teeth.'

This was harder to dismiss than it had been in the morning. Since then he had become less secure about his hair and teeth.

God, my face in the bathroom mirror!

He examined the letter and noticed it seemed different in some way.

There were more words than before.

He read it again.

Sure enough, after the last sentence—

If you wish to appeal against our decision, then please phone this office to make an appointment with me as soon as possible.

—he saw a postscript that, somehow or other, he had missed that morning—

Please note, our phone line is open twenty-four hours.

He mused for a some time before he went to the living room and called the number.

The other end rang.

A brisk voice answered, 'Symmonds's office. Who's calling please?'

'Hello. I'm in receipt of a letter from your department.'

'You received a letter from us?'

'Yes, I got it this morning.'

'And who are you?'

'Sorry. Matthew Gunovski.'

'Gunovski? Oh… So what is it you want?'

'I—' Matt was momentarily confounded. He had wanted to query the meaning of the letter, but the owner of the curt voice obviously believed there was nothing to discuss.

'Yes?'

'I… Er… I wish to appeal, I suppose.'

'Do you? Then why have you left it so late?'

'Your letter only arrived today.'

'You said you received it this morning.'

'Yes, but I had to leave for work. Really, unless I go to work, how shall I pay your taxes?'

'Mr Gunovski, I have to pay tax too.'

'Of course, of course.'

'This isn't the number to call about your taxes.'

'No?'

'However, if you wish to lodge an appeal, I can help you, if you really want to be helped.'

'Yes, I want to be helped. That's why I'm phoning.'

'Then may I suggest you come in person – right now?'

'Right now?'

'Yes, now, Mr Gunovski. This instant. The office is open.'

'Don't I have until tomorrow?'

'*Tomorrow?* May I be so bold as to impress upon you the gravity of your situation, Mr Gunovski? Yes, you have till tomorrow to appeal – in theory. But other appeals are lodged all the time. Limited resources constrain us to handle clients on a first-come first-served basis.'

'How about an email?'

'You could, but I don't know anyone here who ever reads them.'

'Oh, for heaven's sake.'

'And for that reason, I urge you most strongly to come immediately and present your appeal in person to the Secretary.'

'That will be Mr Symmonds?'

'Philip Symmonds, yes. He's available tonight. But I cannot say with any confidence that he'll be available tomorrow. Which in any case is too late.'

'But, *this* minute? Straight away? Is it really so… It all seems a bit desperate.'

'Come now, Mr Gunovski, there is still hope, I assure you. My name is Paul Williams, Mr Symmonds's secretary. Secretary to the secretary – that's me. Come right away. We'll talk. It's for the best. I'll do everything I can. Be brave. Don't' lose heart. Trust me, you will never forgive yourself otherwise.'

Five

Matt's satnav directed him out of the cramped, orange-lit streets of the suburbs and away into the darkness of the countryside.

He drove fast, eager to launch his appeal as soon as

possible. He passed through several villages, slowing down for the sake of speed cameras and then accelerating away from the little islands of illuminated silence. About an hour later, he was passing down an unlit road. On the right ran a sandstone-block wall, eight or nine feet high. The satnav indicated a right turn and, at last, an entrance appeared.

Tall ironwork gates stood wide open.

From there he followed a long and winding gravel drive. The loose pebbles pinked against the side of the car. Giant trees, Yews and Cypresses, brooded on undulating moon-silvered lawns. The estate must have been ancient. Matt expected to arrive at a sprawling country house, instead, the drive terminated in a miserable patch of gravel over which a lamp flickered on top of a slanted metal pole. No building of any sort was in view, just a row of tall black conifers guarding the edge of a wood.

He parked and climbed out. The air was piercingly cold and the silence was complete, without even the ubiquitous sough of distant traffic. His mobile (on which he'd put *The Department*'s number) could not pick up a signal and he looked around, baffled as to how to proceed.

Then he caught sight of small sign, which was mounted on a stump at the very edge of the lamplight.

He took a closer look and found nothing more than a crudely painted arrow that pointed at steps made from wood and packed earth. These rose between two tree trunks and disappeared into utter darkness. After a moment's hesitation, and as he saw no other way to go, he began to climb.

The steps soon gave way to a rough, stony path, which rose as it ran to the right. Matt realised he was climbing a wooded hill. The trees began to thin out a little as he progressed. Going by the general slope, he estimated the hill to be of considerable size. Some fifteen minutes later he had to pause, labouring to regain his breath. Through a tangle of moon-frosted branches, he could just make out a section of the grounds he had driven through, already far below him.

The cold made standing still uncomfortable and although he hadn't quite recovered his breath, he set off again.

Moments later—

Boosh, Boosh, Boosh

—the night air boomed. The tops of the trees thrashed about. He raised his arms and cowered. Outlined against the dusting of stars a gigantic bird passed overhead. An instant later—

Boosh, Boosh, Boosh…

—the thunderclap beat of its wings reverberated into the distance.

In the silence that followed, the dark wood all around became sinister and threatening. And yet, to his surprise, Matt was not daunted. He realised that a still more elemental fear had been stirred within him by the letter from the *Department of Hair and Teeth*.

Twenty minutes later, he arrived at the crown of the hill.

The trees had gradually given way to a large desolate area in which a collection of unimpressive buildings stood apart from each other. Even by the thin moonlight they looked dilapidated. Still, they were not abandoned. Faint lights could be detected here and there, and the network of paths between them had been kept clear of weeds. The largest building lay to his left and had the shape of an old aircraft hanger. A haphazard stack of metal containers were heaped in front of it. Curiously, along the eaves were a row of ached openings, about six feet wide and three feet deep, which were too oddly positioned to be normal windows and which, in any case, had no glass in them. They emanated a dim, yellow electric glow. But such a place could scarcely be an administrative block and so Matt followed the asphalt path to the next building. He came upon a door beside an illuminated window, on which a white plastic sign had been screwed at an annoying angle. He could just make out what it said—

The Dept. of Hair and Teeth

He turned the handle.

Locked.

The window was glazed with frosted glass. Nothing could be clearly discerned through it.

He saw a doorbell button half hanging off the wall and he pressed it. An electric buzz reached him from a far-off empty room. Thirty seconds passed. He pushed the button again. And again.

He could not stand there any longer – the cold would not leave him in peace. He set off to find another entrance.

Circumnavigating the building, he came to other doors, all locked and unmarked. Any windows were secured behind rusted metal shutters. An oppressive silence constrained him to walk softly, like an intruder.

Having circled the complex, he arrived at the aircraft hanger again. In coming at it from another angle, he spotted a door and this was open and lit by the dim yellow light he had seen earlier. Matt knocked once and entered a room that was the colour of old dust. Everything – a wooden table, an antiquated phone, scratched filing cabinets and rickety chairs – were the same dull grey.

There was a communicating door, on which was pinned the notice—

Recollections of old black-and-white films suggested to him that this room had once been in use during the Second World War. It looked like it had been left untouched ever since.

He tapped on the door and, getting no reply, opened it.

Beyond lay the hanger proper.

He took a few tentative steps inside sniffed at a foul animal odour.

The cavernous space was unadorned and empty apart from two rows of crude stalls. These were nothing more than horizontal staves of wood, about six-feet long, supported by four-foot high posts. A scattering of filthy straw covered the floor. Bare light bulbs cast a weak yellow glow over the scene.

No sooner as he had taken these few details in than a shadow shifted to his left and a large form appeared from the dark corner of the hanger.

The thing hopped with great agility along one of the staves, positioning itself so as to get a better look at him.

It was a giant bird. Five feet high. And because it was perched on a stave, gripping it with reddish talons that were like crooked hands, it loomed eight or nine feet into the air.

Transfixed, Matt stared. The creature's mottled feathers were so fine they were almost fur. Its underlying shape gave the powerful impression of deformity and where its beak should have been, there was nothing but a gaping black hole, lined by wicked little hooks. Worst of all were its eyes. They glared at him. But they were not the eyes of an animal. They were lit by consciousness and a furious malice.

They were the eyes of a man.

Matt could not move.

As he watched, the creature's chest began to inflate,

growing and growing till its rotten feathers parted to reveal blue, leprous flesh.

He gasped, 'Oh God.'

The thing answered with a shuddering groan—

Hurrrruhuhuhuhuhuaaaaahhhh

— of loathing and fear. No sort of bird sound. It came from a human windpipe, grafted deep into cold-blooded flesh.

Matt felt his insides dissolve.

Then he was running. He was out of the building within seconds. His legs did all the thinking for him and he hurtled into the darkness like he knew where he was going.

Seconds later, a great weight smashed into him and two incredibly powerful arms clamped themselves around waist. He screamed as he was brought down with a bone-juddering crash.

Six

Two military-style men took him into the administrative building. They led him down an anonymous corridor to a door marked *Visitors* and allowed him to enter by himself.

The room was featureless, windowless. Just a couple of dingy easy chairs and a low table on which a coffee percolator chuckled to itself.

Matt glanced back. His captors stared at him impassively from the corridor. They had ordinary faces that showed no sign of aggression and he wanted to say something to them – just to hear them talk. He opened his mouth to speak.

One of them leaned forward and closed the door.

The heat! Suddenly he was so exhausted that he

dropped into one of the chairs and his vision glazed over.

'Are you all right?'

A man was standing over him. Handsome and aged about thirty. He wore an immaculate pinstripe suit.

'Oh, excuse me.' Matt sat up in confusion. 'I don't know what happened.'

The man leaned forward and offered him his hand.

'Paul Williams. Secretary to the secretary. We spoke over the phone.'

'Of course! Hello! Matthew Gunovski.'

'I guessed as much,' Paul smiled and took the seat opposite. 'What happened?'

'Actually, I'm rather cross, you know.' Matt noticed his voice was reedy.

'Oh?'

'I had no idea where I was going. And when I got here, no one answered the door. And then, when I had a look around... Well, it's a bit unnerving in the dark, isn't it? And I got... I got manhandled. My side aches. It's not on, is it?'

Paul was alarmed. 'You're not hurt?'

'No, not as such.'

'I really am very sorry.'

'But that's the thing. There's always someone apologising who can't do anything about it.'

Paul gestured helplessly. 'But as you can see, we're dreadfully underfunded. With the recession and the cuts and all that, we're reduced to a skeleton crew. Blame the Government, that's what I say. But don't say that I said so.'

'This is really a Government department'

'It wouldn't be this shabby otherwise.'

'Do they... Do they experiment with animals here?'

'Christ, no. Why do you say that?'

'I thought I saw something.'

'You said you got unnerved in the dark.'

'That's right. I got spooked. And the cold. It's very cold out there.'

'Would you like coffee?'

'Yes, please.'

Paul stood up and busied himself at the percolator.

Matt said, 'So anyway, about my appeal.'

Paul turned and flashed him a grin. 'You're lucky. Not everyone gets the opportunity to appeal. Honestly, it's better than winning the lottery.'

'In what respect?'

Paul handed him a tin mug full of brown liquid and sat down again.

'Well, I admit you'll get no money out of it. Still, money isn't everything.'

'And yet we spend all day getting it, whether we want to or not.'

'True, but money isn't the *real* problem you're having at work, now is it?'

Matt swallowed. 'What do you mean?'

'We're in a similar position, you and I.'

'Which is?'

'This is between us, you understand?'

'Sure.'

'Progress in my career is also being blocked by an old boy in charge. You've got Allen, I've got Philip. Philip Symmonds.'

'But he's the man I need to see. The Secretary to the Minister.'

'Yes, but he's so *old*, Matthew. He belongs to another era. His whole mind-set is geared to slowing down the pace of change. But we need *change*. Change we need. Change is the challenge and we have to meet the challenge. We don't want people like him, outmoded and slow, sticking around for years and years. He should retire. The sooner the better.'

'But first he should look at my appeal, right?'

'He *should*, yes. But you're only here at all because I went out of my way to select you. And I've bent the rules to do it. Don't worry, I have the support of the Minister for Hair and Teeth in this matter. You see, if Symmonds were left to his own devices, he wouldn't select anyone, except once in a blue moon. And that's not good enough. By the way, I'm really glad I picked you, Matthew, because I think you deserve the opportunity.'

'Well… Thanks, Paul.'

'Sure. But, I do have to tell you, it's not going to be easy. Symmonds will find any excuse he can to squash your appeal. I guarantee it.'

'But that's not fair.'

'Of course it's not. It's way out of line. That's why I wanted to see you tonight. It's because the Minster himself is here. If you appeal directly to him, in person, then he has the right to overrule Symmonds. You see, we're going to have to circumvent Symmonds for you to have any chance whatsoever.'

Matt looked down at his mug of weak coffee.

'But if Symmonds is supposed to follow procedure, like you say, then maybe I should see him anyway.'

He glanced up and caught something hard and watchful in Paul's soft, brown eyes.

Clearly discomforted, Paul's gaze roamed the room.

'As I told you, Matthew, he will reject your appeal.'

'And yet, if I'm caught not following procedure, that's a reason to reject my appeal, isn't it? I think I need to see Symmonds, just to be safe.'

Paul stared at him helplessly and silently mouthed, *Okay*.

Seven

He led Matt from the waiting room to the end of the corridor and around a corner, where instead of the stark, bone-coloured walls and scuffed linoleum-covered floor of everywhere else, they stepped into a world of lush, deep-pile carpet, tasteful wallpaper, old oil portraits mounted in gilded frames and glittering glass chandeliers.

'Wow.'

'Wow indeed. This is the management section.'

Paul stopped at a finely polished oak door, on which gleamed a large brass plate engraved with—

P. Symmonds, FsRd BSc Udh

Leaning forward deferentially, Paul tapped at the door, opened it and ushered Matt inside.

He entered what looked like a private ward of a hospital.

Beside the bed, an old man in pyjamas, bald and shrunken, sagged in a wheelchair, with his head lolling on quaking shoulders. He seemed to grin up at Matt who, in confusion, muttered, 'Sorry, someone's made a mistake.'

He heard the door close behind him.

The old man giggled, and spoke in a piping, tremulous voice. 'That's the biggest understatement I've heard in my life.' His withered chest shook with mirth. 'And maybe it is also the very last ludicrous remark I shall ever hear.'

'Oh, I'm sure it won't be,' Matt said gamely. 'You'll last a good few years yet.'

'Will I?'

The old man fixed him with watery glare. The rims of his eyelids were falling away, revealing pink flesh.

'Sure you will. You'll bury us all.'

'And why would I care about any of you? I'm the one who faces imminent annihilation. Your joke is inane.' As the old man spoke, Matt realised that he was not laughing, but rather shaking with sobs. 'You ignorant jackass! Why did you come here to talk your rubbish? You don't know anything! Everything you say, or do, or think, will be rubbed out and replaced by the idiocies of the next jackass. That's okay. But why *me*? Why should *I* be ruined and replaced like this? Oh, Christ. I can't get it out of my head – I'm going to die. Die! They'll throw me into a hole and I'll rot to nothingness. It's the worst, the most horrible nightmare. Horrible, horrible! And it's happening to *me!*' His quivering voice cracked in a wail of despair. 'Meeeeeaaaaanoooo, no, no, no… Aaaaarrrgodgodgod…'

Matt stretched out a hand.

The old man stared back in terror, threw back his head and shrieked.

Matt broke for the door and ran down the corridor.

'Hold up,' Paul was calling after him. 'What's the matter?'

Matt stopped and turned. 'You damn well know what! He's insane!'

Paul hurried over and gripped his arm. 'But I told you, he's not able to do the job anymore. I—'

'For God's sake!' Matt pulled away. 'It's outrageous. He should have been retired years ago.'

Paul waved at him like a hypnotist.

'Matthew! Listen to me! Listen! I told you there was no point talking to Symmonds. I told you. Remember?'

Matt responded with a brief nod.

'There. That's better. Let's calm down now. We will sort it out, I promise. Only, we have *got* to go see the Minister. Yeah?'

'The Minster?'

'Yes, the Minister. Come on, old son, be brave. It's the only way you'll get your appeal through the works.'

Matt still had that hideous scream ringing in his ears.

'Can he really help? The Minister I mean? Symmonds made it sound…hopeless.'

'Trust me, Matthew, the Minister can help. He really can.' Paul glanced at his watch. 'But we're losing vital time. We need to hurry. I'm sure I heard his pilot warming up the helicopter.'

'*Helicopter*?'

'The Minister's a busy man, Matthew.'

'But I need the loo! It's the coffee. I can't wait!'

Paul scowled. 'For heaven's sake… Look, all right, down there.' He pointed to the other end of the corridor. 'Then come back and stay here! I'll go nab the Minister and then we'll come fetch you.'

Paul set off at a jog.

Eight

Matt pushed open the oak door marked *Executive Washroom* and hesitated. He found himself confronted by the hunched back and shoulders of a man in a pinstripe suit who was bent over a gilt-framed mirror. The mirror reflected fat fingers tenderly prodding a receding hairline. A single jet-black eye stared straight back at him.

Matt averted his gaze and hastened into a cubical to relieve himself. His mind was in such turmoil that during the interval he managed to forget the man outside and was surprised when he stepped out to see him still at the mirror. He could not avoid acknowledging him as swilled his hands at the next wash basin.

'Evening.'

The man looked down at him. He was at least a foot taller than Matt, and Matt was six foot.

'How do you do, young man. Are you my new pilot?'

The man's voice had a rich, mellow timbre. His face, which Matt couldn't help studying, was a leprous white and far too mobile.

'No. I can't fly a helicopter.'

'Ah. So what's your role here?'

'I'm actually trying to lodge an appeal.'

'Then you must be Mr Gunovski.'

'Yes.'

The man thrust out a huge hand for Matt to shake. 'Delighted to meet you. Charles Coulomb. The Minister.'

'Ah, the Minister! Paul said—'

'You've seen Paul?'

'He's gone to find you.'

'But you've very cleverly found me first. What has he told you about the job?'

'Nothing about a job. I'm here to—'

'You see, Matthew, the Department only grants remission to people who take up a position with us.'

'I've got a job… *Remission*?'

'This is more than a job, Matthew. I am asking that you serve your country. The Department has been in severe decline ever since the War. The Second World War, that is. There's a deal of catching up to do. Join us and you will play a vital role.'

'I'm not attracted by Government work. I'm a scientist not an administrator.'

'It's not admin work. It's so much more interesting than that.

'But still—'

'It's like no other job you could conceive of. At least learn about it before you dismiss it. Anyway, aren't you looking out for a new role?'

'Well…'

'Come, let me show you. But first – cheer up! We're not dead yet.'

They left the washroom and down the corridor they reached a utility door that opened into a kitchen. Matt noted the swatted flies on the white gas cooker. A Vim-smeared oblong steel sink sat below a wire-glass window and next to that stood a peeling, discoloured door.

The Minister unlatched this and pushed it open onto freezing blackness.

'Into that good night we go,' he said, allowing Matt out first.

Matt found this was the very door at which he had tried to gain entry on first arriving at the Department. The sound of the tinny, electric bell came back to him and the vision of himself shivering there as a humble, cowed supplicant outside a sordid, deserted kitchen roused his indignation.

'I've noticed something about the present Government, Mr Coulomb.'

'Oh yes?'

'They're very good making me feel second class. It's almost like they assume I'm a complete sap.'

'You're annoyed,' Coulomb looked down at him. In the weak glow from the kitchen window, his half-lit face had the dull sheen of old aluminium. 'Everyone's annoyed by the Government. I suppose you feel that we take too much tax in return for very little. Well, I for one am not about to treat you like a complete sap. I'm going to be completely honest. The fact is we're struggling with a dire legacy. We are paying dearly for our victory. But come with me now, it'll be easier to explain if I show you.' He put a heavy arm around Matt's shoulders and began to walk. Matt was obliged to accompany him.

They went directly to the hanger, the door of which was still ajar. Coulomb lifted his arm from Matt's shoulder to let him to go first. But Matt hesitated.

'Why do we have to go in here?'

'So that I might explain everything. What's the matter? It's just the changing room. You won't have to use it more than once.'

Matt steeled himself, went in and once again surveyed the dusty office.

Coulomb went to a metal cabinet, out of which he drew a foul-looking feathered costume. Matt recoiled.

The Minister smiled ruefully.

'Well, yes, the uniform is rather poor.'

He draped the costume over the desk and took two objects from the cabinet. They were each a foot long, slender, slightly curved and apparently carved form ancient bone. They were both fluted into an open triangle at one end with a row of tiny holes around the rims. At the other end they were smoothed to points that terminated in miniature tools. One was a hammerhead and the other a forked hook.

They had a repulsive quality, like dirty old prosthetics.

Coulomb casually handed them to Matt.

Matt put his hands behind his back.

'They look antique,' he said, pulling a face. He couldn't find anything better to say about them.

'They are. But you won't break them, you know.' Coulomb smiled grimly. 'They can't be broken. Go on, hold them.'

Matt reluctantly reached out. At the merest touch he snatched his hand back.

'Ugh. *Vile.*'

Coulomb arched his eyebrows and laid the carved bones on the table, beside the costume. 'I suppose they take some getting used to.'

Matt scowled at him. 'This place stinks. You can smell the dust.'

'But it has an interesting history. Did you know that General Nolcraft de Breed ran *Operation Hip Crumbler* from this very room?'

'I'm not a student of the Second World War. Anyway, if it's of such historical interest, why isn't it better preserved?'

As Matt spoke, he noticed how the fleshy face of the Minister looked appallingly coarse in the light from the bare light bulb.

'I'm sorry to say we can't afford to throw money at every deserving cause, Matthew. Anyway, there are already lots of museums around.'

'But then, this place isn't a museum. It's still in use, isn't it?' Matt pointed at the door that communicated with the rest of the hanger. 'I was here earlier.'

'Were you?'

'I wasn't trespassing. I was just trying to find the reception desk.'

'But I don't disapprove. It shows initiative.'

'I went through and I saw…a man, I think. He was wearing one of these things. But…'

'Yes?'

'Well…who was he?'

'I don't know. Whoever he is, he's better than whatever he was.'

'He must have been a pretty bad way before.'

'Like us all! All of us are in a bad way. Sad and rotten. Don't you think about it too? You're a nice enough looking chap, but you are going to die. And, before you die, you must decay.'

They're all obsessed in this place, Matt thought. 'Everyone does.'

'No! Those who take this job don't die. They live for as long as they wish to. They are immortal.'

'Oh, come off it!'

'Scoffing won't help you in thirty years time. Where will you be then? What will you look like? Life,

Matthew, for as long as you want it. That is the reward. No career on earth can give you that. And, in return, all that you have to do is agree to a few modifications. They're virtually not worth mentioning. Minor, but necessary physical adjustments.'

'*Physical* adjustments?' Matt took a step back. 'I think not.'

'You'll have nothing painful to go through. Nothing in any way detrimental to your health. Listen, your good looks seem like an awful lot to lose now, but just think long term. At least you'll still be around. Alive, Matthew. Just imagine cheating death! The thing I've always noticed about death, especially while attending funerals – and as you get older, Matthew, you will be attending many funerals – the thing I've noticed is that there is simply nothing left to say. They are gone and that is that. I loathe funerals. Burying the smelly thing is nothing but an unpleasant and unedifying chore. Sounds heartless, I know—'

'Yes.'

'—until you really think about it. Because, given half the chance, any of the dead, no matter how they once cared for you, would rise up and rip your life away. They greedy swine. But then, can we blame them. Death is dreary.'

'Life too can be dreary.'

Coulomb grinned. His teeth seemed to join from top to bottom, like a grill.

'Paul thought you would be exceptionally well qualified for this job.'

'But I'm not.'

'Oh, but you *are*. You have an incentive. You desire one whom you will never possess. She eludes you, Matthew. She always will. But know this, there are other pleasures of the flesh to be had.'

Matt stared at those teeth. 'You what?'

'You'll derive a far greater satisfaction from of this job than she could ever give you.' Coulomb's black eyes shone. 'Imagine visiting them…in their graves. The triumph of it! Just think! You'll be alive. Alive! And no matter how handsome and strong they were, those that sneered at you, those who rejected you, they will be nothing but dirt below your claws.'

'Claws?' Matt turned away.

Coulomb gently touched him on the shoulder, and he span back round. 'Power is ugly, yes, but always preferable to weakness. I grant you they are favoured and fortunate. They will live and love. But that will not grieve you as it must now, for they will be weak compared to you. They will be your playthings. For even while they live and love, you will… Well, just look.' Coulomb indicated the bones on the table. 'Can you see what these actually are?'

'No.'

'No? Well, they are beaks.'

'Beaks?'

'Not real beaks, true. They're artificial – carved eons ago from the skeleton of a monstrous beast. The last of his kind.' Coulomb ignored Matt's incredulous laugh and pointed to the one fashioned into a miniature hammerhead. 'This little thing is for gradually loosening their teeth. The other – do you see the hook here? That's for hair. You choose one strand of hair, tug on it night after night till it comes free, then move on to the next and then the next and then the next and – as the years go by – the fellow becomes as bald as an egg.' He grinned and winked, 'Or *she* does. And toothless too. So, there you are, Matthew, that's us. *The Department of Hair and Teeth.*'

Matt looked at the bones and looked at Coulomb.

He burst out laughing.

'Sorry, but I think you're quite, quite mad.'

Coulomb wasn't the least disconcerted. 'It's late. You are tired and cold. As for me – well, leave my sanity out of it for the moment and consider the post itself. It's not mad at all. It happens to be crucial. True, the work can be a little slow. We generally go at a methodical pace, so that over the weeks and months and years the clients never notice that the grave is yawning beneath their feet. And yes, there's a degree of monotony too. Still, you can alternate between their teeth and their hair—'

'Stop, please.'

'Oh, I agree. What we do is a terrible, terrible thing. Please don't imagine that I enjoy the suffering. I didn't get into politics to hurt people. I wanted to do good. And still do. But in office one is stymied by budget cuts, confronted by the unpalatable realities. I realised all too soon that hard choices had to be made.'

Matt shook his head wearily. 'What you talking about now?'

'The hard choices.'

'Choices about what exactly?'

'Very well, I'm going to be forthright. Don't quote me though.'

'All right.'

'You see, because of the decline of the global economy, we simply don't have enough money to pay pensions indefinitely.'

'That old story! God, how often have I heard that being spun. You, the Government, never has enough money, apparently. Thing is, I'm working like a galley slave and what do I get for my taxes?'

'Healthcare, free at the point of delivery, a viable infrastructure, schools and sickness benefit, not to mention the active and professional defence of our great country by our dauntless soldiers. And so on and so forth. But you're right – public services are suffering. We are forced, year on year, into making ever deeper cuts. Even if the economy does revive, we shall be unable to return to our previous living standards. Let me ask you, Matthew, why is this?'

'Because you lot couldn't run a bath properly, let alone a country?'

Coulomb revealed his grill-like teeth in a smile. 'No, no, no. The problem is the unsustainable longevity of our population. Scientists have pushed back mortality rates to a point where the country is overburdened by old age pensioners. People who cannot actively contribute to the economy, but who nevertheless require the bulk of the resources that the economy generates. After the devastation of the Second World War, Western governments were naturally eager to promote ideals. They cherished a vision of a future where people lived long and productive lives. But that idealism has crashed into a new global reality. China, India, Brazil, they're all lining up to overtake us. Why? Because they age and die faster than we do.'

'Absurd.'

'But it is true! They're not sinking beneath a pension debt. We must bite the bullet, realise that life was never going to be a rose garden, and reverse the profligate advances in the average life span.'

'Amazing,' Matt exclaimed, 'so yet again, it's all the fault of the average working man or woman.'

Coulomb was finally rattled. 'That's right, everyone's an expert when it comes to politics. I shan't waste my breath labouring the point. We have too many old people in our country and we have to speed up the natural process of getting rid of them. If you have a better idea, then you're perfectly entitled to stand for Parliament.'

'But—'

'Look, I like you Matthew and I agree it's not your ideal job. But really, no job is perfect. And when you're here, you'll be making a real difference. And the personal benefits remember, are unmatched in any other sector. So, think about it, will you? Can I ask that much? Please?'

Matt stared intently into the ghoul's face and said, 'Can you answer just one question?'

'Ask as many as you please.'

'Do I owe any money to the Department? I'm happy to pay, if I do. I've always kept up with my taxes.'

'Money, Matthew? We won't take *that* from you.'

'I'm tired. And it's freezing here. I have to go to work tomorrow. So…'

'Of course, of course. I've detained you long enough.' Coulomb handed him his card. 'This is my direct number. Call me if the penny drops. But only if it drops within the next forty-eight hours. Remember, I can't do anything for you after that. After that, you'll be on your own. And consider this – while our department is one of very many, it is by far the least unpleasant. There are far worse and what they do is unspeakable. If you're not on board with us, they'll be contacting you in due course.' Coulomb sidled up and placed a massive hand on the small of his back. 'But, Matthew, they won't be offering work. They'll be coming to *collect*.'

Nine

Matt woke and put his hand out to kill the alarm before it could talk to him.

As he did so, he noticed a white card on the bedside table—

Charles Monmoulth Coulomb, Minister of Parliament 3999867845773.

So it wasn't a dream. But it wasn't real either. Some kind of psychological test? Yes, he could imagine that. A Government job in a secure laboratory manufacturing chemical weapons. They'd want someone who wouldn't be fazed by bizarre events. Well, maybe he'd consider it, but really, Government jobs didn't pay that well. Yesterday he'd been thinking about Germany, but how about China. The far East. That would impress Melissa more.

While he drove, his mind roamed free. He saw himself as the head of Chongqing's biggest fertilizer plant. *Celestial Chemicals Inc.* And as befitted his position, he would have a ten-bedroom house with a swimming pool in the basement and a helipad on the roof.

Ten bedrooms! Surely he could get Melissa into one of them?

…Sorry, Matt.

A poor drudge without a single helicopter to his name. Well, no wonder Melissa had felt so sorry for him. Not any more. He would put the record straight. Neither of them need suffer any longer.

Dreaming, dreaming, dreaming…

The exquisite images, the tantalising prospects were only mildly disturbed as he turned into the car park of *Acerlo Synthetics* to find that once again his favourite parking place was occupied by a ruby-red *Mercedes* sports car.

This time however, as he parked next to the waste bins, he was smiling.

He sauntered through the front entrance and found himself in the midst of an excited, chattering crowd. For a split second he entertained the crazy notion that he was being thrown a surprise party.

Oh my! What could it be? A long-service award? Chemist of the year?

Happy Birthday?

Allan was suddenly standing in front of him, flushed the colour of a boiled lobster. Much wine had been added to this dish and he was even wearing his best silver-sheen-effect suit, like he was wrapped in foil to keep the flavour in.

'So, you've finally rolled up?' Allen's jocular voice carried the tang of alcohol. His eyes twinkled.

A glance the man's shoulder revealed Melissa and Gideon standing a little way off. They were laughing happily together.

Matt examined his watch. 'As it happens, I'm on time, as usual, Allen.'

Allen was grinning. 'Actually, you're twenty-three and a half hours late, Matthew.'

'Pardon me?'

'Almost a day late.'

'Today is…Wednesday.'

'Today is Thursday.'

'Can't be—' But as Matt spoke, he realised that he could not have felt as refreshed as he did this morning after a mere two hours sleep.

He had slept for a whole day and night!

Rather than meet Allen's eyes, full of rheum and superiority—

You wouldn't think the two could go together, would you?

—Matt cast his glance around the crowd. 'What's going on here?'

'Um? Don't you know? Melissa and Gideon are tying the knot.'

'Tying the what?'

'The knot. Getting married.'

All at once, Matt was juggling hard to keep all the bits of himself together.

Allen would *not* stop grinning. 'Has it come as a shock?'

Matt swallowed in a dry throat—

Click!

'Oh, not really. They were made for each other.'

'You think so too, do you?'

Matt looked at his watch again. 'Well, I'd better get on.'

'Not joining us?'

'I have several experiments that have been running overnight.'

'Two nights – and a day, actually,' Allen said. When Matt simply stared at him, he added, 'Is there any chance the experiments can wait a little longer? You see, it would be a big, big help, Matthew, if you could collect an order for us. Vital chemicals are required.'

'Sure.'

'The solvent in question is Champagne from *Threshers*.' Allen's voice squeaked with delight at his own wit. 'We're imbibing plain old wine at the moment. You don't mind, do you? Melissa normally volunteers, but—'

'Of course I don't mind. It would be a pleasure.'

Matt drove to the nearest village.

Like all UK villages, it had been overdeveloped into an ugly little town. The sleety wind bit at him as he walked from the desolate car park that some supermarket had slapped over the village green. He passed by an all-too typical random pick of single mothers, purse-lipped pensioners and convex or rotund youths, unemployed because they were too stupid to serve in *Micky D's* and arrived at *Threshers*, the off licence, where he paused a moment to consider the hollow-eyed spectre staring back from the shop window. His reflection. It must have been a trick of the light, but he seemed to have turned utterly grey.

Dazed with misery, he went in and felt no relief at getting out of the cutting wind. The shop keeper, a plump, dough-faced man in his thirties, was reading a book at the counter. He did not glance up.

What surprised Matt was that he could smile and speak in a cheerful fashion.

'Nice to be able to read while you work.'

The clerk raised his eyes. Two muddy puddles. His hair was as insubstantial as a brown mist. The slightest breeze might blow it away.

'It's *Asimov*.'

'Is it? I used to like him. As a kid.'

'Me too. As a kid. But I was just checking something... Do you know the trouble with science fiction?'

'No, I don't.'

'All the stories are set in a time, when, by definition, the reader is stone cold dead.'

Matt emitted a chilly laugh. 'Yes, that's true, isn't it? Very true. Well, well. That must be why I don't read science fiction anymore. By the way, I'm here from *Acerlo Synthetics*. Collecting a case of Champagne.'

'Ah.' The shopkeeper flinched as if jabbed. 'I have the case in the large cooler, as requested.' He half turned. 'How's Melissa?'

'*Melissa*? She's...very well. Do you know her?'

The man turned back.

'She usually collects the wine orders.'

'That's right. She does. Always volunteers.'

'And I know her well as a friend, as a matter of fact.'

'Is that so?'

'Oh, we were a bit of an item a year or so ago, when

she first started at *Acerlo*.'

'An *item*?'

'Yes, you know, we had some fun together.'

The shop keeper produced a baggy smile.

'How about that…'

'What's the matter?'

'Nothing, nothing. I'll pass on your congratulations.'

'What for, exactly?'

'She's getting married.'

'You're kidding.'

'I was shocked too, but here I am, collecting the breakfast-time champagne. We like get the celebrations over as early as possible at *Acerlo*. Then it's back to work for everyone. They'll only stop, or start, rather, come the honeymoon. I mean Melissa and Gideon. That's the lucky fellow's name.'

'Never heard of him.'

'Don't worry, you'll be glad to learn that she's picked the right guy for the job. Gideon's marked out for the top. You know the type – *full* head of golden hair, sparkling array of teeth, ruby-red Mercedes. So, like I say, I'll be sure to pass on your congratulations.'

Ten

Matt dropped the case of champagne at the *Goods-in* entrance at the rear of *Acerlo* and asked the postal clerk to take it to reception. He went to the laboratory.

Someone was waiting for him.

Lithe and svelte, topped off with a debonair mop of thick, blond hair—

'Hey, Matt.'

'Morning Gideon.'

'Don't mind me, I'm just looking for some peace and

quiet.' His perfect teeth gleamed in a smile.

'You've come to the right place. By the way, congrats.'

'Thanks.' Gideon's dark-blue eyes flitted over the laboratory equipment with distaste. 'Tests, tests, tests.'

'Want to help me collate?'

'God, no.'

Frowning, past caring, Matt leaned back on the nearest table, folded his arms and looked Gideon over with genuine perplexity.

'Why, Gideon? Why did you become a scientist?'

'Why? Oh, I suppose I was pretty good at it. Science, I mean. I had a gift, of sorts.'

'You took five years to finish your PhD.'

Gideon chuckled. 'Thing is, I had certain extracurricular interests that took me away from the labs. I didn't say so at the time, but I did some acting.'

'You did?'

'I've been in a few films. Very, very minor roles, I hasten to add. I was in a band too. *The Stuarts*.'

'I haven't heard of them. But then, I'm not that keen on music.'

'Not keen on music?' Gideon was astonished.

'No. I'm keen on science. In fact, science is my life. If I were interested in music instead, I should have heard of *The Stuarts*. Perhaps'

Gideon's face fell. 'No, we never did quite break through. We came close though.' He shrugged – although his shoulders did not rise as high as they should have done. '*Que sera*, eh? I can't complain. I had another career to go to, as it turns out. So here I am.'

'Which career would have you preferred?'

But Gideon was too wily for that. 'I don't believe in alternative histories, or futures.'

'You were fated to become a scientist, then?'

'Evidently.'

Looking at Gideon's thick mop of hair, Matt remarked, 'And yet fate is often cruel.'

'Is it? Fate's been pretty generous to me.'

No doubt he alluded to Melissa. Perhaps Gideon had come to gloat. Perhaps he knew about the conversation between him and Melissa the day before last.

Matt avoided those watchful blue eyes.

'Well, I'd better get on. I'm lagging behind.'

'Not coming for a drink?'

'Problematic when working with dangerous chemical. Still, thanks anyway.'

'No worries.'

Matt turned away and began to attend to the equipment on the table. When he turned again, Gideon was gone.

He stared dumbly, feeling his self-confidence ebb away. The idea of getting a job in China revolted him now, because he'd be living out there with ninety-nine billion people he didn't want to be with, while the one he did would be here.

But what then, if he didn't leave?

There would be the build up to the wedding and a big send-off party. Melissa and Gideon would depart for…the honeymoon.

Don't want to think about that.

After the honeymoon, there would be another party. A welcome-back party. Then another party, when Allen had promoted Gideon. Another when he had promoted Melissa. There would be endless parties. But none for him. And so, instead of ever becoming his lover, Melissa would become his line manager and Gideon – well Gideon was going to end up running the whole company.

And would Gideon keep him hard at work?

You bet!

Matt just knew that smirking bag of cherry blossom would be on his back day and night. And as he toiled for the Gideon/Melissa complex, he would burn with the consciousness that every drop of his scalding sorrow was a piquant sauce for their eternal happiness.

Matt noticed that he was breathing through his mouth. His heart was racing. The laboratory walls were closing in. If the future was *this* bad before it had even begun what would it be like when…. Oh God, the injustice of it was going to absolutely kill him! And it was indeed so unjust. Allen, Gideon and even Melissa would be nothing without the products that he had developed after years of solitary toil and study. And yet, here they were, reaping all the rewards.

I know, it just isn't fair, is it? Sorry, Matt.

That voice!

He couldn't stand it any longer. His despair and self-pity gave way to rage. *You have stolen everything!*

He went to the nearest computer terminal and plugged in a flash drive he kept on his key ring. Within minutes he had downloaded all the research data from the central database.

Soon enough Acerlo was going to find another company seriously undercutting their prices.

It just isn't fair…is it Melissa? Hope you all find another job soon… Not!

The lab technician arrived moments after. Bantering cheerfully with her in a way that was most uncharacteristic, he spent the rest of morning setting up the next batch of tests for her to perform. Now and then he would break out into brittle laugher.

'Did you have some champagne, Matthew?'

The technician was staring at him from behind a titration stand.

'Your diagnosis is correct.' He checked his watch.

Twelve o'clock – already. 'That's why I'll be working from home this afternoon. If anyone wants me, let them know.'

When he got back to his apartment, he noted that it had never looked so small and tatty. All the fabrics were nylon and all the metals aluminium. The white goods were nothing but a load of Chinese rip-offs. Cheap and nasty, because cheap and nasty was all he could ever afford.

Chinese rip-offs? Hey, don't knock the people who're going to make you rich.

The phone bleeped.

Insanely, he had the sudden conviction that Melissa was calling him.

She had changed her mind!

Life bobbed back into view.

Still not drowned!

'Hello.'

'Hello, Matty?' It was Abigail. 'I just called you at work.'

Matt hadn't thought about Abigail once during the last forty-eight hours. For a split second he wondered why she should ever call at all.

Then he remembered.

This librarian was his girl friend.

'There was a leaving party. I came back early.'

'Leaving party? That's nice.' She was assuming (Matt knew) someone had retired. Deep down, Abigail longed for the mellow comforts of old age. Day trips to market towns, afternoon TV, the central heating on in summer.

He blurted, 'I'm thinking of striking out too.'

'What?'

'There are jobs going in the Far East. China. Chongqing.'

Abigail laughed. 'Really?'

'Why? Don't you believe me?'

'I suppose so. But you're talking about the other side of the world.'

A chill went through him. The world. That big, lonely sphere. His fate lay at its far end.

'Let's go live there,' he pleaded. 'Both of us. Let's just leave.'

'What do you mean?'

'Go to Chongqing.'

Again, that laugh of hers.

'What for?'

'To live!'

'Live? In Chongqing?'

'Yes, that's what I'm saying.'

She began to sound less tolerant of his absurdity. 'But Matty, we can't.'

'Of course we can. It's not the *moon*.'

'But – it's not *here*.'

'Here? There's nothing here.'

'Our family, our friends.'

She meant *her* family, *her* friends.

'We'll make new friends. New job, new places and new people. I've got intellectual commodities I can sell. And we could start a fam—'

'My job's here.'

'Like I say, money won't be a problem.'

Abigail's voice soothed and cooed, as if to calm a decrepit old man mouldering in his Bath chair. 'Matt, we're a bit too long in the tooth to go and live abroad.'

'Christ, we're not!'

'Oh, Matt, what's the matter, really? Tell me.'

He opened his mouth. No words came out, only the breath of his body as he deflated. His eyes closed up.

'Nothing. I'm a bit out of sorts today. Sorry. Look, I don't think I'll be up for the *Women's Institute* lecture tomorrow.'

She was alarmed. 'Aren't you well, sweetheart? Shall I come over?'

'No. A bit fluey, perhaps. Honestly, I just want a rest.'

And yet he *did* want her to come over.

Tears started into his eyes. But not out of love for her. Rather, speaking to Abigail had brought him to his senses.

He had been reacting to events and got all fired up. Lost his scientific perspective. A maelstrom of emotion was not appropriate to a mild-mannered chemist. Underneath, he was not so different from Abigail. And so he wept, because he knew full well that he simply didn't have the guts to avoid the humiliation of working for Melissa and Gideon. To do so would entail taking a one-way journey to Chongqing.

Like a Zen 007, eh?

No, he wasn't one of those. He wasn't capable of becoming a big shot on the other side of the world. He quailed at the very idea.

His tears came faster.

'Matt?'

'I'm going to bed now. Sorry, I'll call tomorrow in the morning.'

'You sure?'

'I'll be here, sweetheart.'

Eleven

Matt woke in the night, hardly able to breathe. His chest was gripped by an agonising constriction and a blinding pain stabbed at his temple. He was either having a heart attack or a stroke. Or both.

Or maybe it was just the booze.

He didn't normally drink, but today of all days had surely been the optimum one to begin his alcoholic decline.

He threw out an arm, knocking off an empty whisky bottle from the side table before he could fumble the lamp on.

The light blazed and he found himself looking up at a dirty mass of feathers towering over him. Claws the size of man's hands were clamped wickedly into his chest and high up, near the ceiling, the beast's head was twisted away from the lamp, as if the light were a blinding torment.

Matt screamed and twisted convulsively. His thrashing arms battered the beast away to the left and it let out a squawk and landed on the floor with a soft thump. It couldn't have weighed more than a few pounds.

Matt scrambled backwards out of bed and thrust himself against the wall. The filthy thing righted itself in the same instant and glared at him from across the bed.

Frozen, Matt could only stare back, his heart pounding against his rib cage. The thing's wary eyes glowered with such a hate-filled animus that it transfixed him to the spot.

It was waiting for his next move.

Matt obliged by sliding a little closer towards the door.

The thing crouched in readiness. As it did so, Matt spotted something hanging from the creature's disfigured beak.

A single dark hair!

He automatically put a hand to his temple.

'That's mine! Mine! You filthy…!'

The beast honked with derision. Its eyes twinkled with

gleeful malice.

Looking into those eyes, Matt gasped with sudden recognition. 'Paul – it's *you!*'

Paul let out a shriek of rage and shame. He stretched wide his loathsome wings, filling half the room. Matt cowered, his arms flung across his face. Paul launched himself into the air and flew across the room with a single, ear-splitting wing beat and vanished under the door, gliding effortlessly through a gap less than an inch wide.

Out in the hallway the flimsy letter flap rattled and—

Utter silence.

Matt was left trembling, hunched up on the floor.

As the minutes passed, he became more and more aware of his thumping hangover. The pain finally forced him to get up and venture to the bathroom.

He took some *Alka-Selza*.

Turning to the mirror, he was appalled at the sight of his bleary, bloated face. As a rule, drink held no attraction for him. For good reason, he saw now. That bottle of whisky had wrought manifest damage. Fleetingly, he comforted himself with the hope that what he had just seen was an alcohol-induced nightmare.

But he had not forgotten the Minster's words and he leaned closer to the mirror to examined his temple…

He yelped with indignation.

'What? No!'

His hair had visibly receded.

He had been violated!

Oh, but that such a foul, squalid, furtive operation should be sanctioned by the Government was beyond endurance.

This is an outrage! Where's that swine's card?

'Hello, Matthew.' Charles Coulomb's rich and supple voice answered at the first ring.

'God damn you,' Matt shouted, choking back his sobs, 'haven't I paid enough down the years?'

'Now, calm down.'

'What for? Your wretched undersecretary, Paul, has just been sitting on me, yanking out my hair!'

'I'll ask you keep your voice down.'

'It's *obscene*.'

'I thought I'd explained all that. Paul's only doing his job.'

'No! It says in the letter I'll lose my hair over next twenty-three years. He's going too fast. I'm half bald already!'

'He's annoyed with you, that's why. You didn't take the job. Philip Symmonds is a wily old dog. He's been holding up recruitment for personal reasons. He doesn't want anyone working on him, you see. But then, out of the blue, he says, *Yes, we're way behind and there's no time to waste and we have to recruit from within the Civil Service*. And *POW* – Paul finds he's been signed up. He had no choice. It was in his contract all along. So Symmonds has got his thrusting, upcoming rival put out the way. Cunning, what? You have to admire him, old Symmonds – he knows how to keep the younger generation down.'

Matt was holding his hand to his naked scalp. He cried out in despair, 'But Paul has to stop. He *has* to!'

Coulomb was stern. 'No, he doesn't. He's decided to fast-track you and that's entirely his prerogative. You see, it's another excellent perk of the job and I'm sorry I didn't mention it before. Not only can you select your own clients, you can fast-track them too. Help them along the way and reduce the burden of an inflated population even more quickly. The country benefits tremendously.'

Matt struggled to get the words out. 'But I didn't do anything to him.'

'Well—'

'I'll kill him! I'll wait up every night!'

Coulomb spoke with restraint. 'Do you know what our motto is, Matthew?'

'No.'

'*Death Conquers All.*'

Matt's voice dropped to a whisper. 'For God's sake.'

'Remember the teeth. Paul can swap beaks, and in a couple of years, believe me, you'll be both bald and toothless. Just like Symmonds, eh?'

'Stop, stop, stop – Oh, you son of a bitch!'

'No! You stop! Hold your peace for a moment.' Coulomb waited for Matt to get his snivelling under control and continued in a tone that was firm but fair. 'I'm only giving you the facts, brutal as they may be. But let's not give up hope. Like many in the Executive, Mr Symmonds has his own agenda, as I explained, and what it amounts to is thwarting Government policy just to keep himself from his ultimate quietus. For some time now, my colleagues and I have felt the need for a new methodology. The need for *extraordinary* measures. Are you listening?'

Matt was oozing tears. 'I want Paul to stop,' he blubbered.

'Yes, yes, Matthew, I understand. Come now, let's show some backbone. If you'll listen and let yourself be guided by me, I think… Well, this is strictly between us, do you understand?'

In response, Matt mumbled incoherently.

'Good lad. So, strictly off the record, I can tell you, Matthew, that I've recently set up a recruiting programme for a *New Model Flying Core*. We've put through emergency legislation and I have obtained extraordinary powers to bypass the Executive for the foreseeable future.'

'I don't understand—'

'Modern medicine, Matthew. It's been an absolute disaster for the country. For the world. People are being kept alive way, way beyond the term of their economic usefulness. Well, I suppose I've said all this before, but we really, really need *more* decay and death, not *less*. And the upshot of that is I can now offer you another post. Same job, but in a brand-new air division.'

Matt grasped the opportunity with pitiful eagerness and gratitude.

'Oh God. Yes. Yes. That would be fantastic.'

Anything was better than death, wasn't it?

Except, just then, a thought struck him.

Sniffling, he humbly added, 'Though, on the other hand, sir, I was thinking of going to China to work. I could get a job there and if I were out of the country, then wouldn't that mean I wasn't a burden anymore?'

'I think you'll find,' Coulomb said stiffly, 'that in all likelihood you'll be back in a few years to claim your pension. That's why we maintain fleets in all our embassies, to take *care* of the expats.'

Matt whinnied, 'God damn, you just can't win—'

But at the same time, he recollected his last conversation with Gideon. Wasn't the fellow so very proud of his thick golden mop of hair? And then, there was that wide grin of his! Wasn't it just plain chock-a-block with white teeth?

Sorry Matt.

He saw Melissa now with his mind's eye. She had appeared at Gideon's side.

They fell into a lingering embrace. But that wasn't enough for them, was it? They turned to stare at him and to watch dispassionately as his body withered and crumbled.

It just isn't fair, is it? Sorry, Matt!

No!

Matt heard himself murmur, 'Okay, I'll do it.'

'Pardon?'

But he instantly had doubts.

Hadn't Paul looked so indescribably hideous? Nothing was left of his humanity apart from those hate-filled eyes.

'I mean,' Matt said weakly, 'what if I agreed to join the *New Model Flying Core* sometime in the future. Perhaps.'

'But you must decide *now*, Matthew. Go on, 'just say, *Yes* and there'll be nothing else for you to do, except wait for us to contact you in a due course. But in the meantime, might I ask if is there anyone you happen to know – one, or perhaps two people, who have a full heads of hair and a beautiful teeth? Person or persons who it would be an absolute *delight* to work on? A pleasure to put on the *fast-track* to annihilation?' Coulomb's voice dropped to a whisper. 'Well, is there, Matthew? Is there?'

'Oh yes,' Matt murmured.

'What did you say?'

'Yes.'

'Good man! You've made the right decision.'

'No! Wait!'

The connection went dead and—

Blam! Blam! Blam! Blam!

—someone started hammering at the door.

UPDATOR

One

Friday night.

Vincent (young chef) met Sylvianna (young hairdresser) at *Yu2*, a club in London's West End.

Vinny was six foot four, toned, buff and beautiful. He looked like one of those lantern-jawed aesthetes who sulk at you from *Gucci* ads.

And Sylvianna wasn't that bad looking either.

So, what else was there to say?

After midnight, they exited the hot, crimson interior of *Yu2* and drifted up Oxford Street, pursued by the ribald cheers and highly witty remarks of their respective crowds. Meanwhile, very, very dark Sub Saharans circled around them hissing, *Minicab, minicab, minicab…*

But don't worry, they caught a proper taxi instead.

Destination?

Sylvianna's cute little apartment out in Earl's Court.

'Want coffee?'

He nodded, but only managed a sip before his lips were required elsewhere. And his hands too. Soon enough, he was busy, busy, busy undressing her.

'I like a bit of rough,' she laughed. 'Rough *and* ready.'

Vinny's busy fingers froze.

What did she mean by calling him *rough*?

It couldn't be the way he was undressing her. When it came to the undoing of buttons and clasps, Vinny prided himself on undressing women with as much care as he undressed himself. Never in his life had he yanked anything off. He removed it. Folded it. Hung it up in the wardrobe.

It was no good, Sylvianna and him could not move forward till he had got to the bottom of this.

'What do you mean, *rough and ready*?'

Sylvianna answered in a husky whisper.

'Whatever I mean, it doesn't matter.'

She nestled a little deeper into the smoky-grey cushions of her powder-blue sofa and closed her eyes – waiting for the bliss to begin.

Vinny couldn't get over how perfect her face was. Skin that was smoother than porcelain. So utterly unblemished it looked unreal.

As a matter of fact, compared to her he probably did look a little bit rough.

'Okay.'

He recommenced the unfastening of buttons.

Some were small, others were tiny and they all took a remarkable amount of itsy-bitsy fiddling to make free. Then came straps, hooks and eyes. Then clasps of some description, and…another row of buttons. And behind them lay fasteners. And then…

As he worked, ever more feverishly, Sylvianna heaved many a full-throated sigh, just as if he were already caressing and manipulating flesh rather than textile.

The minutes passed and the clothes were piling up beside the sofa. Layer upon layer of them. She might have been dressed for a Siberian winter rather than a London nightclub.

The breakthrough came when Vinny was confronted by a set of frilly laces. Sylivianna's shapely torso was bound in a corset. A nice, sexy one too. Fabricated from intricately patterned material and edged by rinky-pink ribbon.

Vinny took new heart and did not delay in the untying and drawing out of laces that was required to attain his ultimate goal. He soon had the two flaps of the corset uncoupled and, opening them like the jaws of a clam, he found…nothing was inside.

Sylvianna chuckled softly to herself, as if revelling in his confusion. He raised his staring eyes to her face and watched the smirking head come loose and roll off the sofa.

Kudunk!

The skull thumped the wooden floor and—

Rukka-Rukka-Rukka-Rukka-Rukka…

—rolled away.

Stupefied, Vinny turned from the skull to the headless carcass, just as it reached up and enfolded him in its arms.

He let out the most Goddamn awful scream…

Two

…and woke with a start.

His naked terror abated in the bright, morning sunlight that filled Sylivanna's tastefully decorated bedroom.

But naked terror was immediately succeeded by acute embarrassment. Had his lunatic scream frightened Sylvianna out of her wits?

'Oh.'

He was alone in bed. And the rest of her apartment was filled by that air of suspense left by someone who should be there but wasn't.

Vinny peeled the sheets from his clammy skin and got up.

'Woh there, what the hell is this then?'

What he meant was, *Good heavens, I'm feeling a trifle peaky. Why on Earth would that be?*

A most pertinent question, seeing that he was a health nut and always woke up feeling tiptop. Unless he was hung over, of course. But that didn't happen often, and definitely not this morning, because he had drunk only orange juice last night. He had an evening shift tonight and when he had an evening shift he always stayed off the booze.

So he *wasn't* hung over, and yet, he *didn't* feel tiptop.

This was a mystery.

The malady was all the more disquieting because he couldn't name it. All that his groping mind could fetch out of the medical dictionary was the phrase *off colour*.

That said, *off colour* was a peculiarly apt diagnosis, because he did have this weird feeling like he was coated all over in a grey, unwholesome muck.

Grey, unwholesome muck???!!!

He *really* didn't like the sound of that.

Easy, guy. Take a nice warm shower. That'll fix it.

Vinny pulled his shorts on and ventured out of the bedroom.

A note lay on the kitchen table—

At work til 4. Make yurselv some brekky, Love Sylvianna.

Oh, that was sweet of her…writing a note and all.

After his shower, he decided to leave a note in return just to be polite—

Soz I didn't wak up. I was ok for brekky, but I hadda showa instead. It was great!!!!

This was Vinny's sixth effort. Chin resting on knuckles, forehead corrugated, he brooded now over the possibility that Sylvianna might think he meant the *showa* was great, rather than the *sex*. He wanted to let her know, in a nice way – a way that didn't shout it – that the sex had indeed been great.

He glared the words.

Why *wouldn't* they say what he wanted them to say? Or rather,

Why the hell didn't she wake me up?

His knockout smile could have done the talking.

He took another piece of paper—

Cheers! I'll call after work.

He almost added—

Cuddunt hang on til 4 cuz I gottu meet up with a mate this morning,

—but didn't.

Three

'Hey, hombre!'

Fahah, his mate, was waiting for him in Marble Arch Station, their usual rendezvous point.

'Hey, sorry, I'm late. I was—' Vinny made a deft little punching action in the air.

Fahah grinned.

'Nice one, bro.'

Fahah looked a couple of years older than Vinny, but at twenty-seven he was actually a couple of years younger.

Or rather, he had always looked a couple of years older till today. As they ascended the resonating steps of the station concourse and joined the swirling crowds down a sunny Oxford Street, Vinny noticed with interest that Fahah's light olive skin had never looked so fresh. Furthermore, his black hair, cropped close, didn't look any thinner. That was most surprising, because ever since he had known him, Fahah's hair had been getting thinner every day.

'You're looking very well, my friend,' Vinny remarked.

Fahah put on a mock English accent, 'Thanks, old chap.'

'No, honest.'

'Must be something I'm taking.'

'Yeah? I wouldn't mind some myself. I can't lay my finger on it. I'm not feeling sick or nothing, but I ain't feeling buff neither. Not buff at all.'

'It's you paying for your pleasures, innit?'

Vinny considered this possibility. Good, clean sex wasn't harmful and he didn't do any other sort.

Nah.

He let his gaze wander around Oxford Street. The bustling pedestrians looked so happy and the shop windows sparkled in the sunshine and the traffic had the gaiety of a huge fairground ride and yet…and yet he just didn't feel a part of it.

His mind drifted and he recalled the strange dream that had woken him with a scream that morning. He was about to mention it when he noticed Fahah, who was usually so chatty and buoyant, had lapsed into a thoughtful silence of his own.

'You're quiet, man.'

'Eh? Nah, I'm just so impressed. Third time this month – you're a machine.'

He laughed.

Fahah owned a strange laugh. It seemed like a thing separate from him, like a sort of pet. The sound of it was half growl, half cackle. Both fiendish and lovable at the same time. Perhaps because it had Fahah's soft-brown eyes, which were always gentle and often a little sad.

Better get it over with, Vinny told himself.

'How's Gab?' He asked.

'Oh, she's being… I don't know – what does she want off me, eh?'

Vinny shook his head and commiserated with a threadbare smile, knowing that Gabriella, Fahah's ex girlfriend, didn't want anything from Fahah. And even if she had wanted something, something like a silver bracelet, say, or a holiday break, Fahah could not have supplied it.

He hadn't worked for over two years.

And this was partly Vinny's fault.

You see, they'd met up and become bros while cheffing at the same restaurant. Vinny had quit the place, because the restaurant was shit and he'd got a better job at a better restaurant. Like a good and faithful bro, Fahah had followed him. But Fahah should have stayed put, because, with the best will in the world, he was a shit chef.

But how did he manage to get a job at Vinny's new restaurant, eh? Him being shit and all? Well, Vinny knew Fahah's limitations and he hadn't put a special word in for him with the management. But it turned out he didn't have to. Fahah had a talent for something other than cooking. He had been born to sell (Vinny was always saying, *Do sales, man, you'll fly!*) and he was so good at talking that he didn't even have to know what he was talking about to make people buy into whatever he was saying. Thus it was that Fahah had talked about his cooking tasting great and he had convinced the management that it would taste great, but what he couldn't do was talk his food into tasting great.

And the management had axed him after a week.

That was cruel and harsh and Vinny felt like he ought to quit the restaurant, with its better pay and better prospects, just to show solidarity with his good bro…

…two years later, Vinny was still at the restaurant and Fahah was still looking for another cheffing job. But why, when he really couldn't cook? Well – and this was seriously unlucky for Fahah – Gabriella, the girl he loved above all others, had a penchant for chefs (as Vinny had ascertained for himself) and her brief relationship with Fahah was nothing more than an amazing testament to his persuasive tongue.

She was a nice girl – sort of – and she never actually said, *Fuck off, loser!* She let her utter indifference do the talking.

'Have you heard off her this week?'

'I phoned.'

'Yeah? What's the news?'

'Plenty, as it goes.'

Fahah didn't expand on this and Vinny didn't ask him to.

They turned off at Bond Street and entered Soho, bantering non-stop.

By then, Fahah was looking a little grey. Like many intellectuals, he was low on physical stamina and both talking and walking for a full hour had drained him.

Vinny said, 'Let's dine at *Bungies*, coz. I need to chillax and get an energy boost before we look round the shops.'

Fahah smiled at him with his gentle eyes. 'Ah, very well, amigo.'

In *Bungies*, a cellar café, Fahah groaned with relief as he sat at one of the tables. Vinny joined him, after standing in the queue to buy coffees and cakes.

'So anyway,' Fahah asked, a cheeky grin revealing that the caffeine had revived him body and soul, 'let's hear the lastest story.'

'Last night? Her name's Sylvianna.'

'Interesting. Is it like you'll be seeing her again?'

'Funny thing is, I don't know. I woke up this morning and she'd gone off to work. She just left a note to say, *Eat.*'

'She's feeding you already. That's a good sign.'

'Ha! Anyway, I wrote a note back. I said, *Thanks for everything, I'll call after I've finished work.*'

'So, you really like her, then?'

'Too early to say. Anyway, I should have said I'd call after *she's* finished work, because I finish after midnight. Though perhaps I should have said, *Call me* instead and then she could have called any damned time she liked.'

'I'm detecting this feeling that she's under your skin, bro.'

'Not really. But it's funny how she didn't wake me up.'

'She wants you to stick around.'

Vinny grinned. 'Maybe she was just scared in case I got going again. I am a woman-destroying machine – according to you.'

Fahah pulled a pantomime face of disgust. 'I was joking. Anyway, you're going to have an empty tank, draining it like this.'

'Nicely put, coz. Still…I really do feel a bit off-colour.'

Fahah's gentle gaze filled with concern. 'Still feeling shit, coz?'

'Not one hundred per cent. Know what I'm thinking? I'm doing too much overtime, innit?'

Fahah thought about this and nodded judicially. 'You do look worn. Yeah, I would say, *No!!!!* to the management, if I was you.'

'Sure I should. But guy, they pay so good.'

Fahah's soft gaze took on a more melancholy cast.

'Oh, but you're right,' Vinny went on quickly, 'your

health's more important than money.'

Fahah brightened. 'Strange you should say that, hombre – putting your health first is the basis of my whole philosophy.'

'You think I should take some time off?'

'Should you? Course! Like I say, you're definitely looking rough—'

'*Rough*? You didn't say, *Rough* before. You said, *Worn*.'

'Easy, dude, easy. You was the one saying you wasn't feeling so good.'

'Well I don't feel *rough*. It's not that bad. It's like a general iffyness. I can't say what it is, exactly. Could even just be in my head.'

'It's both, bro. It's your body *and* your mind. What they are both saying is, *Slow down, Vinny!*'

Fahah was wearing his widest grin and Vinny broke into a smile. 'I'm outnumbered then, ain't I?'

They started on their cakes. Then they just mellowed out, sipping coffee. As soon as the cups were drained, Fahah said, 'Shall we get going now?'

He tired quickly, but he also revived quickly.

They cut through China Town and headed into Covent Garden.

Vinny had a yen to update his loafers.

They drifted from one boutique to the next, Fahah talking fast. As a born salesman, he couldn't help plunging head-first into the role of advisor and extempore shop assistant, leaving the real shop assistants to stand around and watch him, like they were staff he was training.

Vinny didn't mind. Fahah had a real nose for quality. And the more out-of-reach the goods were for him personally, the more discerning he became. He picked out a pair of loafers that were perfect for Vinny. Then, five minutes later, he spotted a pair of jeans to go with the loafers. Vinny had never suspected that he needed new jeans too, but he had to agree with Fahah that this pair of jeans were so excellent they made the pair he was wearing seem shabby. *Rough*, even.

After a couple of hours, during which Fahah talked Vinny into renewing his current shirt, sunglasses and man bag, they found themselves on the Tottenham Court Road (*the* street to pick up one's hi-tech) and, as luck would have it, the latest *iphone* had just hit the market. The *i21*. True, Vinny's *i20 phone* was still pretty amazing of course, but times had moved on and it was no longer as new as his loafers, shirt, jeans, sunglasses and man bag.

They milled around the all-white interior of the *Apple Store*, where the silvery machines seemed to float on their Perspex stands.

Meanwhile, a loud silence emanated from Fahah.

He was immune to *Apple*. In fact, new technology in general simply bored him. For the first time that day he commented on the price of the goods being perused.

'Why's this shit so expensive?'

'R and D costs, innit? And you pay for style too.'

'But this thing looks like the old one.'

'Does it, Fahah?'

Oh no, this time the master was wrong. The slickness of the case was definitely more slick. The screen didn't have billions of colours – it had trillions. And *Apple* had made their phone slimmer and lighter than ever before… It looked just like the pill that would cure him.

In other words—

He *had* to have the *i21*.

And he couldn't bear to wait. Not even to spare his friend's feelings.

You see, the new *i21* easily cost more than Fahah had to live off for a year.

After the purchase, Vinny saw that Fahah was exhausted again and so he steered him to a small Italian place, between Carnaby Street and Soho, where they dined now and then.

Sipping coffee and waiting for their rabbit loins, Fahah grew less waxen and he took a look at the *i21*.

'I see people patting away at these things,' he mused as the glowing screen illuminated his face. 'But a phone's a phone, innit? Hey, that's a point – you could call Sylvianna now.'

'Who?'

'Sylvianna!'

'Oh yeah. Her.'

'Didn't you leave a note to say you'd call after she finished work?'

'I did, yes. But—'

'Vinny – it's five. Her hairdressers' would have shut. Call her now.'

'Hm, why not? But I'll transfer everything first.'

'How's that?'

'Take the data over from the *i20* to the *i21*. I want to call from the *i21*, don't I?''

Fahah nodded, but his eyes had glazed over the instant the word *data* had left Vinny's lips.

'Well okay, I'll transfer later.'

He called Sylvianna's number from the *i20*.

A man's voice answered. His petulance squeezed his words up tight. His, 'Hello, can I help?' came out as a monosyllable.

'Hey, it's Vincent here, I'm actually calling to speak to Sylvianna.'

'No, man, she's gone out the shop to get some stuff.'

'I see. Well, I'm sort of up town if she calls back—'

'Maybe not. She's gone to the chemist. It's like a cold or something.'

'Oh, that's a shame. Sorry to hear that. Say – *I'm sorry to hear that*, will you?'

'Yeah.'

'Not too bad, is she?'

'Nah.'

'Just a cold?'

SIGH.

'Yeah.'

'Okay! Cheers!'

'Sure.'

The connection dissolved into the ether.

Vinny and Fahah looked at each other for a moment and then burst out laughing.

'What's going on?' Fahah asked.

'A gayboy's answering her calls, that's what's going on.'

'But she ain't well, he says?'

'It's a brush-off story, innit? Well, I hope it is. Makes you think though. What if she really *is* sick? I didn't use nothing last night…and I felt iffy first thing, didn't I?'

'Hey, hey, don't worry. She's just dropping you, like you say.'

'Yeah, you're right.'

And yet… And yet, being dropped wasn't so good either.

Rough and ready, she'd said.

A shadow must have crossed Vinny's brow, because Fahah said, 'But that doesn't mean you should let yourself be dropped, guy, if you like her. Maybe she wants you to keep trying. She's testing you. And it may be worth it. Okay, you might get a knockback, or two, but what I always say is, *It isn't what you* DO *you regret, it's what you DON'T do.*'

Yes, Fahah did often say that.

Vinny decided to give Fahah some sound advice in

return.

'Perhaps. But every now and then, *not* doing something might be better. Maybe trying to be with Sylvianna might turn out futile.'

'Futile?'

'I mean a complete fucking waste of time.'

Fahah's thoughtful frown brought his eyes closer together. 'But as it says in the good book, *Who dares, wins.*'

'But what if you do win? Have you considered what happens then? The ladies – so many of them require constant care and attention. Having to give constant care and attention means you don't live for yourself.'

'True…'

'Me, I've already got a full-time job. That's the way I see it. I've got enough demands on me.'

'But this Sylvianna, she just went off to work and left you there to sleep it off. No fuss. No hassle. Perfect trust, man. That's so rare.'

'Yeah, she was pretty rare.'

'There you are.'

'Good looking too.'

'Of course.'

'Self supporting. She's got her own place and she doesn't ask for nothing, 'cause she works.'

'Fantastic.'

'And frankly, when I said I'm a chef she wasn't the least impressed.'

'No kidding.'

'So…would you like her number?'

'*What?*'

'Sylvianna's. Or we could all meet up, maybe, for a drink, and I could introduce you and everything. You two might hit it off.'

Fahah was incredulous. He spoke softly, as if to a

child who'd had a bang on the head.

'I couldn't do that to Gabriella.'

The pasta dish arrived. And after that came the rabbit.

By the end of the meal, which Vinny was happy to pay for, evening was drawing on.

They trailed back down to Marble Arch, chatting all the way. The crowds were thinning, but just a little. The sun was low. Its balmy light troubled Vinny with an undefined sadness. Something about time. Something about yet another day passing into night, never again to return.

They paused near the sonorous entrance to the underground and watched the tourists streaming out of the earth. Some formed knots and drifted off uptown, talking loudly to each other. Others were like single atoms and shot off in all directions.

The laughter, the shouts, the swarming traffic that pounded around Hyde Park Corner – it was the stuff of life itself and it made the air throb.

How wonderful that throb was! How lovely!

And yet even while absorbing the marvellous ambience, Vinny still couldn't shake this dismal feeling. The feeling that everything around was inevitable and everlasting – except himself.

'What's up, bro?'

'Eh?' He turned and found Fahah staring at him curiously. 'Oh, I was just thinking.'

'That's why we're both so thin, bro. We think. The brain burns calories like nothing.'

'The thinking diet… You know, you could sell that, Fahah. Honest now, I'm going to say this just once more, I swear, but I know, absolutely *know* that if you give sales a chance, you'll break out and fly, man. *Fly*.'

Fahah produced his widest grin and most fiendish cackle.

'When you say that, I always say, *Leave it alone, don't I?*'

'No need. Like I say, I ain't going there again.'

'Am I saying, *Leave it alone*, this time? Did you hear me say that?'

'You just did.'

'Na, na, nah, I didn't really.'

'But—'

'What I'm saying is, maybe I'm ahead of you, eh? Maybe I *am* going into sales.'

Vinny stared and then laughed.

'No way! You're getting a job now?'

'Hey, coz – gotta go.'

'But really? Why didn't you say before?'

'Because it's got to be a story worth telling, innit? So I'll be telling you about it soon enough.'

'Yeah? Right, right, right. Hey, friend – see ya!'

Cackling in reply, Fahah disappeared down the vaulted stairway of the tube.

Four

Back in his Holborn apartment (an unmarried uncle had helped him buy it), Vinny placed his shopping on the sofa in the living room and sighed with relief. Carrying all that stuff had become a chore.

He glanced around him.

He'd had the place redecorated last month. It had cost an arm and a leg, but at least anyone could see that the decor was of a higher quality than Sylvianna's.

However, his silent appreciation was disturbed by the near-palpable quietude that had accumulated in the rooms during his absence. And it had not been dispelled by his entrance.

He threw open the window, let the breeze flap the curtains, and turned the television on to add some background noise different to the airy thrum of the city. The TV's soulless exclamations – the noise that fills the ever-widening void between the ears of the world – followed him around while he stowed his new things away.

He glanced at his watch.

Still an hour to go before work.

Plenty of time for a shower.

He stripped and was about to take his watch off when he noticed the damnedest thing.

Somehow, he wasn't satisfied by what he saw.

The watch on his wrist. It… It…

It looked like it needed *updating!*

But how come? He'd only bought it last month. And Fahah had been on the scene too, directing as usual. He was the genius who'd spotted the perfect model and negotiated the price down. He'd even persuaded the shopkeeper to put a better strap on it for no extra cost. Yes, Fahah had done everything to get Vinny the optimum watch – except pay for it.

Vinny wondered briefly if Fahah's exquisite taste had finally let him down. The watch really didn't look right on his wrist anymore. He ran his forefinger along the curve of the face. But no, Fahah's exquisite taste had not let him down. The watch was great – there could be no denying it.

And so, the problem had to be…had to be…his wrist!

His wrist?

No way! This is crazy. There's nothing wrong with my wrist.

There was nothing wrong with any part of him. He could see that for himself in the mirror. And Sylvianna could vouch for him too. She wasn't alone, either.

Change the girl's name once a fortnight and Vinny's story wrote itself.

But maybe that was part of the problem.

I've been going too fast, that's what it is. Doing my head in. Too much serious fun. And too much overtime. I need to take a break.

Actually, as he saw from his watch, he needed to get ready for work.

He hopped in and out the shower and kitted himself out in the new jeans and shirt.

Meanwhile, a game-show audience hooted and whooped on the television. He plopped himself down on the sofa for ten minutes. Tonight's host, Brandon Juste, was looking particularly glossy and smooth, despite the fifty years he'd graced the planet.

No, the truth was Brandon looked better than glossy and smooth. He looked downright perfecto.

That was odd.

Why?

Why? This was a HD TV, that's why.

The years on Brandon's back should be showing up in fine detail.

Vinny could well recall the changeover to HD in the dim and distant past and he was pretty certain that, like all the other sun-dried old fruits on TV, Brandon had been as raddled as a prune. And his eyes had been weary unto death too. Sure, his eyes were still like totally dead, but they were no longer dull. They were shiny.

Know why that is, guy? Brandon's a star and he gets star treatment, that's why. Special drops for the eyes and surgery for the complexion. Loads of botox. You need that dirty medicine to keep your TV career rolling.

Just then the camera cut to a quick shot of the audience. In that split second, Vinny saw they all looked perfecto too. And so did the contestants. They were as finely polished as marble. Ugly as sin, to be sure, but not flawed and blemished and gouged like they used to be.

The television was getting on his nerves. He offed the thing and phoned for a taxi.

'It'll be five minutes, sir.'

In the hallway, he pulled on his brand-new loafers and stopped dead, transfixed as he stared down at them.

Now what?

It was like with the watch. Something wasn't quite right.

As he examined the loafers, wondering what was wrong, the answer came to him, *Ping!* like the explanation had been texted into his head.

The loafers were *too good* for his feet!

Vinny was shocked. Appalled. Disturbed. How was his watch doing? He glanced at it.

Damn.

Still too good for his wrist!

What is this craziness? What's going on?

Getting a bit flaky now, Vinny gave himself a diamond-standard promise to take it easy this Sunday. Give the relatives a miss and mellow and chill. And from now on he'd definitely cut back on the overtime.

If I didn't buy so much crap, I wouldn't need to work overtime in the first place, would I?

His taxi was waiting for him in the street.

Five

The restaurant where Vinny worked, *The Depot*, was converted from a Victorian warehouse that stood alongside the riverbank in Mortlake, west of the city. The bar and extensive dining area overlooked the Thames through a row of huge windows. In that part of London, the riverbanks were still lined by mature trees, and these were gilded now by the rays of the setting sun.

Vinny sat at the bar – there weren't any evening diners yet – and ordered coffee from one of the waiters, a very tall, blond South African of about twenty. If any of the other chefs had ordered at the bar, they'd have got a pout off this guy, but Vinny was the second head chef. A rising entity. He got served straightaway.

The waiting staff were bustling around, setting out the cutlery and napkins and little bowls of green and black olives. Their conversation (still relaxed at this time), together with the merry *Ching!* of metal on metal, echoed pleasantly in the capacious space of bare-brick walls and polished-oak floorboards.

Vinny always relished the ambience of the yet-to-be-filled restaurant. The melancholy of the afternoon had been exorcised and the liveliness of the evening had yet to begin.

He sipped his coffee.

'Nice to get away from the ubiquitous blaring television.'

Eh?

The guy talking to him sat a couple of bar stools away cradling a bottle of imported beer. Vinny could have sworn the bar had been empty. Well, that was just a gross failure of perception – this guy was far too solid and vivid to miss. He was one of your bright young things of yesteryear who had gone well to seed. Over forty by now, Vinny reckoned, his chiselled features just-about poked through the old-dog fat.

'What blaring television?'

'The one that isn't here,' the man said. 'You starting your shift now?'

'How do you know I work here?'

The guy pointed at the hatch behind the bar with the

end of his beer bottle. 'Seen you through there in the kitchen. Me and my current missis came here to eat a few weeks ago. You the head chef?'

'Sure I am.' Vinny smiled.

'No, honest,' the guy smiled back. 'You seemed like you were in charge of the kitchen. Or at least the little square of kitchen we could see from here.'

'I'm the second head.'

'Yeah? This place has a nice atmosphere here. I like it.'

'I like it too.'

Someone switched the lights on and Vinny glanced round at the row of windows. He liked to see the last of the daylight mix with the muted luminescence of the electric lights.

The guy glanced round too.

'Beats working in an office, all right. Do you create the meals?'

'Some of them. This place is part of a chain. A small chain. There are two other restaurants. The management lays down the general style.'

'Would you like to run your own place?'

'Why – you got one needs running?'

'I wish,' the guy flashed some expert dentistry. 'Though since you come to mention it, I do happen to be head hunting.'

'How's that again?'

'You're not interested in acting, or anything like that, are you?'

'What makes you think I would be?'

'A lot of waiters are just resting actors. It's well known.'

'I'm not a waiter.'

'Of course not. Respect. As for me, I'm a partner in a film company.'

Vinny scrutinised the guy. 'No kidding.'

'We make infomercials. And edit documentary stuff for some of the TV channels.'

'Sounds cool.'

Though, of course, telly's a load of shit.

'To be honest, it's nothing to get excited about – I mean the gig that I'd like to offer you. It's a few days work at most. But, we could use you. We really could. Not acting as such. You just have to appear.'

'Appear?'

'That's it. See, you got the right sort of face.'

'I've got the right sort of face…for what, exactly?'

The man fished out a business card.

'For this project. It's not a big deal. You just have to turn up and we'll arrange the rest. We're based in New Oxford Street. Check us out on the net. That's me, Ethan Wiseman.'

Vinny read the card—

Ethan Wiseman, Calilope Camera Ltd.

From the corner of his eye he noticed couple of waiting staff were hovering nearby, all ears.

He grinned.

'Can you promise me I'll be famous?'

'No.' Wiseman took a swig of beer and stood up. 'But it's a paying job. Interested?'

Seeing Wiseman was about to go, Vinny said. 'Could be, if I don't have to do nothing – strange.'

'Don't worry, you keep your clothes on. Look, I gotta shift. Sorry. Can you come up to the office? Soonest is bestest.'

'I'm off work tomorrow.'

'I'm glad you're interested, but tomorrow's Sunday. How about Monday?'

**

The first thing Vinny thought about when he woke up next morning was his new career as a celebrity chef. He was bound to have one. He was younger and better looking than any of the celebrity chefs up there already. And he was a superior cook too. No doubt about it.

Okay, Wiseman had in no way suggested that the shoot would involve food preparation, but once everyone saw how much the camera loved him, they wouldn't be able to keep his talent off the screen. It'd be perverse – a crime even – not to hand him a daytime slot.

But hold on a sec. Looking fantastic was essential, but it wasn't everything. He also had to be sunny and upbeat, like the rest of them. And to be sunny and upbeat he had to *feel* fantastic. But, as a matter of fact, he didn't feel fantastic.

He felt stale.

And worn and frayed around the edges.

Rough, even.

If anything, worse than he had yesterday.

That ain't right. What's going on with me, eh?

Well, for a start, he couldn't blame work

Sure, the restaurant had been busy, but nothing out of the ordinary. He hadn't even hung around after the last order, as he would most nights, enjoying a chillax at the bar while the rest of the staff sweated over the cleaning up. Rather, he'd called a taxi straightaway.

Restless night?

Nope. He'd slept like a log. Fatigue was Fahah's diagnosis, remember? And Fahah knew less about medicine than he did about cooking. No, what ailed him was this lurking sense of not being at ease in his own skin.

It sounded physical, but now that he came to analyse it, Vinny started to think that his malady was wholly mental. His mind was overworked, not his body.

I was on the right track last night. I've got to ease up on the accelerator. Chill. I've got to have more ME time. Got to do nothing for a spell. Like Fahah. He doesn't do squat and he's getting to look better all the time. If you're stressed, it shows in your face, doesn't it?

It occurred to him to check whether or not the stress was showing in his face now.

Okay. Stay calm. Let's just take a little looksee in the bathroom mirror...

Not such a good idea, Vinny!

He took a step back and cussed.

His celebrity-chef career was crashing and burning before his eyes.

A sound night's sleep had left his face looking... flabby!

There was no mystery here, however. He tended to pile on the pounds when he wasn't careful to keep up with his exercise routine. Seems his Sunday-morning jog couldn't be put off for a single second longer.

He pulled his running gear on and left the apartment.

It was half seven and the streets in Holborn were pretty quiet. He walked towards the City, which was almost deserted at this hour. Good for jogging. Also, night had left the air crisp and cool – that was good for jogging too. He looked up into the milky blue river of sky that ran between the City's stone facades and drank in the calm.

There, he felt better already.

When he reached St Paul's, he set off at a steady pace down Cheapside and turned off left down Ironmonger Lane before he got to Bank, circumventing the station by threading through the narrow and ancient side-streets of the venerable *Corporation*.

Poc, Poc, Poc, Poc...

His light, rapid footfalls on the paving stones echoed down the narrow alleyways. An occasional pigeon or two fluttered amongst the copper roofs. He passed the familiar old wooden doorways, which he only ever saw firmly shut and counted them off as he followed his favourite route.

He came out onto Old Broad Street, from where he put on a sprint in the direction of Liverpool Street Station. The pavements would be crowded there and as soon as he came within earshot of mechanical and human traffic, he turned off towards Throgmorton Street.

The noise of the world retreated again.

The city was so fresh-faced this morning. Every door handle, brass name plate and engraved window looked like it had been polished just moments before.

Vinny thought that perhaps he too felt a little fresher.

The cool morning air cleansed him.

The blood rushing around his veins was driving the morbidity out of his system. He was on his way to being bang up-to-date again. In step with the boundless march of progress—

What's that sound?

Prickling with instinctive alarm, Vinny stopped and cocked his head.

He could hear a distant and indefinable noise rising and falling with the restlessness of conflict.

Is that a riot?

The idea of taking a look flitted through his mind.

A riot. That's like history in the making. I should go look.

On the other hand, the sound had a menacing edge that he didn't like one little bit. And too, he seemed to recall from school that history had sounded dead dangerous. A massive number of people got blown up and splattered in history.

I can always catch it on the telly.

It was time to head home. He wanted to shower, change and take a leisurely stroll up town before it got overstuffed with tourists.

His trainers slapped the pavements—

Sploc! Sploc! Sploc!

—more urgently than before.

He expected to leave the riot well behind in seconds.

It shifted.

The noise circled round to his right, moving with amazing speed. It seemed closer. And shriller. He could pick out individual high-pitched squeals and screams. It didn't seem possible people could make such sounds.

He slowed, uncertain.

The noise swelled with shocking power and force. A lunatic cacophony.

And it came from right around the next corner.

Hair standing on end, Vinny flew in the opposite direction and darted down the first alleyway he came to.

The rioters seem to pour into the street behind him, just as he disappeared from sight. He could hear their bodies. Thousands upon thousands of smooth, glossy and...*hollow* bodies. They slithered, insect-like, against each other in a frenetic, swarming torrent. He saw them with his mind's eye. Long crawling things, gold-coloured and of exquisitely fashioned ugliness. He saw them so vividly they might have been creeping over his brain. Giant locusts with human faces.

It wasn't the screeching of rioters he'd heard, but the scritching of gigantic bugs.

Vinny had never run so fast in his life.

His every step covered six feet. He bounded down one

side-street after another, wrenching his ankles and knees
as he barely slowed to take corners. He had no idea where
he was. In a narrow alleyway between towering stone
walls, he juddered to a halt and—

NO! PLEASE!

—fell to his knees.

The swarm had split in two and he was trapped.

He closed his eyes and curled up into a ball. He could
hear the glossy mass sweeping towards him, countless
claw-like hands scraping at the stone paving and hard
jaws snipping at the air in anticipation.

Slam!

The alley reverberated.

And then…

Silence.

Vinny opened one eye.

A porter in a black suit was emerging from a doorway,
wheeling a sack trolley loaded with grey boxes. He did
not look at Vinny, not because he was ignoring him, but
because his indifference to a fellow human being curled
up and wailing on the ground was complete.

Vinny climbed to his feet. His legs felt like rubber. He
turned and jogged shakily away, in a hurry to be
wherever real people were.

Seven

New Oxford Street.

Just before ten-thirty, Monday morning.

Heavy traffic had already warmed and thickened the
air with exhaust fumes. Motion and noise were
everywhere. Vinny stepped out of the ceaseless flow of
pedestrians and stood at the narrow, scruffy doorway that
stood between two shop fronts. He double checked the

address.

This is it, all right.

The anonymity of the doorway was not encouraging and Vinny was already in a low mood. While walking from his apartment in Holborn, he had noticed everyone he passed appeared more functional, sleeker and polished than he did, despite the fact that he wore his new loafers, his new shirt and had the *i21 phone* in his pocket. The phone in particular was not helpful. It did not make him feel young, sleek and modern. Quite the reverse. Like when a old fucker drives a shiny new sports car and it highlights how wrinkly they are.

Not that Vinny blamed his *i21*. The phone was honestly trying its best. Rather, he reproached himself for working too hard over the past few months and getting himself into an overripe state, just when he needed to look like a prototype celeb at the top of his game.

Too many shifts, guy.

That was also his explanation for the brain crash he'd experienced during yesterday's jog.

That had been worrying trip, to put it mildly.

No worries, though. He had a true believer's faith that becoming a celebrity chef would solve all his problems.

Vinny went though the door and mounted the grubby stairway. On the first landing, he came across a woman sitting on a packing crate with a laptop on her knees. In her twenties, dressed in baggy retro gear and indefinably dirty, she gave him a toothy smile.

Because she blocked the way and because she looked like she owned the stairs, he didn't feel he could get past her without an explanation.

'I'm looking for Ethan Wiseman of *Calilope Camera Ltd.*'

'Is it Vincent?'

'Yes.'

She pointed up the next flight of stairs. Vinny stared at the well-gnawed fingernail doing the pointing.

'Keep going till you see… Well, you can't miss the office. Eth'll be expecting you.'

'Thanks.'

She opened her legs wide to create a gap and he edged past, his crotch almost nuzzling her snout.

'Hope you get the…job.'

Vinny climbed four flights and found Ethan Wiseman waiting at an opened doorway. Dressed all in black he looked like the oldest teenager in the world.

Hey, Vincent. Come in.'

'Thanks.' Vinny noticed how weak his voice sounded compared to Wiseman's Climbing the stairs had winded him. Just like he wasn't hundred-per-cent fit.

He sat down on one of the two chairs in the cramped office. Wiseman sat opposite. Their knees almost touched.

'You all right?'

Vinny had winced as he sat.

'My legs are killing me.'

'Strange, so are mine.'

'Jogging?'

'Christ, no.'

'Well, I was. I was jogging yesterday.'

Wiseman shook his head slowly, like he just couldn't picture it. 'Why?'

'I jog every Sunday, if possible.'

'You're pretty fit then, apart from your knees?'

'My knees are A1 too…in general.'

'Really? Well, it just shows – you can never tell by appearances, can you?'

'How's that?'

'I just never assumed you were an athlete, that's all. Don't worry, it's not relevant. In fact, looking at you now, I don't think we even need to do a screen test. We're good to go. Can you free up a few days over the next fortnight – starting tomorrow?'

'Wow, just like that?'

'Can't you manage it?'

'I suppose… Yes, sure I can. But don't I need some preparation first?'

'Preparation? Like what?'

'I dunno. Don't I need to learn a script?'

'You mean lines? No, Vincent, you don't have to say anything. And the director will talk you through the scenes.'

'What scenes?'

'What scenes? Hm, let me think…well, one scene's in a suburban kitchen. A normal kitchen in a normal family home. At breakfast time. Your wife will be there, and kids, I suppose. And she hands you a letter. You open it and read it. Silently. And frown.'

'Frown?'

Wiseman nodded.

'Frown. You just have to frown. It's not classical acting or anything. Then another scene is where you're walking in the park, on your own, and another is where you're in the doctor's surgery. You have to look concerned, but calm. I mean when you're listening to the doctor. Calm because he is very decent and humane. And so is your wife.'

'What does that mean, humane?'

'Frankly, I don't know. But it's in the script. The director will know, that's the main thing. Getting back to the story, last of all, you're sitting up in a nice, comfy bed, in pleasant surroundings, and your family's crowded around you. Lovingly. And that's that.'

'Why am I in bed?'

'Well, Vincent, it's because you're dying.'

These words stabbed at Vinny like an icicle. A big one. And even though there wasn't any icicle really, the sensation was just as unpleasant.

'I'm not doing it.'

'What? But Vincent, it'll be easy! No acting at all. You don't have to thrash about in pain or nothing. It's a promo for the *Mortlake Hospice Trust*. The last thing they want is anyone thrashing about in pain. They want to keep their clients reassured about the…process.'

'So I get a letter and I'm dying, and then I die in bed. Is that it?'

'Not quite. You never actually die, you're only ever dying.'

'Stop saying that – it's depressing.'

'No it's not. That's the point. It's going to be reassuring. That's the objective of the film – to reassure. You're on your own at first, dying. Yes, that's bad. But then you're dying with the help of the *Mortlake Hospice Trust*. And that's good.'

'No, it's not good.'

'It is… Well, not in reality, I suppose…but then this isn't reality we're talking about, is it? This is just a promotional film and you are only acting. After a fashion.'

'What I mean is, it's not good for me. Where does it lead to, this promotional thing?'

Wiseman's eyes went from side to side. 'I don't know. Where should it lead to?'

'To other stuff in front of the camera.'

'Stuff?'

'Celebrity chefs are all over the telly, aren't they? So I thought, *Why not me too?*'

'Ah, got you. You mean TV work… Um, well, you never know—'

'Come off it! I'm going to be dying in bed. Who

wants someone like that cooking for them? Cooking's about life, innit?'

Wiseman absently scraped a thumbnail over his pointy chin.

'You know, I think you're right about that.'

'So why pick me for this job? Why not a mortician? It wouldn't damage his career, would it?'

'I've tried morticians and none of them look the part. Too rosy cheeked and too ugly. You have just what we're looking for, Vincent. You're a good-looking chap for a start. A real poster boy. But that's not everything. Poster boys are ten-a-penny. What you got is this extra ingredient that makes all the diff. You give this impression of…like not being very well.'

'But I am! I'm A1 fit, me.'

'I said it's an impression. An illusion. This is a promo, Vincent. *Mortlake Hospice Trust* can't enhance their image with an actual dying person. They don't want someone who looks shit messing up their advertising. That's what you've got – this genius gift for making the terminal condition look great.'

Eight

At the restaurant. The end of the afternoon shift.

Vinny went into the tiny changing room and pulled off his chef whites. He was dumping them into the laundry basket when Charles, the small, dapper manager, stepped in and beamed at him with a Vietnamese-French smile.

'Hey, Vinny.'

'Hey.'

'How things going, then?'

Charles was so small and self-contained – he didn't crowd even in a confined area like this. His presence was

composed of high status and intelligence – classy stuff
like that.

'Why? What's up?' Vinny asked.

'Why should anything be up?'

'I don't know. You've never come in the changing
room and asked me how things are going before.'

'Always a first time.'

'Yeah… But, what's up?'

'Nothing! You're doing a fantastic job. As always.
Thank you.'

'Oh.'

'What, you don't believe me?'

'Yes. Why? Shouldn't I?'

'You got some worries, maybe?'

'Nothing to drain my brain, no.' As Vinny spoke, he
found himself yawning like a hippopotamus. 'Excuse me.
I'm feeling a bit tired.' He began to drag his shirt on, one
of his very best, which had become limp and dull in the
sultry summer heat.

'You've had a few days off, here and there.'

'Oh, on account of having things to do.'

'No colds or anything?'

'Nah. I'm not suffering from nothing except this
humidity. The kitchen's at max temperature.'

'That's true.'

'But so long as the customers are satisfied…'

'That's true too. But then, I don't think about the
customers *all* the time. That's putting the horse behind
the cart.'

'Is it?'

'Sure. We're got to feel good about working here
before people will feel good about eating here, no?'

Vinny nodded, wondering, *What horse? What cart?*

'It's a matter of ambience.'

'*Ambience*.' Vinny grinned. 'You know, that's your

most favouritest word, innit?'

Charles smiled happily.

'I'm glad to say it is.'

Vinny gradually stopped grinning. Once again, he wondered what the hell this conversation was about. 'You don't think I'm spoiling this ambience thing, do you?'

'Nooo – I wouldn't say that. But, I have to say, I see more than the average customer sees. Or even the average waiter, for that matter, and I have to say, you *do* look a little…preoccupied.'

'Oh, *that*. I didn't want to mention it, but when I had my days off, I didn't go dry-slope skiing, like I told some people. Between me and you, Charles, I was doing a little bit of film work.'

To Vinny's surprise, Charles looked seriously interested.

'That's *incredible*, Vinny.'

'Is it?' Never had Vinny heard the word *incredible* pronounced with such solemnity. It was like a judge intoning *Wowser!* to pass the death sentence.

'Do tell. How did you get into that?'

'I was, um, talent spotted.'

'Really? Where?'

'Oh…that's a long story.' He didn't want to say that he was talent spotted at the restaurant. 'And the film was only this promo-type thing and a lot less exciting than you'd expect. The whole thing only took a few days. I finished with it last week, which was a relief.'

'Was it? But still, you're an actor now, Vincent.'

'Not so much an actor. I didn't have to say nothing.'

'You were an extra?'

'Ah – no, I was the main dude.'

'The main dude? And you didn't have to speak?'

'Another guy did the voice over.'

Charles smiled politely. 'You say a promo. What were

you promoting, Vinny?'

For the life of him, Vinny couldn't think of a single credible alternative to the filthy truth.

'*Mortlake Hospice Trust.*'

After an inscrutable pause, Charles said, 'You've surprised me, Vinny. What a dark horse you are. Working for a charity and that.'

'Yes, it is a charity, actually.'

'It's great work you're doing. I know from personal experience.'

'You do?'

'My grandmother.' Charles said, hastening to make clear that his *personal* didn't mean him personally. 'She needed palliative care towards the end.'

'Ah, I'm sorry to hear that,' Vinny said absently. 'By the way, I never went anywhere near the *Mortlake Hospice Trust* itself. I was in a studio in Syon Park. So I haven't brought nothing back with me.' But as he spoke, Vinny had an all-too vivid recollection of lying in that bed—

my death bed

—and how twitchy he'd got. Sure, it was in a studio. But even so, everyone had treated him like he really was dying. And they all kept saying how good he was at it too.

Well done, Vinny! The more you do it, the better you get. Now one more time, eh? Final take—

FINAL TAKE?

Charles nodded sagely. 'I've heard making a film is slow work. Still, how amazing you are, Vincent. Why didn't you tell anyone?'

'Well, it's a sensitive subject. All the waiters want to be actors, don't they?'

'Ah, I see.'

'I thought they might get jealous.'

'Yes, yes, I think you're absolutely right about that. Yes indeed. I'll keep mum about it, don't worry.'

'Thanks, I won't.'

They laughed conventionally and Charles retired from the scene, only to make an unexpected come back just as Vinny was exhaling with relief.

'I completely forgot why I came to see you, Vincent. Your friend's in the bar. Fahah.'

'Fahah?'

'He's in the bar.'

'That's a first! He hasn't been back since he left. He used to work here, Charles, before you came.'

'No kidding? Great! Where's he working now?'

'He's not really working.'

'Oh? Well, we do have a line-chef vacancy coming up —'

Vinny was suddenly jigging on the spot.

'No way! Charles – I'm not putting him down or nothing, honest, but cooking is not at all his strength.'

'Oh. Right. I see.'

'It's a massive shame though, I'm not saying it isn't. He's like a great guy.'

'Of course he's a great guy! You're mates.'

They left the changing room.

Nine

Charles headed into the office and Vinny crossed the courtyard and went into the dining room.

Fahah was standing alone at the end of the bar.

'Hey, bro.'

Fahah turned and grinned. He growled his fiendish laugh.

'Hey, Vinny, my man.'

'How you doing?'

'Not bad. Not bad at all, amigo.'

'What can I get you? Want a *Daniels*?'

'Just an orange juice, my friend.'

'Orange juice?' Vinny had been appraising Fahah's broadly smiling face. It had never looked so spic and span. 'You in fitness training, or something?'

'No need. I'm fit enough. What do you think of the suit?'

Vinny hadn't had time think about the suit. Fahah's suit made it clear he was here to find a job.

'It's the dog's bollocks, coz. You look like you standing for Parliament.'

'Ha!'

Vinny motioned to the waiter behind the bar and got served fast.

'Mind if we sit? I've just finished a shift.'

'No probs.'

They sat at one of the rough wooden tables beside a broad window. From there they could look over the Thames. The dining room was full of afternoon sun. The bubbling conversation of the last of the lunchtime diners and the chiming counterpoint of cutlery and glasses created all the ambience Charles could have wished for.

This was, of course, Vinny's favourite time – when the restaurant was winding down before the evening service. He delighted in chillaxing here as he watched the Thames flow beneath the billowing tresses of the ancient willows.

And now Fahah was spoiling it, because any minute now he'd ask Vinny to put a word in with the boss so that he could have his old job back.

'Nothing's changed here, man,' Fahah marvelled as he gazed around with his kindly eyes. 'And yet it feels like I've been gone centuries.'

'Well, in restaurant years you might as well been gone centuries. Things change triple fast in this trade. Sure, it looks the same, but the new owners, I swear, they got no soul. Private equity. They're squeezing the staff to death and cutting costs. Long term, they'll run it down and asset strip, or some shit like that.'

'That's what I thought. It's all tired out, man. This place needs a total refurb.'

'What? No way! Or rather, I see what you mean. But still, as they say, if it ain't broke, don't fix it.'

'They say that, do they? You should tell them it needs a refurb. After a good refurb they'd get more customers, innit?'

'We're already rushed to death and—'

Don't tell him Charles wants to recruit more staff!

'—and we are at max capacity in the kitchen already. We couldn't squeeze another body in there to save our lives.'

'Sounds like they need a bigger kitchen.'

'Bigger kitchen? Like at *Micky D's*? This place is all about quality, coz.'

'Yeah, yeah, yeah, yeah. You got a point. Small is beautiful. But what I'm still saying is, with a refurb, this place could be a lot more beautifuler.'

Talking of a lot more beautifuler, Vinny took a rest from putting Fahah off asking for a job and instead just looked at the guy. In the benevolent noonday light, Fahah gleamed like he was straight off the *Bentley* production line. His usual sallow look was OUT and honey hues were IN. And he had more hair than ever before. Vinny narrowed his eyes. No – he could not see a join. That hair was growing fresh.

No doubt about it, Fahah was no longer on the wrong side of *drained and bald*.

You didn't reverse time like this by sitting around on

welfare, did you?

And then, look at the suit. He couldn't afford that, unless…

'Oh my Lord, Fahah – you've already got a job.'

Fahah grinned, nodded and savoured the moment. 'And you want to know something even more amazing?'

Vinny shook his head..

'It's a job in sales.'

'In sales!' Vinny's cry was a heartfelt protest at the bleeding obvious.

'Just guess what it is I'm selling.'

'Nah.'

'Go on.'

'Okay. Selling financial products?'

'Nope. Can't you work it out?'

'You like sports. Is it sports equipment?'

'I'll tell you, then – it's a health treatment.'

'Tanning, is it?'

'No, it's much more medical. I didn't mention this before, but a few weeks ago, before we last met up, I was watching films all night long and I just felt so shit and in the morning – late morning – I took a stroll to buy the groceries and I cut through the market and I ran into Gabriella and her mom.'

Vinny had trained himself to be upbeat about Gabriella. 'That was nice.'

'No, guy, it was nasty. I'd been up all night, and I was wearing the old running bottoms I've had for years and they're all baggy now and I hadn't shaved and I looked like complete shit. And Gab and her mom – they're so cool. You never know what they really think. They're chatting and being polite. But then, I catch a glimpse of myself in a shop window, because we're standing outside this kebab house and I see myself looking so skank. And I know then that's how they must be seeing me.'

'Looking skank?'

'And you know what the worst of it was?'

Vinny shook his head.

'Gabriella said, *Take care of yourself now*. Like she really meant it. Only, not like she meant it before, see. This time it was like, *Take care of yourself*, when you're talking to a guy on his deathbed.'

Vinny's heart missed a beat. 'That's a strange thing to say.'

'She didn't say it, but I knew she thought it. That's how *rough* I looked. Man, I'm telling you, after that, I staggered back home like I'd been punched in the head. But then, I couldn't sit still neither. I was pacing round and round, and the room wasn't big enough all of a sudden. The only way to escape was to go up to Hammersmith, to the *Pertemps Agency* there, and get a job.'

'And you did it. You went in and sold yourself to them. I always said you could sell anything.'

'It wasn't easy. At first they said they had nothing just then, but they'd put my name on file. But I wasn't having that. They would need to call the police to get me out of their office. In fact, I expected them to. I was like out of my mind with ambition and determination. I *told* them there was a job for me. They looked at me then and said, *Well, we got this commission-only job. In sales*. Okay, I didn't want to work in sales, and not for commission only either. Everything was wrong. But the thing is, I couldn't say, *No*. It was my one chance. And as it goes, I said, *Yes*, even before they could explain what the job was.'

'You crazy? It could have been the worstest thing.'

'The worstest thing was seeing Gab feeling sorry for me because I looked so *rough*.' Fahah's soft brown eyes ran curiously over Vinny's outer edges. 'But anyway, it's *E. T. C.*'

'Eh? What is?'

'This job is with *Epigenetic Treatment Centre Ltd*. Up in Epping. I went that same afternoon, straight from Hammersmith Station, using all the money I had for the groceries.'

'Awesome, Fahah. In the morning you're in the Bush and by the afternoon—'

'I had a job in Epping.'

'In *E. T. C. Limited*. I can't get over it. So how's it going?'

'I've been learning the trade.'

'You don't need to learn, Fahah. You're a natural.'

'*Know thy product*, that is what they say. What I had to do was try the treatment myself. For free. Well, I have to pay them back later, innit? So, the thing is, I do the treatment myself and then when I'm selling it I speak from experience. See? I demonstrate the product.'

Actually, Vinny had already begun to think there was something a little too good about how Fahah looked.

Unnaturally good.

'Are they into plastic surgery?'

'What? Not at all. I wouldn't do that shit.'

'No, course not.'

'It's based on – organic stuff. It makes you feel more… better.'

'More better? How?'

'It's hard to say. That's why this job's harder than you'd think. But looking at me now, don't you see that I'm… more better?'

'You do look…um, refurbed.'

'And that's why I am getting more and more customers. You know, Vinny, looking at you now—'

'What?'

'It wouldn't hurt to try it yourself, would it?'

'Nah. I wouldn't.'

'Remember, it's what you don't do that you regret, not what you do do. That's what I always say.'

'I know.'

'Looking back, when you're lying there in bed for the last time, because it's your death bed, you need to be able to say, *I did that shit, all right!* Don't you think so?'

'This is new, Fahah, all this talk about dying.'

'Okay, okay, not to overstress it or nothing, but while it's hard to imagine that day will ever come, it will. And sooner than you think.'

Vinny smiled sourly. 'How soon is last week?'

'How's that again?'

'Um, just a joke.'

'You shouldn't joke about your health, Vinny. You're burning the candle at both ends. Sure, you're experiencing all the benefits of that now, but what about later on? You need to act today, while you still have time. What you need is the general pre-disease cure. And trust me, guy, when you take it you'll feel so much better about yourself. And when you feel better about yourself, then you'll start to feel better about your environment and everyone else in it. This thing I'm talking about is better than a cure. It's an all-round improver. See too, I can get you a to-the-bone deal. It's a course of ten treatments. I can hand you the first session free, and then I can cut a deal for you on the rest. Listen up, Vinny, you'll get the rest at a *fifty* per cent discount. *Half price.*'

'Oh yeah? So how much is it for each session?'

'Ninety-nine, with the discount.'

'That's steep, for…fuck knows what.'

'Organic pharmaceuticals, that's what.'

'So now I know, eh?'

'Trust me, this shit works, whatever it is.'

Vinny smiled.

It ain't the shit that works, it's your golden tongue,

Fahah.

'Look, you ain't going to get ripped off. I can guarantee that, because the first treatment is free, no obligations. Okay? Then it'll be your decision, isn't it? And it'll be the right decision too, because, Vinny, you can't fool yourself, even some of the time. And because I know you're not going to fool yourself even some of the time, I say here and now that I'm willing to bet good cash money that you'll go back, again and again and again.'

Vinny placed his hands together and gave a little bow.

'Wow, Fahah, that was great. Total respect. I'm really impressed. You was always meant for sales, innit?'

The space between Fahah's eyes narrowed. The sure sign that he was lost.

'Does that mean you're going to try it?'

'This shit of yours? Nah. So have you told Gabriella the good news yet?'

'Gab?' Fahah shook his head. He was even more lost now.

'Coz – about your getting the job! Didn't you tell her?'

'Oh, I see. Yeah, I told her over the phone.'

'And?'

'And? Well, I ain't got much to say. I told her and she was really glad for me. Actually, she said we should meet up for a coffee.'

'Result!'

'A coffee at *Dunkin' Doughnuts*. She came with a friend, of course, which I expected. They was on their way to aerobics, so they couldn't stay long. You know the routine. Anyway, I'm just chillaxed about it and I say even before they get a chance to, *Nice to see ya, but gotta go.*'

'Good for you. Play it cool. You got to let the new you sink in.'

'It sank in instantaneously, bro. She calls me the next day. Virtually serving it on a plate for me.'

'You're saying you're back with Gabriella? No way!'

'You got it in two, Coz. No way.' Fahah couldn't help smiling. A cold, all-too-perfect smile. 'Trouble with Gab is, she's gone well to seed. Right down the slippery slope. Strange how I didn't see it before. But honest, bro, she looked shocking in the harsh light of *Duckin' Doughnuts*.'

Vinny stared at him. 'You're saying Gabriella's not good enough for you now?'

'It's cold, but this is the killer fact of the matter, Vinny – since I've been having these treatments my standards have skyrocketed. She just looks so damn *rough and ready* these days.'

Ten

The reflection of Vinny's face floated like a jellyfish in the carriage window. Behind the jellyfish, the houses and gardens that reeled past were so neat they appeared computer generated. In fact, even the clouds, so pure white and evenly suspended in a uniform blue sky, looked modular, like they'd been pressed out of fresh plastic.

And then the other passengers – didn't they look fabulously slick? He felt grainy and rough even compared to that grandmother type over there in the opposite seat. Why did she have to sit close enough to make him look as mouldy as her old dad?

When the train finally trundled into Epping Station, Vinny was first out the carriage and ten minutes later he was walking down the high street. He glanced into the shop windows as he passed by, trying to like what he saw, but the existence of new fashions and new devices no longer stirred any interest. Rather they stirred painfully melancholic thoughts about his mortality. Ever since playing a terminally ill man he had gone downhill fast. In what way, he still could not define, but he'd gone beyond wondering what was wrong with him.

He wanted a cure.

And here, in a boxlike and anonymous building down a quiet side street, he found *E.T.C. Ltd.*

The name was etched milkily into the plate-glass doors.

He stepped through onto an expanse of blond pine flooring that was punctuated by a few blocky easy chairs in prime colours and an olive-green reception desk

No one was in sight and he couldn't hear a sound. The world might well have ended the moment he walked in.

The muted pastel surfaces, bathed in a pale and diffuse luminescence, instantly filled him with indefinable dread.

This place had something wrong with it. Almost a smell. A stink that made him think of squashed insects.

He reacted without thinking and turned to leave.

'Pardon me?'

He looked around. A lady in a navy-blue business suit stood behind the reception desk. She smiled at him. Her eyes were black and shiny.

Like beetles.

'May I help you please?' Her intonation, though musical, was wrong. Each word was articulated separately, as if plucked from other people saying other things.

'I did have an appointment. Fahah, I mean Mr Hauzee, arranged a meeting with Dr Beriscoes. However—'

'Oh yes, the free introductory session.'

He noticed her ovoid face did not move, apart from her lips, which were large and scarlet.

'Yes, but—'

'Your name, please?'

'Vincent Iqbal.'

'Of course, Vincent. Take a seat please. Dr Beriscoes will be with you directly.'

'I don't—'

'Ah, here he is.'

Another voice, deep but smooth, said, 'Mr Iqbal?'

Vinny pivoted round.

A small man, wearing a formal blazer, was standing right behind him. He had a fatherly face bronzed by the sun and wrinkled by a warm smile. His black hair was threaded by grey and the irises of his brown eyes were ringed by white age.

'Mr Iqbal?' The man asked again, quietly amused by Vinny's surprise.

'That's me.'

'Juan Beriscoes, MD. Welcome.' He thrust out a gnarled hand for Vinny to shake. 'Please, let us sit for a moment.' He indicated one of the sofas.

As they sat together, Vinny glanced back and saw that they were alone. The woman at the reception desk had disappeared again.

Dr Beriscoes settled close beside him.

'Take heart, young man, Let me assure you that the treatment will ease you symptoms considerably.'

'And what are my symptoms, would you say?'

'Ah, but you present the syndrome in its most unmistakable form. Yours is a general feeling of discomfort with your environment, no?'

'Well—'

And not even your personal possessions – your clothes, wristwatch, loafers – not even these bring total pleasure any longer. There is always a tension between you and them. And sometimes there follows a crisis. Am I not right?'

'Could be.'

'Perhaps the anxiety spills out into bad dreams, or even,' he gave Vinny a penetrating look, 'daytime hallucinations? This happens when the sufferer is intelligent and sensitive in nature.'

'What is it called, this syndrome?'

'But you will not find this on your mobile phone. *Google* doesn't know about it yet. It is a very, very obscure condition. Not rare at all, mind you – but the fact remains that the usual medical practitioners will not be able to diagnose it. He, or she, will ask, *How do you feel?* And you will have to say that you feel fit, because you are. You are indeed fit – I can see that. Yes? Don't you keep yourself in shape and eat well?'

'Sure.'

Dr Beriscoes shrugged. 'So, what can your doctor say except that you are healthy?'

'But then, I *am* healthy.'

'So if, like your doctor, I say, *Go away with your mind at rest, for you are hale and hearty*, will you go away with your mind at rest and enjoy your life?'

'Yeah,' Vinny said weakly. 'I mean…'

'Do you enjoy your life, Vincent? Do you? Do you really?'

Vinny felt tears start into his eyes. 'I've stopped enjoying life, it is true.'

Dr Beriscoes's knobbly hand settled over his and squeezed it. 'There, there.' The hand was withdrawn. 'So! Let us get to the bottom of this problem. Let us face it, and name it, and shame it, eh?'

Vinny nodded and he hitched a gulp. 'Yes.'

'First let me give you some unexpected news. You are fine! Yes, you are fine. But still, something is wrong. But what? What is it that is wrong?'

'Yes, what is it?'

'It is this – that everything *else* has changed, except you. Everything else is getting better. But, you, Vincent, are not. You are getting left behind. And this, my friend, is what makes you so feel bad.'

Baffled, Vinny searched the bronzed face. 'Everything else has changed for the better?'

'Yes. Everything is improving, is it not, Vincent? The jackets, the shirts, the loafers, the sunglasses, the watches, the phones. Everything's being upgraded except—' Dr Beriscoes paused for effect. 'The *thing* inside them!'

'The *thing*?'

'You, my friend. You. You have become dated.'

Vinny bridled. 'Hang on. That doesn't seem right. I'm only twenty-nine. That's young.'

'Ah, but you are an *old* twenty-nine.'

'Twenty-nine isn't old.'

'I said, an *old* twenty-nine. Different thing. A few decades ago, you would have looked and felt like a *young* twenty-nine. Not anymore. You have not kept up with the times.'

'I truly have, you know. I'm not wearing anything more than three months old.'

'No, no, listen to me, please. I said, *YOU have not kept up with the times*. As I have already told you, everything else is moving forward, getting upgraded. It is you who is out of fashion.'

'What you're saying is crazy.'

'Is it? Then why are you here? Isn't it because your friend, Fahah, was an old twenty-seven once, but isn't anymore? You have seen the difference, no?'

'Well, yeah. He *looks* better…'

'You imply perhaps he is not really better?'

'That's right! You've got it. I knew there was something wrong about this improvement in Fahah, and now I think I got what it is. See, it's like this. I look a little rough and ready, sure, but that's because I actually do something. And I'm good at it, too. I've got experience. And I don't see nothing wrong in looking like you got experience. It's not like with the *iPhone*, the loafers and the wrist watch. They lose their value when they get a bit worn and scuffed. My looking a bit worn only shows I've learned something. My value's gone up. And anyway, what's the point of the watch or the *iPhone* without *me*? Nothing. They exist for me, not the other way round.'

Vinny stood up.

Dr Beriscoes looked disconcerted. 'You are not leaving, are you, Vincent?'

'Yes. But thanks for the introductory session.'

'That wasn't the session. That was the chat.'

'Thanks for the chat then. It's been a big help. From now on, I'm happy to let nature take its course.'

'Nature!' Dr Beriscoes jumped up. 'Don't you realise that if you let nature run riot you will be rendered utterly defenceless against the *Hursborg's Syndrome*?'

Vinny shook his head. 'Who's what now?'

'Professor Hursborg is…the one who discovered it.'

'But what? What did this Horseberg discover?'

'Come!' Dr Beriscoes beckoned Vinny over to a cleverly hidden sliding door in the nearby wall. He drew it aside to reveal racks and shelves of clothing and snatched up a random item – a pair of grey slacks. He stretched them wide before Vinny's horrified eyes.

'Look! Elasticated tops. Permanent crease!'

'Allah!'

'You can say that again. But would you like to know something rather interesting?'

'I'm not sure.'

'You'll be wearing a pair of these one day. And sooner rather than later.'

He fluttered the slacks under Vinny's nose.

Vinny took a step back.

'No way!'

'Yes! You won't be able to stop yourself.'

'I tell you now, I swear, I will never in my life wear such things.'

'Oh, but you will.'

'Okay, okay, when I'm as drastic as ninety-nine years of age.'

'Long, long before that. Don't you see? This is what I have been trying to tell you. Your possessions already look too good for you. I'm right, aren't I? But it's only going to get worse. Much, much worse. Why? Because everything's being updated faster and faster. Soon, very soon, the shirt, the watch, the loafers won't be mildly unpleasant in the way they remind you of your mortality, they will become utterly unbearable. This is the *Hursborg's Syndrome*, as identified by Professor Sarius Hursborg of the *Hursborg Institute*. The future is not going to be kind. The future is cruel. You cannot allow it to overtake you. Not without suffering severe consequences. Do you want to live in Hell before you even die?'

'Of course not.'

'Then consider the alternative. Professor Hursborg's methods are controversial, but they work, and if you don't undergo treatment, I tell you, Vincent, you'll be pulling these on within a decade.'

Dr Beriscoes waved the slacks at Vinny again.

'Stop doing that!'

'You won't be able to bear anything else next to your skin. Anything else will be *torture*. Grey slacks. Grey checked shirt – tucked in. That's the future.'

'It doesn't have to be.'

'You're right. You could take the treatment.'

'No, wait a bit. Let me think.'

'But there's no time. It's urgent.' Dr Beriscoes clutched the slacks tight, like they might fly off and attack Vinny. 'Beyond a certain age, the treatment becomes problematic. It doesn't work anymore.'

'At what age?' Vinny searched Dr Beriscoes's craggy face – the treatment had obviously come too late for the good doctor. 'Fifty – sixty?'

'No, Vincent…*twenty-nine.*'

This had Vinny popping with indecision.

A last-minute offer!

He ran his hand through his hair.

'I don't know.'

'No, you don't. It may already be too late for you. At least if you try the free session you will know whether or not there is still hope. If there is, then at least you can decide about continuing the programme further down the line.'

Vinny just couldn't make his mind up.

'Well, you have come all this way,' Dr Beriscoes cajoled, 'why don't I show you around? A quick tour, nothing more.'

Against his better judgement, Vinny said, 'Yeah. Okay, then.'

Eleven

Dr Beriscoes, conducted him to the other side of the reception desk. The glass partition behind it was divided into two overlapping sections that created the illusion of a solid wall, but there was a gap between them through which the receptionist had appeared and disappeared apparently from thin air.

They went through and met further partitions of

frosted glass. They were arranged like a maze. Vinny had to follow the Doctor closely so as not to get lost. Turning this way and that, they came to a solid, red-painted door. Dr Beriscoes pushed it open.

'After you, sir.'

Vinny stepped through into a large, lofty room. The rough block-work walls were painted red, like the door. Buzzing fluorescent tubes were suspended from the ceiling by chains. The floor was bare, dusty concrete. Here and there, tapestries hung from the walls. They depicted stylised tropical scenes in which large round eyes peered out of masses of luxuriant foliage. In the middle of the room stood two objects. The first was a massive block of silvery metal, about six feet square, into which had been cut the shape of a near-horizontal seat. The other object was a truncated pyramid, eight or more feet high. Its peculiarly irregular sides met at the top in a clear-glass funnel that was large enough to sit on. The body of the pyramid was made of metal, enamelled dark green. It bore a gold-coloured dial and a bank of switches. Running up one of the pyramid's faces was a steel ladder.

Vinny stared at this monstrosity and was put in mind of a magician's stage prop. It evinced the same tawdriness and contrived mystery.

Dr Beriscoes called tentatively, 'Mrs Hursborg?'

Several long seconds passed in silence.

'What's wrong?' Vinny asked in a hushed voice.

'Mrs Hursborg seems to have left us.'

'Good.' Vinny turned to go.

'Ah, Mrs Hursborg!'

A short, stout late-middle aged woman had appeared from behind one of the tapestries. Evidently it concealed a door.

'Juan,' she exclaimed, 'this is pretty poor timing. I've been waiting and waiting.'

'I know, I know, but— '

'Well, you *do* know, that's the point. If you were the one carrying it you wouldn't be so slack, believe me. It kicks terribly.'

'I'm sorry, I really am. It's my fault. You see, I kept this young gentleman talking.'

'You should chat less, Juan. I think it may be too late. It's gone off.'

'What a shame!'

'Well, as it is your fault, you'll have to arrange another appointment for the poor man.'

'That's the trouble, he's already twenty-nine.'

'Twenty-nine!' Clucking, Mrs Hursborg approached Vinny, her face full of motherly concern. She wore dark-blue skirt and jacket and brilliant-white shirt – the sort of pristine uniform sales ladies wear at perfume counters. Her skin had the texture and colour of yeast and she had a whirl of grey-blue hair that might have been spun from fibre glass. Her eyes were quite colourless. 'I'm so sorry dear, I wasn't made aware that this was an emergency.'

Beriscoes said, 'This is Vincent Iqbal. Vincent, Mrs Hursborg.'

'Hello. Pleased to meet you, Mrs Hursborg.'

'What a nice young man.' She shook his hand. 'You know, I think there might just be a chance. Sarius and I were running behind schedule last night. And mental attitude is important. It helps that you want to do the right thing.'

'I'm not doing anything,' Vinny said.

'But you don't have to do anything, dear. Just take a seat, lie back and—'

Click!

The door.

Vinny turned to see that Dr Beriscoes had left the room.

He wondered how he would find his way back through the glass maze.

'But I'm only here to have a look round.'

'You can look around as much as you like – afterwards. Please, let's hurry now. Remove your jacket and sit back on the chair.'

'What for? I mean, what are you going to do?'

'Shine a light into your eye. The *Kronoscope* will give us an immediate answer as to whether you're treatable or not.'

'You're not taking a blood test?'

'Vincent, we're not going to take anything *out*. All you have to do is sit. It takes mere moments.'

'That all?'

'That is all. And it's free.'

'Well—'

Mrs Hursborg took his jacket. 'I'll hang this up. Could you settle down on the chair? Lie back and relax.'

'Okay, okay.'

Vinny stretched out on the metal chair while Mrs Hursborg put the coat on a hook beside the door

He heard her muttering to herself, 'Tsk, tsk, *twenty-nine*.' She came back. 'I know it's not very comfortable, but it's not for long.' She opened one of the faces of the pyramid and he saw that it was merely a cabinet with two shelves inside. On the top shelf was a glass sphere, surrounded by a mass of pipe-work. On the shelf below was a mounted drum of clear plastic tubing and next to that what looked like the wizened corpse of a small animal. Mrs Hursborg took this and placed it over her face.

It was a mask.

From the centre of it protruded a grotesque snout of grey skin. A black lens glistened in the tip.

'What the hell is that?'

Mrs Hursborg's voice came out snorkly.

'The *H.S.D.*'

She stroked and massaged the snout and the lens glowed green. The green of decay.

Pretending he wasn't jittery, Vinny said, '*H.S.D.* – that doesn't tell me anything.'

'The *Hursborg-Syndrome Detector*. I'm just going to look into your left eye.'

She leaned over him and brought the lens close to his face.

'Ugh, what a nasty thing!'

'It cost hundreds and hundreds of thousands to build.'

'You'd never guess.'

As the glowing lens drew near, Vinny began to detect a pattern forming in the murky glass.

'See anything?'

'No… Wait, yeah. Oh no! So sick!'

The pattern had resolved into a gaping mouth, stretched so wide that the skin was beginning to rip as it crammed into its naked throat a filthy, squidgy, jellied living lump – a bulbous and finny, spiked and fluted incarnation of smelly, nauseating deformity.

'What is it, Vincent?' Mrs Hursborg's voice had a mocking quality to it. She found his repugnance amusing.

'I can see your horrible, horrible mouth, Mrs Hursborg.'

'That's not my mouth…it's…yours.'

'No! No it's not! Agh, *vile!*'

'But what you see – and I can see it too – is your mouth as it is revealed by *Zeta-Theta Light*.'

'Give me a break!'

'You see yourself, Vincent, consuming the putrefaction of time.'

Mrs Hursborg stood upright and lifted off the mask.

'That nasty thing I saw ain't me.' Vinny tried to sit up.

The metal was so slippery he couldn't seem to get purchase.

'Don't you want to know the result of the test?'

'Could you give me a hand here. I'm sliding about…'

'The *H.S.D.* gives you just *one* star out of five. We need to act immediately. Lie still please.'

'But I've seen enough!'

He scrabbled at the metal but it was smoother than ice. And even colder.

Mrs Hursborg passed her hand along the side of the chair and a huge and invisible weight pressed upon him. It was like a pane of glass squashing a fly. He could only just breathe.

'Stop it… Being crushed… Killin' me…'

'It's temporary. We can't have you jerking about, Vincent.'

Mrs Hursborg climbed the steel ladder on the side of the cabinet and stood astride the glass funnel on the top. Balancing precariously, she hitched her skirt to her waist, exposing bare withered flesh. She squatted down and out came a cunt, as dry and fat as an old hornets' nest.

It pulsed and it quivered and then it—

Splosh!

—split, releasing a sopping mush of bright pink that filled the glass funnel.

Vinny was screaming.

The abortion glooped down into the glass sphere inside the cabinet.

'Allahu Akbar! Allahu Akbar! Allah! Allaahhaa!!'

Something was moving in the filthy pink mess. A round, insane eye slid in and out of view, and then a scrabbling claw.

Gore running down her legs, Mrs Hursborg tottered down the ladder.

'Please…let me…go,' Vinny sobbed.

'A minute more and we're done.'

She threw a switch. A machine in the cabinet hummed into life and an ear-piercing shriek of pain came from the glass sphere as the contents swirled.

The monstrosity was being liquidised.

Mrs Hursborg unrolled a length of clear tube off the drum in the lower shelf of the cabinet. It had a wicked needle at the end, which she held up to examine. The pink pap raced along the tube and began to ooze from the tip of the needle.

'No, no, no, no!'

She thrust the needle into his arm.

'Gak!'

'I realise it might be little prickly, Vincent, but in thirty seconds you'll feel like a new man.'

The door burst open.

'Mrs Hursborg!'

'Juan! Wait – I'm almost done.'

'But Mrs Hursborg!'

'What is it?'

'*Professor* Hursborg!'

'Sarius? What's happened?'

'*Astra Zenica* are going to sue him.'

'My God! Again?'

'He's on the office phone.'

'Coming! Coming!'

Mrs Hursborg bustled out.

As the door slammed, Vinny grunted weakly, 'Wait …please.'

The pump in the cabinet hummed.

A dreadful coldness was creeping up his arm and into his chest, spreading out and driving daggers of frost into his stomach. He could see his bones turn into shiny metal. He became a skeleton of chrome, vibrating in agony. His flesh turned white, flaked off and fluttered down into a black, screaming abyss.

'Huh, huh, huh, huh fuggha! Hak! Aak. Uagh! Gaaaaahhhaa… *Aaaaaaagghhaaaaaa!!!!*'

Twelve

Vinny felt great – just great!

He'd woken up back in the reception concourse, stretched out on one of the blocky sofas. Mrs Hursborg and Dr Beriscoes were staring down at him as if they couldn't believe their eyes. And when he sprang up and told them how grateful he was for the treatment, it was like they couldn't believe their ears either. In fact, they seemed like they couldn't believe he was there at all, still talking to them.

'If this is how you feel after the free trial, the rest of the treatment must make you feel like freaking Muhammad Ali!'

Mrs Hursborg and Dr Beriscoes exchanged a significant look.

'But you don't feel, um, *freaking* now, do you, Mr Iqbal?'

'No, Mrs Horseberg. Not quite there yet.'

'Any pain?' Dr Beriscoes asked.

'Just a little stiffness. The next treatment will nail that, won't it?'

Dr Beriscoes favoured Vinny with a taut smile. 'Certainly will! *Ahem*, that said, however, we won't set the next appointment just yet. Everyone is a little bit different and you, being all of twenty-nine, need extra time to allow your system to calm down. For this reason, we think that we should give you another six months.'

'Really? That long?'

'Trust me, I'm a doctor.'

'That's right.'

'And *we'll* contact you, Mr Iqbal,' Mrs Hursborg said. 'Won't we Juan?'

'Oh definitely. No need to contact us,l Vincent. We'll be in touch. You see, you are a…*special* client now.'

'One of the discerning few, eh?' Vinny said drily.

Mrs Hursborg and Dr Beriscoes chorused brittle laughter.

'Exactly!'

The laugher stopped.

'Well, Juan, I don't think we should detain this young man any longer.'

'So many things to do, eh, Vincent?'

'Not really.'

'Us too, us too. Not a minute to spare.'

He found himself being hustled to the door.

Dr Beriscoes stuck his head out and glanced up and down the street.

'All clear. The sky I mean.'

Vinny glanced up. 'No, looks like rain.'

'So it does. I'd hurry straight to the station, if I were you, Vincent.'

A firm hand on the small of his back directed him out onto the pavement.

Vinny heard Mrs Hursborg whisper, 'Think he'll get there before it starts?'

Dr Beriscoes instantly shut the door and Vinny did not hear what the reply was.

What did that mean…?

Looking around, he saw with boundless relief that everything appeared to be its old self again – only more so. More rugged, more grainy, more real. The clouds didn't seem to be pressed out of pure and clean plastic anymore. They were grubby. Yes, it might indeed rain soon.

Ah – she meant will I get to the station before the rain starts. Bless her!

He walked away from *E.T.C. Ltd.*

Reaching the high street, Vinny saw the gloss that other people had acquired recently and which had made him feel so rough in comparison was gone. Or rather, *he* was the glossy one now. He thought back to Sylvianna and, in his memory, she appeared coarse skinned and oily haired.

In fact she looked… rough and ready!

Bitchin'!

He couldn't get over it. He just felt so superb. Perhaps a bit stiff – that was all. A Sunday morning jog would soon loosen him up.

He dawdled to observe the shoppers more closely. Strange, despite their humdrum, creased and greasy faces, they seemed to be favouring him with mocking smiles.

Huh, what's the joke, suckers? You're the ones who need the treatment now.

That said, he did feel he'd like to sit and take a coffee now. A chillax, in other words. The treatment had been by no means unradical, eh? No need to hurry. He wasn't nearly as busy as Hursborg and Beriscoes had insisted he was. And as for the rain – he couldn't care less. He wasn't that *old* yet.

As it goes, he wasn't even an *old* twenty-nine anymore. More like a young twenty-one.

Wait till old Fahah sees me.

Just then, he was passing by the display window of a fashionable clothing outlet. The mannequins were sporting a new line in casuals that caught his eye. His own attire, he noted, had not kept up with his treatment. His jacket in particular had fallen behind the times.

A far, far more desirable jacket was on show in the window.

Vinny wandered into the shop and began to stroll between the racks of clothes. He couldn't see the jacket hung up anywhere and he called to a shop assistant in the next aisle to ask for it.

'Excuse me, I— Oh.'

Vinny found he'd mistaken a dummy for a real person.

Staring into the blank face, he hesitated. The thing wore such an arrogant scowl.

Vinny smiled. *Hey, guy,* you *the man!*

Before the dummy had a chance to answer, a man strode right up and stood right in front of him. Vinny got a real close up of the bald, bespectacled face, all sweaty and red and truculent. What was this character and his laughably dim shirt doing in an emporium of youthful attire like this? He looked like an accountant or… Ah, that's right, he must be the manager. Just the person after all.

Yeah, I've seen this shirt…

Vinny was speaking, but his mouth didn't move and no actual sounds came out.

The man turned away and yodelled oh-so-wearily over to the other side of the shop. 'O Anth– o–ney!'

'Yes?'

A lanky, scrawny young man came into view. Receding chin and two long front teeth. Like a rodent's.

'Can you tell me something, Anth-o-ney?'

'What?'

'*What?* What is this doing here, that's what.'

The manager pointed a finger at Vinny, without turning back to him.

'Hm, I dunno.'

'*Dun-no*? You didn't put it here – is that what you're saying?'

'I didn't put it there.'

'But I didn't put it there either. So who does that leave?'

'Ashleigh.'

'Ashleigh? Oh, right, *Ashleigh*. But Ashleigh has gone to lunch and when she went to lunch this wasn't here. Mystery *not* solved.'

'Maybe it just got delivered.'

The manager stared. 'You joking?'

Was he joking? Anthony looked like he was thinking it over.

The manager expelled a whinnying sigh.

'Can you just move it? *Plu–eeeze*?'

In reply, Anthony stepped forward, placed his knobbly hands around Vinny's waist and lifted him effortlessly into the air.

Hey!

'Hey!'

Anthony turned.

'What?'

'Where are you going?'

'Er – to put this in the window?'

'Did I ask you to put it in the window?' A delayed answer suggested that Anthony was thinking again. The manager almost fainted. '*No, I didn't* – those are the words you're searching for. And we're not putting it in the window because… No, never mind, I'll tell you now in order to save time and for future reference. Ready?'

'Yeah.'

'We're not putting it in the window because it's wearing wick clothing that we don't sell and it's got a stupid grin on its face. So – take – it – *away*.'

'To the stock room?'

'Wrong!'

'The basement?'

'Kerrr–rect!'

'Okay.'

'D'hokay!'

Anthony carried Vinny to the rear of the shop.

Put me the fuck down, you rat-faced son of a bitch!

The shiny interior of the shop gave way to bare concrete walls and floors. The concertina metal door of a service elevator yawned wide.

Put me down!

Anthony held Vinny aloft with just one arm as they entered the elevator. He turned and yanked the door. It crashed shut so hard it should have fallen to bits.

Asshole! I'm not going to ask again!

The elevator sank and when it stopped, Anthony wrenched the door open again. The thing just about held together.

Dumb fuck…What's going on?

They entered a cavernous space – more unadorned concrete. The corners were filled with shattered office furniture and cardboard boxes that spilled coat hangers and paper drifts. Anthony headed straight for a green door and opened it. A low energy bulb automatically flicked on and revealed a tiny room half filled by a throbbing air con pump.

Anthony put Vinny down, facing him.

They stared into each other's eyes.

'Where the fuck did you come from?' Anthony said. But it wasn't a question directed at anyone else but himself.

Vinny was most unhappy. He hadn't been happy since he'd come into this shop. Surely this was a hallucination.

As Vinny watched, Anthony raised his knuckly hand and worked a stubby forefinger absently into one waiting nostril.

Disgusting drongo mother…

Anthony signed happily as he wiped what he had

excavated onto Vinny's lapel.

You dirty bastard! I'll kill you!

The *dirty, disgusting, drongo bastard* turned away. But he paused at the door to contemplate Vinny with a curious frown.

Then he shuffled back and deftly turned Vinny around to face the bare wall.

Vinny heard the door being pulled open behind him and then the wheeze of the automatic door-closer.

After a minute (an interval set by a Government energy-saving directive) the light—

Click!

—switched off.

SMITH VERSUS JONES

One

Steve was a shade late home from work.

Home was the neat suburban house at the end of Orchard Drive, a well-tended little cul-de-sac where nothing out of the ordinary ever happened.

The main streets were a different story.

Just a minute before, he had been forced to swerve and mount the pavement to keep body and soul together. A huge van had come from the other direction, dead in the middle of the road. As it roared past, Steve caught a glimpse of—

Beltop & Co, Removals

—emblazoned across its broad flank.

Son of a… I'm going to complain!

But minutes later he was kissing Belinda and he forgot about everything else.

As always, she had been waiting for him in the kitchen with a white-wine spritzer and ice. God knows, Steve was grateful for his white-wine spritzer and ice after nine hours at the office. And yet, after the kiss, he hesitated to sip from the tall, tinkling glass.

'What?' He asked. 'What is it?'

Belinda's delicately featured face tended to display the slightest nuance of emotion and a hint of tension showed in her smile.

'Oh, honey, stay calm… The house has sold. We've got new neighbours.'

'Neighbours?' Steve, a middle-sized and pleasant-looking guy in his early thirties, loosened his tie. Then he slipped it off altogether, like he couldn't breathe. 'Already?'

'Well, it has been empty a year.'

'A year! No way!'

'Don't shout, dear.'

'Sorry… But a year? God, time flies.'

'That's right, dear, it does.'

He took a deep, cleansing breath. 'So, when are they moving in?'

'They've moved in. They're next door now.'

'What?' He was indignant all over again. 'But the *For Sale* sign's still up.'

'No, it's not.'

'I saw it. Just now.'

'Looksee. It's gone.'

Steve went to the living room and craned at the window.

'But I'm *sure* I saw it.'

'Anyway, here's the good news. They seem okay.'

He turned to her. 'How do you know?'

'Oh, they popped round earlier.'

'They've been here? Already?'

'Yep.'

His eyes were drawn to his favourite armchair.

Have the dirty creatures laid an egg on it?

Steve was not what you'd call a social man…

He adored his wife and respected the memory of his parents…and that was about it.

When it came to neighbours, Steve most like the electricity substation that stood behind a tall hedge to the left of their delightful home.

Next best were the retired couple opposite. They were great. They spent so many months abroad, roasting under Spanish skies, that you might as well say their house was unoccupied.

Least loved had been Mrs Oliphant, in the house on the right. An ancient, retired school mistress whose haughty, patrician manner made, 'Good morning!' sound like a curt command.

And Steve had always jumped.

Then she had slipped in the shower and died.

End of term, Mrs Oliphant!

That's what Steve had told himself when he heard the news.

He wasn't mean, you must understand. He didn't shout, *End of term, Mrs Oliphant!* out loud. But he was joyful nevertheless. Because now that Mrs Oliphant was gone, Orchard Drive was a little more like God's own garden.

And who wants intruders in God's own garden?

Alien bodies?

Have the dirty creatures laid an egg on it?

...Steve raised his gaze from his favourite armchair and found Belinda smiling at him.

'Honest, I wouldn't lie,' she said. 'They're not so bad.'

He sighed. 'Of course not. Sorry, sweetheart.'

'They're called Quaid and Katherine Jones.'

'Quaid? Phew!'

Belinda chuckled.

'Just the two of them. At least for now. Katherine's five months pregnant.'

'Oh, that's just great.'

'Why?'

'There'll be months of squalling next door.'

'And there'll be months of squalling here too.'

'Don't say that.' He encircled her in his arms. 'Ours will only cry because of the racket next door.'

She laughed dutifully and snuggled into his chest. After a moment, she murmured, 'They're dropping round after teatime.'

He stood back.

'Bel!'

She couldn't help laughing again. 'Come on, it's for one evening only. They're like us. They're too busy with their own lives to bother with neighbours. And don't you worry, after the baby – their baby – comes, you won't see them at all.'

'No, of course not. That's true. It's the way we all live nowadays, isn't it? In our own private little bubbles… thank God. I'm a silly old martyr, aren't I?'

'Yes.'

They put their foreheads together.

He sighed, 'Flip, I'm dog-tired today.'

'Poor heart.'

'Mind if I sit out a second, for you know what?'

She straightened. 'Tea'll be ready soon.'

'Okay, okay.'

'Ten minutes!'

'Yes, yes, I hear.'

He took his pack of cigarettes from the sideboard, went through the patio doors and sat outside on the garden bench.

This leafy part of Manchester had once been industrialised. A disused railway line ran past the bottom of the garden. It was sunk behind an old hawthorn hedge that had flourished through neglect into a paling of full-grown trees. The dark-green leaves glittered in the low, mellow sunlight and the black, twisted branches were full of birdsong.

The evening chorus in paradise.

A young sparrow flitted onto the scene and hopped across the lawn and Steve's spirits lifted a degree or two. The little birds were always cheerful and busy. Always so happy in their work. When they flew, they almost looked like tiny spinning tops. The sparrow turned into a spinning top now.

He smiled.

On a mission, eh?

His smile was that rare kind that asks nothing in return.

Lighting his cigarette, he let his mind drift…

…back to *Serpinski Gaskets Ltd*, where he had worked for the past seven years – a mere plodder, a turnip, a non-entity amongst equals and a weaver of other people's ideas in the wonderful world of CAD.

Then, about six months ago, a new plodder had joined the firm. Alok Singh. A no-less solid citizen than him. No taller, or shorter. The same age. Who knows, they might even look identical. You couldn't tell, because of Alok's beard and thick spectacles.

And yet, the company boss, Michel Eschops, a dark-haired sixty-year old, who was consumed daily by agonising impatience, had taken an immediate and unequivocal liking to Alok. There was even a rumour that Alok and his wife had already dined chez Eschops, which (Oh, the outrage of it!) meant promotion might be in the air.

And so, because Alok was just as a turnip too, the other turnips at *Serpinski*'s turned a tiny little bit green with envy.

And, of course, Steve should have gone as green as the rest of them.

Except…something wonderful had happened.

It had been a day like any other. Not so long after Alok Singh had joined *Serpinski*'s, as it goes. Steve had been *turniping* at his terminal, when suddenly and without warning he had been inspired by an original idea.

No one else could have been more amazed than he was.

He knew most people get a lucky break once in their lives – he had found Belinda, for instance – but never had he suspected himself capable of having an *original* idea.

Just thinking of it now made him grin.

'Steve!'

He woke from his tobacco trance and stubbed his cigarette out into the old flower pot earmarked for that purpose. Then he ran upstairs to change into casuals. He hated eating while wearing a suit.

They chatted over dinner and Belinda observed, 'You're in a good mood.'

'Yeah? Well, I finally got the final modification drawn up in CAD.'

'Oh, super! Are you sure Mr Eschops didn't see you?'

'No, I was careful.'

'Are you going to surprise him with your idea soon?'

'Not yet. I have to be confident the design speaks for itself. He won't listen to me if I simply try and explain it. I don't think he'd listen to anyone on the team – except Alok Singh, perhaps. But that's okay, Bel, because Alok doesn't have anything to say.'

'Poor Alok. He doesn't have any new ideas of his own, does he?'

'Oh, he has his own qualities…'

Steve fell silent. A most ludicrous thought had just popped into his head—

Without Singh being around, I would never have had my idea…

What an odd notion! And it couldn't possibly be true... could it?

'Steve?'

'Um? Oh, just thinking.'

'What about?'

'About our visitors. I wish I could just unwind tonight. I've been slaving all day and my head's in a haze. Stuff about work keeps bubbling up into it.'

'Don't worry. It'll be a one-coffee visit, I promise. I'll make sure about that.'

Half an hour later came a knock at the door.

The Joneses were calling.

Steve answered and introduced himself to the waiting nondescript couple. The pair of them were well matched. Opposite ends of the same creature. The same mousy-coloured hair and light-brown eyes. Same sized skull – smallish and bullet-shaped.

Steve shook their hands. Cool, limp.

He showed them through.

'We've just been enjoying a stroll.' Quaid spoke without an accent. His origins had been carefully effaced and not replaced by anything.

'Oh yes?' Steve said. Unbidden, the word *foraging* came into his head.

'Scouting the area,' Quaid added, like he was correcting him.

'Still boiling hot out there, isn't it?' Steve said, thinking how cold and clammy Quaid's hand had felt. 'I was cooked in the office today.'

Katherine tittered.

Belinda greeted them with drinks and they all sat.

'Did you like what you saw, Quaid,' Steve asked, 'when you went scouting?'

'Sure,' he smiled. 'Not totally ungreen around here, is it? I like it to be not totally ungreen. I'm a country lad at heart. I grew up on a farm. Although Father wasn't a farmer. We rented it, that's all. Father was actually a doctor.'

'Whereabouts was the farm?'

'Surrey. Near Guildford.'

'I ask because I grew up on a farm myself. Only it was in Greater Manchester. And Dad was an actual farmer.'

'Didn't you want to follow your father in his foot steps?' Katherine asked. She had a high lip line that revealed her bright-pink palate.

'No. I wanted a career in engineering. My brother is working the farm now.'

'You're the black sheep of the family, then?' Quaid smiled.

Steve considered this remark.

Belinda said, 'How about you, Katherine? Did you grow up on a farm too?'

Katherine flashed rinky-pink gum.

'Only after a fashion. The housing estate I grew up on was built on farm fields. And actually, we did a school project about it for history – or it may have been geography, and we learned all about the farm and I found out the farmer had committed suicide and that's why the farm was sold. And the farm house got burned down not long after they built over the fields and now there's a shop where the farm house was and that's called *Fags 'n Mags* because that's all they sell.' She heaved a mechanical little sigh. 'It's a really, *really* sad story.'

'But it's also progress,' Quaid reminded her. They exchanged a covert smile.

Steve glanced at Belinda and said, 'So, Quaid, what is it you do for your daily crust?'

'I'm in packing,' Quaid answered, putting an emphasis on the word *packing*, as if it meant so much more than Steve could ever know.

'*Packing*?' Steve mimicked the emphasis.

'Yes, at *Porgem Packing Ltd*. You wouldn't know the firm. It's not major at all. We're based at the *Graisbourne Industrial Estate*.'

'I've heard of the *Graisbourne Estate*.'

'Doubtful. Just another anonymous nowhere noplace.'

'I may even have been there—'

Katherine piped up. 'Me, I'm an old-fashioned stay-at home. Just a housewife, buttering the crust, rather than earning it.'

'Housework is harder than a lot of full-time jobs, wouldn't you say?' Belinda said.

'Yes, I would say that.' Pink flash. 'Especially if the man doesn't lift a finger at home.' Pink flash. 'Not that I'm judging.' Pink flash. 'I can't, because Quaid's no good at helping out at home either.' Pink flash. 'But at least he tries hard with the doey-uppy work.'

'The what?' Steve queried.

'You know, the renovating. Though for the really, really big stuff we get the builders in.'

'We're having them in next week,' Quaid added. 'Of course, it's going to be a mess. A dreadful, dreadful mess. Dearie me, yes. But that's us, isn't it, sweetness? We just go for it.'

Katherine smirked. 'That's right. We can never wait to get stuck in.'

'And when we do, we really make a meal of it.'

They snickered.

Teeth on edge, Steve said, 'So Quaid, what is it you pack at Porgem Packing?'

Quaid turned and stared at him with his flat, dull eyes.

'Everything. If you've got it, we'll pack it.'

'If I wanted pack a goldfish, for Australia say…?'

Belinda chuckled.

Quaid continued to stare at him. 'Yes, *livestock* of all

sorts…and we can send it much further than Australia.'

'*Further*?' Matt snapped.

It was Katherine's turn to chuckle. She added. 'We don't need our little goldfish packing.' She patted the ugly bump under her breasts. 'Rather he's going to be unpacked soon enough. That's why we need to be extra, extra fast doing our renovations.'

'So you'll be putting in a nursery, will you?' Belinda said, suddenly oblivious to the tension. 'What sort of things do you have in mind?'

Two

Steve looked up from his desk.

'Still here?' His boss asked.

'Um?'

'I've brought this morning's meeting forward. Everyone's waiting.'

Steve accompanied Eschops out the design office and into the conference room. The big windows here provided a grandstand view of the brick and asphalt industrial estate that was the home of *Serpinski Gaskets Ltd*. The dusty sunlight illuminated row upon row of turnips going to seed – the other designers. They were planted in front of the presentation screen. Standing beside the screen was Alok Singh.

Uh?

Why had that particular veg been uprooted from its plastic-moulded chair?

Steve sat and Eschops positioned himself to one side, where he stood with his arms folded over his barrel chest.

'Ladies and gentlemen,' Eschops said, forcing the audience to crane round. 'Alok has come up with a most interesting idea and I thought we all should hear it about sooner rather than later.'

He nodded to Alok.

'Thank you, Michel.' The strip lighting reflected off Alok's spectacles, blanking out his eyes. His heavy beard isolated his red-lipped mouth, which was contorted into a mobile rectangle by nerves.

He cleared his throat...

For Steve, the presentation that followed had the quality of a fever dream.

Why? Well, to begin with, Alok's voice seemed to reverb and echo. Listening to it made him feel like he was flying away to some distant point.

Then he stared to feel intolerably hot. Something was wrong – very wrong indeed. He'd just heard the phrase *contra-inertia gasket release* and now he was perched on the edge of his seat, his heart pounding. Soon, he could see nothing in the room except that twisty-turny mouth, floating in a vast prickly cloud of beard as it hawed and buzzed out details of...Steve's one and only brilliant idea!

The Steve-Smith Gasket Design.

The blood drained from his face and filled his neck, making it bulge. He was prone to flush like this under stress. He itched to pull off his tie, but he wasn't at home now. His bright-pink neck must have caught Eschops's attention, because when Alok wound up, Eschops chose to get his reaction first.

'Mr Smith, what do you think? Is there something in this, or what?'

Steve couldn't stop his rancour oozing out. 'Yeah, there's something in this all right.'

Eschops scowled. He did not approve of Steve's faint praise. Everyone else took note of this and when asked in their turn what they thought they duly strained and strove to discover outstanding originality in Alok's idea.

Not surprisingly, Steve was left out when Eschops picked a team to produce the prototype.

The meeting was brought to a close and Eschops headed back to his office.

The designers, meanwhile, dallied in the meeting room and chatted. Laughed even. Their relief at not antagonising the boss was palpable and their enthusiasm for the project was tempered now that he wasn't glowering over their sweaty heads.

Steve watched for his chance and sidled up alongside Alok.

'Just unbelievable, Alok!'

'Thanks.'

'How did you get it – the idea?'

'How? It was in the back of my mind. Know what I mean?'

'No. Did someone at *Serpinski*'s sort of inspire you?'

'Inspire?'

'Maybe something they said? Something you happened to see on their computer screen, maybe?'

'No, I don't think so.'

'So, it was just lying there, in the back of your mind?'

'Yes. And then, one day, it came to the front.'

'What day was that?'

'Don't know.'

'This week?'

'No, long before then.'

'Have you patented it yet?'

'Eh? Well, I wouldn't would I? The idea has to be finessed. And anyway, it belongs to *Serpinski Ltd*, doesn't it? I suppose Mr Eschops will patent it.' Alok paused to stare at him. 'You feeling all right, Steve?'

'Yeah, yeah. Dodgy takeaway.'

'Oh yes?'

'Chinese.'

'Ah, Chinese I like it! But Mrs S won't allow me touch that shit. She is saying it is like putting wet concrete in your gut.'

'Yes, that's just what it's like. It isn't fair, is it? Shouldn't the person who comes up with the *whole* gasket idea get the credit for it? What you've got here isn't the *whole* gasket idea, is it, Alok? It's just an outline. A sketch. A notion. I can see loads of stuff you've missed out.'

'Really, Steve? That's great.' Alok's eyes roiled under the thick lenses of his spectacles. 'What's them then?' Steve could almost feel Alok trying to leech his brain.

'Well, it's not for me—'

'Don't be so modest, Steve. I'll ask Michel to put you on the team.'

'You're kidding?'

Alok was baffled. 'Kidding? How?'

'I mean, you got the best already. Paul, for instance. That guy's a genius.'

'Of course he is. Even so—'

'Nah. I'd be a dead weight, honest.'

'Quite possibly, but still, think about it, eh?'

'Think about it? Don't worry, I will.'

Steve returned to his desk and scoured every folder and document on the *Serpinski* intranet to check whether his private work had found its way onto the server to become accessible to the turnips. As he toiled, sweating in the celestial light of his computer screen, he cursed himself for not doing the most important stuff at home.

But it turned out he need not beat himself up. He could not find the slightest trace of the *Steve-Smith Gasket Design* on *Serpinski*'s intranet. It had stayed put on his surreptitious flashdrive.

Unbelievable but true – by sheer coincidence Alok had conceived the *Steve-Smith Gasket Design* all by himself. Or at least the outline of the *Steve-Smith Gasket Design*.

And now they had christened it the *Serpinski Contra-Head Gasket Project* instead.

No mention of Steve Smith.

Steve did not like this one bit. Unlike Alok, he did not feel *Serpinski*'s should have automatic intellectual rights to his idea. He had already decided to patent his work before he proposed to Eschops that it might be developed and manufactured at *Serpinski*'s. But he had kept putting it off, because of the costs involved.

More fool him.

The situation was tricky now that everyone in the design department were witness to the fact that Alok had outlined the basic concept.

On the other hand, Steve had developed the contra-head gasket design fully. The *Serpinski* team were still way behind. So, if he patented his design fast, he might have a defendable case if Eschops took him to court.

And yet the cost of the patent would be high.

And so would the court case of Serpinski vs. Smith.

Hmmmm, what to do?

He wasn't the sort of man to throw money around and he was not litigious in any way. However, these were exceptional circumstances. The fact was, he just couldn't let go of the *Steve Smith* bit of the *Steve-Smith Gasket Design*. It sounded too good.

I've got to get that patent.

Only he also had to explain it first to Belinda, didn't he? Naturally that might prove a little challenging. Still, he was pretty sure they wouldn't need to spend *all* the savings she had earmarked for the baby.

Just most of them.

Three

Evening.

He'd turned into Orchard Drive.

Whew, what a day!

You can bet Steve was looking forward to his white-wine spritzer.

He entered the kitchen through the back door, like he'd done every evening for an eternity in God's own sweet garden.

'Hi…'

Eh Where…?

Steve found Belinda in the living room, surrounded by glossy brochures. Brochures for new kitchens. And new bathrooms. And even new conservatories.

Her eyes were bright with excitement.

'I was round Katherine's today.'

'Next door's?'

'She's got some amazing ideas about what to do with the place. Mrs Oliphant had let it get very tired.'

'I remember her saying to me once, *If it's not broke don't fix it.*'

Steve had begun to miss Mrs Oliphant, relative to being stuck with the Joneses. No doubt about now, the cemetery's gain was his loss.

'Lucky thing Quaid doesn't have that attitude, or she'd have to carry on living in a dump. Look what she's going to do.'

Belinda began to take him through the projected improvements that the Joneses would be making to their kitchen. To start with, that is.

Steve positioned himself uncomfortably on the end of the sofa and tried very hard to pay attention.

His eyes kept sliding off the slick brochures like cold fried eggs.

He was only too happy to rely on Belinda's taste in domestic decor. But right now, Belinda wasn't talking about her own taste, rather she was repeating in her lovely voice what Katherine Jones, in her dreary voice, had opined.

With many a flash of rinky-pink gum, eh?

He didn't like the sound of any of it.

'Bel, why did you go over to see her?'

'Oh, she asked me round.'

'You could have said you were busy.'

Belinda looked puzzled. 'I just thought I'd go goggle at what they've got. Out of curiosity, isn't it? Aren't you curious?'

'Sure. But, you know, they weren't very…*nice*, were they? Didn't we say so, last night?'

'Mr Smith! We shouldn't run people down just because they're…people. We shouldn't, should we? We've agreed.'

'You didn't mind my running them down last night after they left.'

'Like I say, I only went round to nose. And I'm interested in what she's planning because we're planning ahead too, aren't we?'

'Yes, yes. The spare room. I'm going to do it up soon.'

'Steve, we've got the money to do a lot *more*. And I thought perhaps they've got the right idea – to freshen the *whole* place up. Before the baby comes along.'

'The *whole* place?'

'Hm.' She nodded emphatically in the way that charmed him so much.

But his chest was tightening up.

'Well, the Joneses have got an excuse,' he equivocated. 'Mrs Oliphant let her place get tired. You said so.'

'Yes, she did.'

'But our place isn't tired, is it?'

'Yes, it is.'

'Oh, come on.'

'You haven't been there. Anyway, the spare room's in a worse mess than anywhere next door. And you've been promising for months.'

'Yes, yes, I know.'

'Don't growl like that.'

'Okay.' He drew a deep breath, forcing it down into his chest. 'You know, Bel, I've got so much pressure on at work, it's ridiculous.'

Belinda frowned out of concern.

'Has something happened? What is it?'

Steve got off the sofa to wrestle with the problem of putting today's calamity into words. He heard the glossy brochures squeak below his feet.

But how the devil could he explain the urgency of the matter?

He could not tell her that Alok had stolen his new gasket design. It seemed the man had hatched the idea by himself. And when she heard that, Belinda would only conclude the idea wasn't as original as he had claimed. Or valuable. Looking down at her now, he saw himself through her eyes. To ask for their savings to patent his design rather than provide for their baby's comfort would look like he was more interested in his own vanity project. No amount of reasoning would ever convince her otherwise.

He sank back onto the arm of the sofa, sitting more uncomfortably than before.

'Nothing really. Just the usual...' He felt her gaze resting on him and he used a fail-safe subject changer. 'I worry, you know, about how I'll cope when... Afterwards.'

Belinda murmured sympathetically, sat closer and stroked his arm. 'You'll be fine. We'll both be just fine.'

'Yes, course we will. I'll start on the spare room. This weekend—'

'But honey, remember, the whole place is tatty.'

His chest – it was tight all over again.

Very wearing, that.

And where my white-wine spritzer?

'It's not *tatty*.'

'Tatty.'

'Not so much as it desperately needs money spending on it, surely'

'Meanie.'

'But—'

'Listen, Stevie, I want to live in a nice place.'

'How is it not nice now?'

'And I don't want our child to have to crawl over debris. Bits falling off everywhere.'

'That's not going to happen.'

'What's the point in your working at all if we don't have a good life here at home?' Her voice was beginning to rise. 'Home is where *I* have to spend all my time, *Mister* Smith. Remember?'

Steve felt his neck glowing. It was going to become permanently inflamed at this rate. The dilemma was cooking him from within, like a microwave oven. Only this oven used the heat of frustration, not microwaves.

And while he was being cooked at full blast by his frustration, he momentarily wondered why he should be a husband and a father rather than a maker of motor engineering history.

The inventor of the *Steve-Smith Gasket*.

'…and the dishwasher keeps packing up, the washer's on the blink, and if we leave things as they are now now, before everything changes, we won't have the time or money to do anything up for another five years and by then we'll be living in an absolute dump…'

He kept saying, 'But it won't.'

Belinda put a cap on that sagacious reply with, 'You just don't care, do you?'

Instead of laughing this off and appeasing her as he might have done on any day but today, he burst into his own tirade.

The sound of his voice, the bitterness of his recriminations appalled him.

It seemed like he had some new active ingredient acting on his emotions – fermenting them.

When all the doors had been slammed and Steve was sitting alone in the living room, listening to the sobs that sounded so remote in the bedroom above, his anger drained away and took his vitality with it. In five years of marriage, he and Belinda had lived in harmony. Even a mild argument had been rare and would leave them both feeling exhausted.

Right now, however, he felt sick.

But then, he had always suffered from this nervous condition that made his anxieties run to extremes. So, as the sound of his wife's sobbing faded away into an oppressive silence and darkness fell on Orchard Drive, Steve became tormented by the notion of a divorce. He sensed, rather than pictured, the solitary, chilly existence to come. Work, home, roads and shops – he had always known, deep down, these were only tolerable because he had Belinda.

There would be no more lingering kisses.

No more white-wine spritzers.

No more Steve Smith, really.

Just an empty zero rolling around the big, frozen sphere that fools called THE WORLD.

He climbed the stairs.

Belinda was lying face down on the bed. Lowering himself down beside her, he began to talk softly, confessing to having no hope without her, telling her she was everything that was important. At that moment, the *Steve-Smith Gasket Design* was of such utter inconsequence that mentioning it would have been ridiculous

After a time, the first words she spoke were, 'I'm sorry.'

Four

That morning, they were closer than ever before.

Steve phoned the company's secretary, Mrs Hatlespalle, to say he'd be working from home and then went directly to the nearest DIY store to buy materials with which to redecorate the spare room. After that, he and Belinda went together to visit the local bathroom and kitchen showrooms.

They lunched at home and for the rest of the day relaxed in the garden, stretched out on recliners. The late summer sun filled Steve's closed eyelids with a living radiance that ever afterwards reminded him of the golden warmth of their companionship.

At work the following day, Alok Singh sidled up to his desk and displayed a signal solicitude.

'Not well, yesterday?'

'Curse of the Chinese takeaway. A two-day curse this time.'

'Ah, that's bad.' Alok spoke without conviction. He hovered. Silent.

'Progressed at all?' Steve asked, watching him. 'Projectwise?'

Alok's eyes roamed restively. 'You mean with the

Contra-Head Gasket Project?'

'Nice title. Sounds good. Dynamic.' Steve glanced at the office clock.

'Steve, what did you think of it, really? Not the title so much as the idea itself?'

'Oh, I'm keen. Dreadfully keen.'

'Yeah?' Alok exuded a clammy melancholy. It was the sadness of a sponge saturated with the wrong sort of water.

Steve contemplated him with moody detachment. He wondered why Alok was as downhearted about taking ownership of the new gasket design as *he* (Steve Smith) was about losing it.

But that was a sore subject. He didn't care to pick at it. Alok's mysterious distress would have to remain a mystery. He had things to do. He had to get busy with being Mr Average again. A solid turnip doing what solid turnips do these days.

He directed his attention to his computer screen.

Alok's supple shadow slipped away.

After lunch, Steve phoned Belinda for a quick chat. Just like old times.

So nice.

Just one teeny-weenie sour note.

Belinda mentioned Katherine.

Apparently, the woman had been around and announced that Quaid had got an unexpected promotion.

Steve dismissed the news in a light-hearted enough fashion. And yet, throughout the afternoon, he was aware of a faint displeasure. Suddenly, he was a trifle *less* resigned about giving up the *Steve-Smith Gasket Design*. He kept hearing Belinda's softly comforting voice telling him that Quaid had been promoted. But telling him that had made her voice less softly comforting.

Hadn't it?

Quaid – that slithery name – had left a trail behind in his mind.

<h3 style="text-align:center">Five</h3>

The first phase of the ruination of the life of Mr and Mrs Smith life played itself out over the next few weeks.

The process was so subtle that he did not consciously observe the Joneses worming themselves into his head. But the day came when he could no longer doubt it. They had set up residence – a pair of smiling tumours.

Howdy, neighbour!

But even then he wouldn't have felt so bad, if only Belinda hadn't kept reminding him they were inside there by talking about them non-stop.

It was driving him mad.

Not that she driving him mad on purpose. She was not really on the side of the tumours. He must try to remember that. She simply wasn't aware that she was feeding them. Fattening them up on a diet of bile and envy. How could she be? In their deviousness, the Joneses had a way of seeming perfectly innocent to Belinda's mind. She couldn't see anything wrong with talking about them, even though, going by what she said, absolutely *everything* that the Joneses ever did was far, far better than anything the Smiths did.

Their success was relentless.

Quaid, for instance, got promoted every other week. And when he didn't get promoted, he came up with a new packaging design that might make him and Katherine multi-millionaires one day.

A new packing design? Why didn't Belinda get all swoony and excited about the good old *Steve-Smith Gasket Design* instead?

Oh yeah, that's right – he'd sacrificed that to improve the kid's room, hadn't he?

Stop that! You made the decision.

Yes, yes, that was true. He had acted nobly. That was good, wasn't it?

And being noble, he couldn't blame her just because his innards were dissolving in gall. Now could he?

But try as he might, he did blame her.

And Mr and Mrs Smith began to bicker.

And once they started a session, it got harder and harder to stop. Belinda could always heat Steve a few degrees hotter by saying Katherine and Quaid were nice people simply getting on with the job of living, and, by the way, doing it so much better than them.

Steve, like the average overheated pressure cooker, would blow his lid, which was costly, because, to mend the damage, he would always agree to match the Joneses's ongoing improvements to their home.

And so, after having redecorated the spare room, the Smiths had to play catch up and improve the kitchen and bathroom.

But the minute the Smiths' kitchen and bathroom were finished, the Joneses added an orangery.

An orangery for the Smiths now? That required a loan. And getting a loan meant that Steve had to bury all hope of ever patenting his gasket design.

God damn you, Bel.

He winced. Clenched his fists.

Stop. What are you saying?

If only he knew. He was just so bone tired. When was the last time he'd had a good night's sleep?

The night before the Joneses had moved in next door, that's when.

There, don't you see? It's not her fault, it's the Joneses. The wretched Joneses. It's their fault. Why can't we see it?

But that question didn't seem to have an answer.

Steve began to feel a dread for the future. Somehow or other he sensed that reality itself would become ever more slippery over the weeks to come.

Six

On the doorstep of winter, just as the Smiths's chilly orangery was being completed, the Joneses decided to rerenovate the kitchen. That is to say, the kitchen was going to be renovated *twice* in one year.

In the solitude of his thoughts, Steve voiced his opinion:

Those crazy bastards!

But through a supreme effort, he didn't set off an argument concerning the sanity of the neighbours. He avoided being openly *negative* about the Joneses these days. Bel didn't like his being *negative*…

…only, the thing was, the Joneses weren't alone anymore.

You see, the Joneses's renovations were always undertaken by *Mothcoat and Daughter Ltd* – a building firm made up of a pack of deformed and nimble creatures that arrived at half-six every morning in a rusty pickup truck. There would be half an hour of shouting in a non-human language before a cement mixer was kicked into life to grind away for the rest of the day.

A little light music to have breakfast by, eh?

This noise sounded like it ought to accompany frenetic activity. And yet, when Steve left for work, the *Mothcoats* never seemed to be doing anything, except nosing through heaps of broken masonry and treading rotted plasterboard into the mud bath that used to be the lawn. A stinking fire was lit out of sight. But the smoke wasn't out of sight. It got in Steve's eyes, in his nostrils, his hair and all over the car's windshield as he drove away.

And Belinda? By rights, she should have been aghast at the noise and the squalor. But no, Belinda showed an infuriating patience with the works next door, pointing out she was the one who had to put up with them.

Just lately, she merely looked at him when he blew his lid and ranted about the disgusting sight, sounds and smells of the *Mothcoats*. Now and then, to his enormous exasperation, she'd point out they had never heard a peep out of the Joneses while they (the Smiths) were having their own renovations done, and for that reason they should be more tolerant.

Meanwhile, Steve would inwardly curse her.

He had been doing that for…weeks? Months?

Cursing Belinda – his wife. How could he? What kind of man was he turning into?

The kind that never invented the best God-damned gasket the world has ever seen…

Oh sure, there would be remorse. He would tell himself never, ever to think these thoughts again. And possibly a full minute would pass before he did.

Was it any wonder they were arguing every night?

He took to fleeing the house, slamming the front door after him and driving off to some nameless place to park up and to wander around in a daze. The relentless traffic, the stream of the other drivers' hard and selfish faces, the aerial background throb of a mechanised city – all these would finally intrude onto his misery and remind him of the dreaded desolation of spirit that lay about him. Ah, the loneliness – that sensation of being slowly electrocuted. He could never bear it for very long. Soon he told himself once again that he must never make

Belinda suffer for what was, surely, *his* problem.

And so he would go home, apologise and, because she was truly a good-hearted soul, she would apologise too… only just a fraction less sincerely than the time before.

Of course, long before now he had noticed how terribly ill she had begun to look.

Bafflingly, she put off going to the doctor, and that caused yet more arguments. He would plead with her, saying that he was only trying to help by insisting she go. In return, she would accuse him of being a bully.

Oh, but how drawn her face looked these days.

Why couldn't she see it for herself?

Her obstinacy perplexed him. It went right against her usual conscientiousness about her health. Only after days of wrangling and begging did he finally persuade her come with him and see the doctor.

The bastard assessed her to be completely well!

Belinda reproached him for the entire length of the journey home. As he listened, his heart felt like a lump of stone weighing down inside him. And her words struck him like blows. There were no more little lacerations these days, only the heavy—

Thunk, Thunk, Thunk

—of an iron rod.

But he was past reacting.

Or so he thought.

Then she mentioned Katherine and Quaid had recently said she looked, *Blooming.*

'Blooming?' Steve bellowed as he swept the car round onto the driveway and wrenched up the hand brake.

Belinda's eyes widened. Fear? Anger?

'And they were right. The doctor says so.'

He spluttered in his incredulity. It sounded idiotic. 'They say you're blooming? I can't… God damn it! Everyone… The doctor and Quaid and Katherine—' He couldn't finish coherently.

'Everyone except you. Keep your voice down.'

It was eight in the evening. The damp of autumn cold had resolved itself on the windscreen like tears. Through these he saw the rubbish heap covering the front garden of the Joneses.

'Don't talk about them anymore,' he hissed. 'Hear me?'

'I don't. I know better.'

'You do? You talk about them all the fucking time.'

'Do I? I didn't I tell you Quaid had another promotion last week, did I?'

He choked. 'Why? Why do you have to tell me this?' His voice whined like a plane going down.

Belinda gaped at him in surprise for a moment. As they looked at each other, it almost seemed they both knew what was happening.

Then the comprehension died between them. Belinda went on like a clockwork mechanism. And so did he.

'And that's why they're now going to redo the living room as well as the kitchen,' she yelped. 'And on top of that, they're putting a king-sized porch on the front.'

Steve tore out of the car and into the house, leaving the door to swing open. He tried to take off his coat, but he was trembling too much to undo the buttons.

Belinda followed, looking more ill and vulnerable than ever. He struggled to speak, desperate to find the words to mend it all.

She looked at him, frankly bemused.

Then she was talking again. Saying that they too needed a porch.

'But the dirt keeps coming in. That's why they've got one—'

He was shaking his head, silently begging her not to talk about the Joneses anymore. He could even see them now …their mouths wide open and their pointed tongues shooting out to pierce his flesh, over and over and over…

He was screaming.

'Stop it! Stop it! For God's sake, shut up! Shut up or we're finished!'

She looked at him in astonishment.

Even then – at the very, very last moment – part of him still lived in her eyes.

He tried to speak, couldn't and…it winked out.

Seven

He was driving to nowhere.

Driving blind.

By one lucky stroke after another he didn't crash.

At last, his good luck brought him to the *Graisbourne Industrial Estate* on the downside of the city.

He pulled up on the wet, black road. The street lamps were spaced wide apart, letting the void of the night sag down between them. He couldn't see another vehicle anywhere, nor hear nothing apart from the—

Plink, Plink, Plink

—of drizzle on the car's tin roof.

Jerry-built warehouse units loomed all around him, deserted and left to dream alone in the ghost-grey of sodium security lights. Tatty signage displayed the company names. *Goobal Fabrics*, *Meebles Electricals* and *Bububen Extrusions*. Over there…yes, he could see the *Tile Centre*.

Of course! He'd been here before. Seven years ago, just after he bought the house, when he was doing a spot of renovation.

So long ago…

Before he had even met Belinda.

Momentarily resuming the skin of his old self, Steve experienced a nostalgia for the poor fellow. Compared to what he was going through now, he had lived once upon a time in a state of blissful happiness.

But wasn't there something else he knew about the *Graisbourne Industrial Estate*? Something pertinent to current circumstances...?

He remembered.

Quaid worked here.

Steve closed his eyes and rested his forehead on the steering wheel.

God, he was so sick of the Joneses. He had tried to escape them and merely ended up visiting the scene of Quaid's endless career triumphs.

All those promotions...

Steve sniffed back his tears, sat up and looked around at the anonymous, rain-swept hole.

All those promotions...here? Who gets promoted every other week in this dump?

At long, long last Steve managed to entertain the notion that Quaid might be a liar. How queer he'd never questioned Quaid's incredible success before, like he'd been hypnotised.

But if I could prove to her that he's a bare-faced liar, then...

Steve started the car and drove around slowly, reading off the company names as he went. There didn't even seem to be a *Porgem Packing* in existence. That was even better than he'd hoped for. The jerk didn't even have a real job.

He was lost in thought and stopped just in time. A row of denuded Lombardy poplars shivered in the headlamps, blocking his way. A dead-end.

As he reversed, his headlamps illuminated the words, *Porgem Packing Ltd* on a rusty sign. Behind it stood the shabbiest, most run-down industrial unit of them all.

So it is real. Okay. Well then, let's just take a better look.

He drove onto the deserted customer car park and stopped beside a metal tank mounted on a girder framework. The wet, black asphalt reflected the light of the security lamps, making it seem like a curved surface. To one side, a tall, blocky hedge of some evergreen shrub, scaly in the dim, motionless light, was breathing in and out.

It's the breeze.

He was standing outside his car now.

A faint but filthy reek circled about in the air.

He went to up the lone door and found a tiny white plastic sign—

Customers

A rotten little thing that was about to fall off the wall.

So tempting jus tot…

He reached out.

Look, Bel, a piece of Porgem Packing came off in my hand.

Was he crazy?. He would look like a vandal. *They'd* win again. Better to bring her here. Show her the reality. They could even go in and buy a cardboard box, eh? Then she would see that in this organisation pushing broom was just two pay grades below CEO. He'd leave it to Quaid to explain his other ten promotions.

You fucking liar.

He was about halfway back his car when a metallic—

Tchlinck!

—made him turn round.

A stocky man was striding towards him from the gaping doorway.

Steve squared up to him and the man instantly came to a stop. His large, blunt-featured face gleamed greasily in the rain-slick security light.

'Want something?' The man barked.

Steve stared at the large medallion that twinkled on the man's bare chest. The ruffed collar of his shiny silk shirt was opened down to the navel of his protruding belly. His tight black trousers glistened. They were flecked by sequins.

'Does Quaid Jones work here?'

As the man shook his head very slowly his dark eyes remained fixed on Steve.

'He told me he worked here.'

'But I should know. I'm the chief executive.'

'He said *he* was the CEO.'

The man's lip curled up and a gold tooth glinted. 'Perhaps your ears need new batteries.'

'Yeah? Well, I'll let you get on. Your chest's getting all damp.' Steve turned away.

'Hey! Come back and say something else. Hear me?'

Steve stopped straightaway and turned, catching a certain look in the man's face. The hate-filled glare of some skulking creature that longs to bite but is afraid to strike openly.

'What you hiding in there? Drugs? Knock offs?' Steve jeered.

'Why? Come to buy some?'

'Buy off you? Scum like you ought to be shut down.'

The man whooped. 'Listen to the hard man! Going to put the world to rights all by his little self.'

'I was thinking perhaps I'd go to the police.'

'No, *I*'ll go to the police. You're the one trespassing.'

Steve took a step forward and the man turned on his heels and walked back with a rolling gait to the door.

'Hold on, big guy, I want to buy after all.'

The man's meaty shoulders shook with mirth 'You're too early.' He cocked his head back when he reached the safety of the doorway. 'So piss off.'

'I'll come back tomorrow and buy a cardboard box off Quaid, eh?'

The man grinned. 'Yes, come soon. But you don't want cardboard. It doesn't burn like old MDF.' He stepped aside and revealed a badly made coffin standing under a spotlight. 'Now this masterpiece was upcycled from Mrs Oliphant's pantry – just for you.'

Before Steve could answer, the man slammed the door shut.

Eight

Steve woke with a start before the alarm could bleep.

Dreams had plagued him all night and they did not fade in the light. He remembered vividly sailing through infinite space to an oil-slick world, where he met an ape dressed as a disco crooner. It had backing singers – and these were a breathing block of scaly tentacles and things that squirmed in a metal tank…

The Joneses.

They had talked all together, their delicate voices scarcely louder than the hiss of fine rain and although the nightmare had made him sweat with fear, he had found the voices utterly compelling.

A gift for you, a Christmas pill to chew…

On and on they had chorused while he shivered with horror and revulsion, knowing they hated him. And yet, when they told him that he was wonderful (sneering all the time) he had become deliriously happy.

Just a dream – forget it now.

He turned to Belinda, who was still fast asleep, just as she had been when he had slipped into bed last night.

She did not stir when he rose.

He dressed downstairs, boiled the kettle and swilled down a cup of coffee.

Then he had to leave for work.

His mind was cloudy with weariness and he let his body do the driving while his thoughts wandered.

The dream sang in his head.

A gift for you…

A gift for you…

…a Christmas pill to chew.

And then, all at once, he remembered what the gift was.

A brand new gasket design!

One that was even better than the *Steve-Smith Gasket*.

So *that's* why he'd been so happy to listen to the warbling of the show-time freak and its friends. They had been telling him about the new design. He remembered now it all now, they way they had chanted just before he woke up—

Steve, you simply must plant it, make it grow.

You are a genius and the world must know.

And just think, Belinda might even love you again…

It's up to you now – end your pain!

What a damn strange thing the subconscious was! But he had no time to think about that now. He had to hurry and give shape to the new design (*think I'll call it Project-X*) in the wonderful world of CAD.

He was in the office…

The air grew clammy

H looked up to see Alok Singh standing beside his desk, holding a mug of tea.

'You have a thirst on you, Alok.'

'It is a very dry office. Have you noticed that?'

Alok's roiling eyes were at rest. They peered at him through thick lenses.

'No. I always thought the damp in this place was the

enemy. The dehumidifier's a Godsend. How's the *Contra-Head-Gasket Project*? Hit any probs?'

'Strange you should ask that, Steven. The *Contra-Head-Gasket-Project Team* and I are totally stuck. It's the *Unidirectional-Raylard Pin* – we don't know what to do about it. We know it has to be different, but…'

'Hm?'

Alok's eyes began to roll and bob. 'I really thought I had it in my grasp.' His tone was accusatory. 'I felt so certain. Now it's slipped away.'

'Yeah, the *Raylard Pin*'s the thing, isn't it? Crack that nut and everything falls into place.'

'You know what, Steve, I reckon you could crack this… nut. And it's not only me that thinks that neither. I mentioned our problem to Mr Eschops in my progress report and he said, *Try Smith, you never know*, and I said, *Sure*, and so, here I am.'

'You're here, yes, but I'm working on this at the moment.' Steve motioned to his computer screen, on which glowed the outline of *Project X*.

'What the devil is that, then?'

'Oh, just some old aluminium manifold design I found in the archive. It stinks.'

'Of course, of course. But the *Raylard Pin* – when you've got time. In fact, any improvements, any ideas at all, really, would be most welcome.'

As Alok spoke, *Project X*, shifted and squelched and quivered inside Steve's head, just as if it were being sucked out like a rotten tooth from its socket. He kept his eyes trained on the screen, the muscles in his face tensing as he strove to keep the top of his skull screwed on.

He glanced up.

Alok was still there. He appeared attenuated. And he swayed slightly from side to side. His gelatinous eyes were bloated to twice their normal size.

'Flipping heck.'

'You all right, Steve?'

He blinked. Alok Singh wasn't attenuated after all. His eyes were bloated only by his specs.

'Nothing to worry about. Just hallucinating.'

'Been on the Chinese takeaways again?'

'That's right. Had hardly had a wink last night. Terrible, terrible nightmares.'

'When will you learn, eh?'

'That's what I want to know. For a start, what am I doing here, working on this thing, when my wife and I need to reconcile our differences. Look, it's three already.' Steve began to log off.

Alok watched him with interest. 'What happens at three?'

'I go home and tell my wife everything's all right.'

'Doesn't she know that already?'

'No. I left home before she woke up. Those nightmares, Alok, they sent me out of the house in a daze.'

'That bad? Maybe the doctor—'

Steve stood up. 'It's not me that needs a doctor.'

'You don't? Who does then?'

'Lots of people. It's a sick world, Alok.'

'Amen to that.'

An hour later, with a large bunch of flowers on the passenger seat of the car, Steve turned into Orchard Drive.

Five rusty pick-up trucks were parked outside the Joneses in a semi circle, like they were Wild-West wagons warding off a Red-Indian attack. They were the most decrepit vehicles he had ever seen. To get round them he had to mount the pavement.

The front garden of the Joneses was worse than ever. Knee-deep in rubble, dented scaffolding poles and rotting plasterboard. Two custard-yellow cement mixers roared on the driveway, splashing wet cement onto the paving blocks that had been freshly laid just the week before.

No one was around at first sight, but as he climbed out of the car, the shadowy figures of the Mothcoats emerged from the grey exhaust vapours of the cement mixers and began to drift around without reason or direction, just like vapours themselves.

Nursing his bouquet of flowers from the acrid atmosphere, Steve headed for the front door.

'Halloo there!'

It was Quaid, poking his smiling face round his front door.

Steve nodded and kept his voice neutral. 'Quaid.'

'Profound apologies about the disarray.'

'Oh yeah?'

'Honest, this is close to the finish, Steve. I've begged Mister Mothcoat and daughter to get shift on, so you can rest in peace.'

Steve felt his neck prickle and fill with blood.

Fuck off you lying toad!

'What was that?'

'Didn't say anything, old *chum*. Well – can't linger.'

'I'm sure you won't.'

Steve scurried indoors.

'Bel!'

His voice instantly sank into the silence of the house and disappeared without trace.

His heart gave a sickening lurch.

In the living room a balled sheet of tissue paper lay on the floor beside the sofa. He looked down at it and knew it had dried her tears.

He didn't dare call out her name again, because this was like a bad dream and his cry might make her vanish.

He ran upstairs.

Empty rooms.

Most of her clothes were missing from the wardrobe and her suitcases were gone. He stood there hopeless for a moment and noticed his hands were empty. He'd dropped the bouquet of flowers somewhere or other.

Nine

Belinda's parents lived in a village that lay just beyond the urban sprawl of the city.

Evening dark had come on by the time Steve drew up outside their redbrick cottage. Winter had dead-headed the roses in the narrow front yard. The transom window above the front door glowed a cosy yellow.

Jeffrey, Belinda's father, a closed-down greengrocer (cheers *Sainsbury's*), appeared at the first knock at the door.

'Steven?'

'How's Bel?'

'Well, she's exhausted. She looks in a right state.'

But Steve was simply relieved that Belinda was here at her parents' house after all. Till now he wasn't sure. Her mobile was turned off and he had not risked phoning ahead in case her mother, Sandra, answered. He wasn't up to dealing with that woman just now.

'I took her to the doctor,' Steve said. 'I virtually had to drag her. She didn't want to go.'

Jeffrey searched his face anxiously. 'What's the matter?'

'Oh, the doctor said there was nothing wrong, but you can see for yourself, can't you? It's not physical, though. It's stress. We've both at our wit's end... The neighbours.'

'The neighbours? Belinda says they're very nice.'

'That's the trouble. She won't say a word against them, even though they've had the builders around for months and the upset and the noise is dreadful. Dreadful. I came home early today and five trucks were parked outside the house. The racket's enough to drive anyone nuts. And I only have to put up with it in the morning and evening. Bel's home all the time. I'm sick with worry, Jeffrey... Is she all right?'

Jeff was shaking his head. 'She's fast asleep in bed. Her mother's watching her.'

'Have you called a doctor?'

'You said she saw the doctor.'

'I want her to get a second opinion.'

'Maybe.' In the semi-light, Jeffrey looked like a talking shadow. 'I don't know what to do, Steve. Her mother said... Well, Bel told her... She didn't want to... She said, she didn't...'

'She doesn't want to see me? Did she say she doesn't want to see me?'

'No, *she* hasn't said that. You haven't fallen out, have you?'

'No, no! Not at all. This is all about months and months of strain. Terrible strain. It's not us, it's the *strain.*' Steve found Jeffrey's eyes impossible to fix. He was begging him to understand. 'The strain of the *neighbours*, Jeff.'

'But she hasn't mentioned the neighbours. Except to say they're very nice. A very nice couple.'

'Yes, yes. I do know she says that.' Steve clenched and unclenched his hands. 'But then, she hasn't a bad word to say about anyone. Which is good. But not always good. Because these people... They *are* to blame, Jeff. They really are. Bel doesn't need a doctor. I know what's wrong – it's the neighbours. Me, I run them down and get it off my chest. But Bel defends them just to live and let live. And that means she pretends all the noise and disruption don't shred her nerves. But they do, Jeff. I know they do. You can see she's not well.'

Jeffery was nodding. 'Don't worry, Steven, we'll get her to see our doctor, I promise. He's good, our doctor is.'

'He's good? That's good. If she explains about the neighbours and if he's a good doctor… Well, Jeff, I don't want to disturb her, but—'

'That's right. Sandra says she's absolutely exhausted at the moment. And the baby. There shouldn't be any drama, she says. And I agree. The baby. It's worrying with the baby. Isn't it, Steven?'

'As you might imagine, I worry too.'

'Oh, of course you do. But don't worry. Perhaps tomorrow… You could phone to see how she is, couldn't you, Steve? And I promise, everything'll be okay. Don't worry, she'll get better—'

'I need to see she's safe.'

'But she is safe – here.'

'Yes, yes, of course she is. I know. I know she is. It's for the best she's away from Orchard Lane. That much is true. Yes, it's true.'

'It'll be more peaceful and restful for her, won't it? But any road up—' Jeff glanced round to be sure his wife wasn't behind him.

She wasn't.

So he spoke his mind.

What was left of it.

'—when the neighbours have finished the work, it'll be okay for her to come back, won't it?'

Steve stared at the shadowy cipher, blocking his way to Bel, and on hearing it speak these words an absolute certainty dawned upon him.

'But, you see, Jeff, the neighbours are never going to

stop. For as long as we live, they will never stop.'

Ten

Although he had never been so tired in his life, Steve slept badly that night. When he woke, the first thing he felt was a stab of despair.

There had been no phone call from Belinda.

Going into work today was beyond him and he called Mrs Hatlespalle, Eschops's secretary, to explain that he was ill and would not be coming in.

Before he could put the phone down, she reminded him that a doctor's note would be required on this occasion, because he had taken two days off sick already this year.

'What?'

'A doctor's note, Mr Smith.'

Steve had not paid Mrs Hatlespalle much attention in the seven years he worked at *Serpinksi*'s. She was an undistinguished late-middle-aged woman. Perhaps he had viewed her with a hint of condescension.

'Well thank *you* very much for reminding me.'

But she had already rung off.

Later that morning he left the house to visit the doctor's.

For the first time in months, Orchard Drive was quiet and smoke-free. The *Mothcoats* and their infernal engines were nowhere to be seen.

He paused to examine the house next door.

The overlarge porch had been completed overnight. Elaborations festooned it. Brass carriage lamps, Chinese bells and iron wind-chimes. The more he looked the more decoration he could see. And even greater changes had been wrought too, things that he had never noticed before. Like up in the roof – two dormer windows with Dutch-style fascia. Surely the day before there had only been one. And that had been plainer.

Am I going mad?

At the doctor's, he didn't have to pretend in order to get his sick note. The doctor took one look at him and wrote one out. Furthermore, he was eager to see Steve again in the event he wasn't any better after a couple days' rest.

'But don't hesitate to come even earlier, Mr Smith, if you feel you have to. We can never be too careful.'

Steve was back at Orchard Drive by twelve o'clock and the *Mothcoats* still hadn't appeared.

He was sitting in the living room, staring down at the carpet.

Perhaps they've finally finished. Perhaps I should phone and tell Bel—

A faint tapping broke the silence of the afternoon.

The door!

Steve bounded up and opened it in a rush.

'Oh.'

He felt himself crumple.

'Steve.'

Katherine stared up at him. She too had been most unpleasantly surprised.

'Hey.'

She leaned to once side to try and look around him.

'I've popped over to see Belinda.'

'She's not in.'

'Oh?'

'No.'

'She's okay?'

'She is, yes.'

She leaned to the other side of him to see if she could get a better view that way.

'That's good,' she murmured. Her dark hair was more lank than usual, revealing her surprisingly narrow cranium.

'In fact, she's better than ever, because she's away from all the noise.'

Katherine stopped trying to nose past him and took a step back to look wonderingly left and right down the street. 'Noise?'

'Yes, that's why she's staying at her mom and dad's. To get away from the *noise*.'

Katherine's lustreless eyes silently returned his hostility. But they also showed something new – dismay. Fear even.

'Really? Then I should phone her. See how she is and say how glad we are she's getting better,' She stared at him and when he did not respond, her gaze wandered resentfully over the front of his shirt. 'But, I don't know her number.'

'Bel needs a long rest and plenty of peace and quiet, so she wouldn't even want a quick phone chat.'

'You think so?'

'I know so.'

'Sounds like you know her mind better than she does.'

'Katherine, I'll pass your message of goodwill on.' He gazed over her flat head. 'By the way, have your builders quit on you?'

He bared his teeth at her in a false grin.

She instantly bared her teeth back.

'They'll return soon, don't you worry. How about you, Steve? You're not at work today. Not well?'

'Very well. Thanks for asking.' He began to close the door. 'Sorry, have to go.'

In the last second before he could shut off her face, Katherine glared at him so hard her eyes turned white.

He wasn't sure, but he thought he heard her hiss.

He went to the kitchen to wash his face.

Do it now.

His hands shook a little as he called Belinda's mobile number.

She had finally switched it on.

Before he could say, *Thank God*, she was speaking to him.

'Why didn't you call last night?' She asked. He heard no recrimination in her drowsy voice.

'Your phone – but it doesn't matter. I came over. I talked to your dad. Did you know that?'

'Oh, I was in bed. I was exhausted.'

'Yes, he said so.'

'I'm sorry, Steve.' Her voice was monotone. 'I didn't just up and leave. I haven't left. Not really…'

'No, I know.

'I called Mom. I don't remember what I said. And then they came over. I didn't ask them to and…I don't know. Mom was crying. I came back with them and just fell asleep.'

'I'm sorry, Bel. You must know I'll… But… It's okay…' He flailed at the thin air, trying to pluck the right words out of it. 'You know, we'll get a porch.'

'Porch?' She echoed, baffled.

'Didn't you want a porch?'

'Not really.'

'But it was the most important thing in the world yesterday.'

'Yes, I suppose… Isn't that strange?' Her voice trailed off.

Steve felt tears running down his cheeks. 'Are you all right?'

She thought about this. 'I feel much better here, Steve. I'm sorry.'

'Is your father going to take you to the doctor?'

'Maybe. But I feel better here.'

Steve's restraint crumbled. 'It's not us, is it, Belinda? Isn't it the house? The…noise and stuff?'

'It could be.'

'Them next door.'

'Yes…it could be them.'

'Katherine was around this morning, wanting your number.'

'What for?'

'Yes, what for? It went bad when they came here, didn't it? Don't you think that, Bel? Wasn't it better before? So much better. Wonderful even.' He was crying.

'Yes, things were good.'

'Anyway, you feel better now,' he went on quickly. 'You're better being away from *them*, aren't you?'

'I feel better here, yes.'

'We can start again, somewhere else. We can move.'

'Move? From our home?'

'To a new home, Bel. That's what I mean'

'I think…' her voice began to float away, 'that I need to rest. We should both rest.'

'I've taken the day off.'

'Yes, you should.'

'You see, I've had an idea. I've got a new project on the boil.'

'Oh. Another brainy idea, Stevie?' She was joking in her old affectionate way. Only, it seemed she'd forgotten to add the affection.

'*Project X*. I'll take it straight to China.'

'So far away, Stevie?'

'Well—'

'Sorry, we can talk after I've stopped feeling tired. I'm really tired now, Stevie. It's too early.'

'Yes, yes, you rest – my love.' In trying to whisper, Steve's voice cracked. 'And – I'll call?'

A moment of silence passed, during which his heart threatened to cave in.

'Yes, yes – call.'

'I love you.'

'Yes – call.'

They disconnected.

Some minutes later, Steve rose from his favourite armchair and went through the kitchen and out into the back garden, where the air was soothing on his face. The sun shone and the day was mild for winter. He found he'd brought along his pack of cigarettes. Dropping onto the garden bench, he lit up and watched his old chums, the little birds, as cheerful and busy as ever. One tilted her head, as if to look back at him.

'We can get through this.'

Steve was sure at that moment that this was true. So much so that his agitation subsided a little. He closed his eyes and surrendered to his exhaustion. At length, he slipped into a doze.

Out on the savannah (beyond the moon-lit, fractured rocks where cold, watchful creatures lurk) a lesser beast cries out in sibilant complaint.

Steve jerked awake.

The *Mothcoats* were back out front and they had started their ramshackle cement mixer.

Steve mumbled, 'Bastards.'

And then, 'Oh, damn.'

His cigarette had fallen from his fingers and burnt out on the patio paving slab. He picked it up. Belinda would hate to see the mark.

He stood up and—

—found himself staring at a floating face.

He let out an inarticulate cry.

The face grinned at him.

'Hallo there!'

It was Quaid, poking his head over the garden fence.

'You startled the life out of me.'

'Sorry…about the noise. Mate!'

Steve hated being called *mate*. A fact he had never told Quaid.

'You're not at work either?'

'Day off.'

'Porgem giving you a rest?'

'I get a day off every month – it's in my contract.'

'Nice of Porgem to give you such a generous contract.'

'It's the standard company contract. I don't know who came up with it originally.' He smiled to himself. 'It is very old.'

'Anyway, give my regards to – *Porgem*. We spoke the other night. Delightful chap. So good to see someone keeping the spirit of disco alive.'

Quaid's grin broadened.

'You're mellow today, Steve. But then, it's such a mild, mellow day, isn't it?'

'Except for *your* noise and *your* dirt.'

'But it's the price we pay for progress – no?'

'I suppose when it's your noise and your dirt you don't feel so bad about it, eh?'

'Can't say I'm in love with the noise and dirt, but then, I'm off to *Elmsdale Golfclub* soon. I joined yesterday. It's so calm and peaceful there. Quieter than most cemeteries—'

'Good for you. But rough on Katherine, leaving her behind in the noise and dirt.'

'She's never complained. And I expect she'll still be here when I get back.' Quaid winked.

'Oh, I wouldn't be too sure about that. She might have been carted off to hospital. She is supposed to be pregnant, after all.'

'*We* are, Steve. It's the modern idiom to say *we*.'

'Not that I take much notice, but I do remember Belinda saying Katherine was five months gone.'

'She is.'

'But that was when you moved in. And that, Quaid, would mean Katherine must be eleven month's pregnant by now – which is impossible, isn't it, Quaid?'

'You are right.' Quaid smiled and his mouth bowed up right across his face, almost reaching his ears. Steve blinked and the smile was gone. 'It *is* impossible. And so that means you must be dreadfully wrong in your recollection of events. Is it a fever you've got? What did the doctor say?'

'What doctor?'

'The one you told Katherine you'd seen.'

'I didn't tell her that. Which means one of you is lying.'

'What?'

'You're *lying*.'

'That's fighting talk, buddy.'

'Yes? And what are you going to do about it?'

In reply, Quaid's bland, doughy face became angular and pointed. The eyes seemed to deflate and turn hard and flat.

'I'm going to be the better man, Steve. The good and decent neighbour you deserve. I'm going to urge you most strongly to get a porch. It's what Belinda wants. You want Belinda back home, don't you? Yes, more than anything, I believe… And so, more than anything, you want a porch.'

Eleven

Steve had been in the living room for an hour, his mind

racing as he feverishly sketched various designs for a porch that would more than match the one next door. But before he could start calling builders, he needed to get Belinda's opinion. He stared down at the phone, wondering what was wrong.

Belinda didn't want a porch anymore. She couldn't even remember wanting a porch.

His ideas for the new porch became jumbled in his mind. The urge to plan, to shop and to purchase diminished and he was granted a brief moment of clarity.

Quaid put the whole idea into my head.

And then,

This is what they were doing to Bel.

He exclaimed aloud.

'What's going on with these people?'

They were hypnotists or something. They had attacked Belinda behind his back and now they were attacking him.

He began to hunt them down.

He found no sign of Quaid and Katherine Jones on any of the social media sites.

He Googled, *How do find out where someone used to live?*

The results included a number of adverts for companies offering tracing services.

He phoned one at random.

A snippy female voice answered, 'Jones and Jones Personal Tracing Agency, how may I help you?'

He jabbed *disconnect* on his the phone. Why had he chosen them? Their name was clear as daylight on the screen, *JONES and JONES Personal Tracing Agency.* Was he so tired he couldn't read properly? Or was the name Jones so bland, so common that as to be near invisible?

Yes, they hid themselves, didn't they? Their nature

was to be evasive and cunning. Like the way they had appeared one day from nowhere – guilefully slithering into paradise while he had been at work... There had been no warning at all.

But no, that wasn't quite right.

Even though that day was an eternity ago, he clearly remembered the removal van that had forced him to mount the pavement because it had been driving in the middle of the road.

And the removal van was in the middle of the road because...

It had just turned out of Orchard Drive!

And as it roared past, Steve had caught a glimpse of—
Beltop & Co, Removals
on its broad flank.

They must have been the firm to have moved the Joneses, mustn't they?

Oh, please, God!

Their phone number and the manager's name, Eddie Davant, was on their web site.

Steve called.

A woman answered. '*Beltop Household Logistics,* how may we help you?'

'Hello, I'd like to speak with Mr Davant.'

'Whom may I say is calling, please?'

Did the receptionist sound exactly like the one in *JONES and JONES Personal Tracing Agency* – or was it his imagination?

'My name is...Michel Eschops.'

'And what is it concerning, please?'

'It's complicated to explain...'

'Pardon?'

'It's the *Revenue and Customs.*'

'Could you repeat that, please?'

'The tax office. I work for the tax department. I would

like to speak to Mr Davant straight away.'

'Please hold.'

Light classical music replaced the voice, a tune that Steve recognised from an advert on television. He refused to let himself think. If he thought about what he was doing, he would founder and go under.

A deep voice lumbered into his ear. 'Hello?' Steve pictured an elephant trying to tip toe.

'Mr Davant?'

'Yes.'

'I'm Michel Eschops, I work for a division of *Experian*—'

'I was just told you worked for the *Revenue*.'

'We are subcontracted to *Revenue and Customs*.'

'You're not actually from the tax office?'

'We're subcontracted to the *Revenue and Customs* to investigate cases of fraud and tax evasion,' Steve said, hoping this guy read the same newspapers as him.

'Do you really?' The tip-toeing elephant teetered a little.

'Oh, we're not chasing you, Mr Davant, let me assure you of that.'

'Of course not.' Davant chuckled from a wide, dry gullet. 'How can I help you then?'

'A very simple piece of information. It may seem irrelevant, or a bit pointless, but you should understand that when we're building a case, we have to double check and reconfirm absolutely every detail of our information.'

'Yes, I think I can see that.'

'So what I'd like is this, to check whether you were hired to move house for a certain Mr and Mrs Quaid Jones.'

'Well, I don't know the name of every client we've had.'

'But you have records—'

'Sure we do. I'd have to ask… May I call you back?'

'No, I'll wait Mr Davant.'

'But—'

'I'm constantly on the phone and I'd prefer to—'

'We could fax it.'

'No, I'll hold. If we need anything in writing, believe me, the *Revenue* will contact you. Or more likely, the police will.'

'The police?'

'Yes, Mr Davant. You see, this is a lot more than simple tax evasion. We believe Mr and Mrs Quaid Jones to be implicated in a…paedophile ring.'

'Oh. Christ.'

'Indeed. They've been using untracked funds to maintain their…ring.'

'Well, okay. I'll have to… When are we supposed to have moved these people?'

'Late August, last year. They now reside at five, Orchard Drive, the postcode is M55 8MN. What I'd like, as a matter of urgency, actually, is their former address.'

A moment passed and then Davant muttered curtly, 'Right. Hold, please.'

Steve sat back and let out a long, silent sigh of relief. He was sweating badly and holding the phone against his ear so hard it hurt.

'Mr Eschops?' The elephant was back.

'Mr Devant?'

'Here's the information. I really hope this helps. I really hope you get those – people.'

Twelve

'I *am* going to get them!'

Steve surveyed Orchard Drive from his front window.

Rags of white smoke flew past from where the wind tore them off a smouldering fire. The incessant rasping chug of the cement mixer had started up again, having briefly fallen silent during his phone conversation. Steve saw now that the Joneses's car was missing from the drive, so perhaps the mixer had been stopped so that Quaid could issue instructions to the *Mothcoats*.

Even though he felt bone-weary, he didn't feel he could delay. This was the first advantage he had gained over the Joneses and he sensed that he hadn't much time left.

In fact, Steve sensed he was fighting for his life.

Soon, the silky voice of his satnav was guiding him to a pretty area on the outskirts of the city, where a village had been swallowed by urban sprawl. The former residence of the Joneses stood out a mile. It was the last house on a neat, well-kept cul-de-sac.

Steve scrutinised the place from his car.

The porch was half the size of the whole house. It had white pillars – both pilaster and columnar – and an elaborate copper cupola, or cage, from which a porphyry statue of baby Siamese twins peeped out with four eyes. The attic had been converted to a third storey and a new attic put on top of that and itself converted, with projecting dormer windows. The whole structure seemed ready to topple over.

The Joneses were well underway in reproducing this monstrosity on Orchard Drive.

However, they hadn't started the garden yet. Steve could see what was to come when he climbed out the car and walked through a phantasmagorical landscape of a sugar-coated fairytale. The centrepiece was an enormous working fountain in the shape of lasciviously entwined cupids, scowling as they vomited water.

He reached the door. Its polished wood and brass

furniture it put him in mind of a coffin. The door button was fashioned as a leering, fat child's face – it had a harelip. He pushed its nose and there came a burst of that flesh-crawling yodelling that obese women did in operas.

A heavy silence followed

Steve – this IS a coffin.

He rang again. Still no answer.

There never would be an answer.

The water of the fountain chuckled and burbled and mocked at his back.

He turned and glowered at the jeering cupids.

I'm not giving up. You'll see. I'll call on every house on the street, if I have to.

He started next door.

This was unremarkable looking. The home of some middle-ranking executive, or a designer for a small engineering company. The tasteful pink and grey curtains were the only hint of individuality.

As soon as he knocked, the door was opened by a dark-haired, willowy woman in her thirties. She wore a high-necked gown of dark-blue silk that reached to her feet.

'I'm very sorry to bother you. I'm looking for Mr and Mrs Quaid Jones.'

The woman had a brisk manner. 'They've gone.' A faint smile played around her lips as she stared at him.

'Gone, yes. Did you know them?'

'Only met them once or twice. Why?'

'Ah, I work for *Experian*. It's a credit agency—'

'I know it is.'

'Well, we're trying to trace Mr and Mrs Jones.'

'Is that so?' Her smile, rather hirsute he now noticed, broadened. 'In the red, eh?'

'Could be.'

She laughed. 'I'm not surprised. I met them once and

– you get a feeling, don't you?'

'You did?'

'Just a feeling. They didn't give us any trouble. As soon as we put the deposit down they moved out of here and we never saw them again. We communicated through our solicitors.'

She began to frown. Steve was looking a bit dumb.

'Sorry, do you mean you brought *this* house off them?'

'Yes. Of course I do.'

'But then—'

'What?'

'The Jones lived *here*? Not next door?'

'That's right.' She placed a slight emphasis on every word. 'The Jones lived here not next door.'

'I'm sorry, it's our mistake. I was given the address for next door.' He couldn't help standing back and looking again at the plain house where the Joneses had once lived. 'This is strange…'

'Oh?' The woman's eyes held him in smiling derision for a moment and then drifted over him speculatively. 'With detectives like you, is there any hope for us innocent lambs?'

Steve shook his head in agreement, his mind elsewhere. 'Do you know the name of their solicitors – the Joneses?'

'No, I don't. They handled the sale themselves. They would though, wouldn't they, being dodgy?'

'Dodgy – yes…'

'I'm entertaining this evening, so…'

'Oh, of course. Sorry to have bothered you. Thank you.'

Feeling washed out, Steve turned away.

'Hang on. You might find out more about them from the Khadars. They were neighbours of the Joneses.'

'I've just tried that house—'

'No, it's empty now. They left a month or so after we moved in, but I've got a forwarding address.'

'Great! I'd love to speak to their old neighbours.'

'It's just Mr Khadar now.' She glanced over at the sugar-coated fairytale garden. 'But I'd get divorced too if I lived there.'

'Can't be nice, having that eyesore next door.'

'Not for long – it's condemned. All those improvements undermined the building's fabric and now the whole thing is coming down.'

Thirteen

An hour later, Steve arrived at the street where Mr Khadar lived.

Large redbrick houses stood shoulder to shoulder in what was an affluent location in Victorian times. Nowadays, the houses were divided into flats. The low walls of the front gardens had been demolished and the earth sown with gravel in order to accommodate a plethora of gleaming cars of silver and white. Like wintertime in metal. The street was perfectly deserted. The low sun reflected dully off dusty windows.

He found the house. Number four.

The arched inset porch was adorned by wonderful polychromatic tiles at least a hundred years old. These had been partially smashed away so that a bank of plastic buttons could be mounted onto the brickwork. The dull-green door was peeling.

The address the woman had given him had no flat number.

He tried pressing a button at random.

In the large bow window to his right, a brown curtain

moved and a gaunt, female face, heavily made up, peeked out, stared ghoulishly for a second and vanished.

The seconds passed.

She was not coming to the door.

He tried another button. After a short wait, a young, blowsy woman wearing a shapeless track suit answered. Her doughy face did not move as she asked, 'What you want?' In a slow voice. But before he could reply, she lost interest and turned away.

'Come in, then.'

'Sorry, where's Mr Khadar's flat?'

She didn't glance back.

'First door on the landing, next to the toilet. Don't use it.'

The bare wooden staircase lay directly ahead of him and ran up into darkness. He climbed the hollow steps and the landing light flickered on automatically, revealing several unmarked brown doors, one of which was opened onto a vacant toilet seat.

Steve tapped on the next door. Craning his neck, he was just able to catch a dimmed voice.

'Come in.'

He stepped into a small, cramped room.

A middle-aged man, thin to the point of being wasted, dressed in old black trousers and tee shirt, lay prone on an unadorned bed. His pool-like, passive eyes stared up at Steve from a dark and unshaven face. Stubble powdered his cheeks with grey. His head was propped up on a greasy pillow, but he lay on top of the sheets and his bare feet pointed large oblong toes up at Steve, who was constrained to stand right at the end of the bed, because the room was crammed full of stuff. The many oddments of furniture were covered in heaps of old laundry and deformed cardboard boxes. The bed itself had been pushed under the sash window. The long, fuscous curtains, sustained by a slight and sunny winter breeze, brushed the man's right arm. In his left hand he held a smouldering roll-up cigarette.

'I'm sorry to bother you. It is Mr Khadar, isn't it?'

The man drew a breath to answer, as if there had been no air in his lungs. His mouth pouted into a square.

'How did you get my address?'

'Your neighbour gave it me.'

Khadar's face contracted in pain.

'Not the Joneses,' Steve blurted. 'I mean the woman who lives there now.'

Khadar glared. 'Really? So what's her name?'

'I never asked. I've just come away from speaking to her. I...' Steve was rattled by the ugly suspicion on Khadar's face. 'Honestly, I'm nothing to do with the Joneses.'

'Yet you know where they used to live.'

'I found their previous address from the removal firm.'

'Removal firm? Ah, I see...' Khadar closed his eyes for a moment. 'So they've moved next door to you.'

Steve glanced round the room and spotted an armchair, the seat of which was covered in a tangled mass of plastic flowers, but the arms were free. He stepped over tattered newspapers and discarded clothes and took a perch. From there he could look straight out of the window.. The upper branches of a bare tree were level with the sill.

'I just want to ask, what can I do about them? How do I make them stop?'

'I can't tell you, because I don't know.' Khadar squeezed out the stub of his cigarette between his fingers and dropped it into a small ashtray that lay beside him on the bed. His hands were long and narrow.

'What happened to you? Did they... Did they cause

your divorce?'

'I'm not talking about that,' Khadar snapped.

This brief emotion drained him. He winced as he swallowed.

'Okay. I won't ask again.' Steve waited patiently. *Just like a supplicant*, he thought

After a moment, Khadar turned to him and seemed almost to smile. 'What I can tell you is that you have commenced a journey that I began myself – oh, let's see… a lifetime ago.'

'A journey? I don't understand.'

Khadar's face, with its large staring eyes and long nose prompted a faint recollection of some creature Steve had seen at the zoo. Maybe a lemur. Or whatever that thing had been with the death-camp stare.

'It's simple. I used to be somewhere else and now I am here. And so are you. You are here on a desperate quest for knowledge and understanding, and for that reason I presume the Joneses have already begun to renovate.'

'Yes, yes, they have.' Steve leaned forward.

'In which case the best advice I can give is – move out before they begin the porch. I don't know for sure, but I sense there *might* still be a chance then—'

'They have begun the porch.'

Khadar's grin displayed the silvery stumps of his teeth. 'Ah! Well… Not good.'

'What do you mean?'

'I mean that's that.' The lemur fixed him in its eerie stare. 'End of story.'

'The damned porch. What has the porch got to do with it?'

Khadar let his hand drop to the floor beside the bed and without looking, he deftly picked up a tobacco tin. Soon, the long, nimble fingers were rolling an attenuated cigarette. As he worked with practised concentration, his shallow breath whistled through his long proboscis. Steve would have to wait for his answer.

'When the Joneses built their porch, and it seemed desperately urgent that you had to have one too, was that, or was that not the last straw? Eh? The final turning point?' He took a ten-for-a-quid lighter from under one leg and lit his crumpled cigarette. He drew hard. The pool-like eyes closed as he exhaled a sigh that sent more of his life up into smoke.

Steve stared at the smoke in dumb misery, remembering the argument over the porch – that was the last time he'd seen Belinda.

But then—

'Wait a minute. You're talking about the porch that the *Joneses* built. But they never built a porch when they lived next door to you. They didn't make any improvements at all, did they? I've just seen that for myself. You don't know anything.'

Khadar held his cigarette in front of his square mouth, as if lost in thought. 'Ah.' He emitted a visceral chuckle. 'Thank you. You've just reminded me of how insane I am.'

The perverse conceit in Khadar's tone irked Steve. 'Is that so?'

'Oh, but I'm afraid you're mad too. Quite mad' Khadar sucked hard on his cigarette again. 'I'll explain. And if you don't believe me, just fuck off. Right?'

'Yeah, right.'

Khadar stared up at the grimy ceiling. The breeze from the stagnant garden rose and fell and the curtains brushed over his right side, back and forth.

'The haven't renovated. They never renovate anything. There are no *Mothcoats*, no building works, no mess, no noise. It's all in your head. Like it was in mine. I investigated. Spoke to people – what was left of them – and I went to see the places were the Joneses used to live. They were untouched. But they were always next door to a condemned house. Condemned because the owners had made so many improvements.'

'Okay, that's what I saw when I went to your old address. But I'm not insane. And I don't think you are either.'

'And yet, if I went back now, what I would see next door, where the Jones used to live, is a gleaming palace of gold and marble.'

'There's no palace, I tell you.'

'Of course not. And yet, I watched them build it. I saw them replace wood with marble, aluminium with silver and finally, they used gold. They built a golden palace, shining so bright it nearly blinded me. Of course I know it's an illusion. You're not telling me anything new. But it doesn't make any difference. I see what they want me to see. And so will you. Not only that, you'll believe in it no matter what I tell you now. And you'll need to keep up with their fantasy. Try as you might, you are doomed to renovate your home to match theirs until your house begins to crumble, crack and fall apart around you. You'll lose everything. You wife, your job – nothing of your old life will be left. But even then, they will not be satisfied. Because when you're sick, when your mind goes completely—'

'I'll end up here?'

Khadar blinked and turned his head on the greasy pillow to look at him. His purple lips twisted in contempt.

'A puny worm like you? At best they will let you rot on a mental ward. What you need you haven't got. Incredible willpower and spiritual enlightenment. To survive, you must join battle with the ultimate enemy. Even with my infinitely superior intellect, I still had to rely on the transcendental teaching and magnanimity of Guru Swabhiguthamarah. It cost me all the money I had in order to partake of his wisdom and learn how to renounce the material world. Sublime renunciation alone can defeat the Joneses. One must enjoy that supreme mastery over the ego that only *I*—' he rose and thrust a clenched fist into the air, '—*Raj Khadar* was superb enough to attain!'

Steve stood up. 'Thank you for your time.'

Khadar looked up at his raised arm in surprise.

'Oh.'

There was a watch wrapped round the stick-thin wrist.

'I see that I am late.' he murmured. 'It is my fault. I should have left before you arrived.' He smiled in pleasant recollection. 'Only, you see, I was in the pub till two last night.'

'Were you?' Steve was stepping over the mess to get to the door.

'Sir – you came in a car, perhaps?'

'Yes.'

'Stop – please. I can tell you more. Come and see me tonight. I'll be in *The Goose on the Green*. It's just down the road. In fact, you can see me there any night. Yes, I would very much like to hear how you are progressing. Meanwhile, is there any chance I might obtain a lift to my workplace? It's not far to drive, but the bus takes forever.'

Steve hesitated at the door. 'Okay. I'll wait.'

'I am highly grateful to you. I will take seconds.' Khadar moved with arthritic slowness. He climbed off the bed, pulled on some rotten trainers, dashed some cold water on his face and sprayed himself all over with *Lynx for Men*. Then he slipped a crumpled check shirt over his emaciated shoulders and was ready.

Steve drove under Khadar's directions through ever

more grimy streets till they arrived at a trading estate. A windy, open place where voluminous warehouses dwarfed the few cars that were parked on their concrete aprons.

'Stop here, please.'

Steve pulled up and looked around. 'You don't work in packing, do you?'

'I'm a cleaner. Thanks for the lift. You were kind.'

Steve yawned. 'I'm very tired.'

'Yes, I know you are. I am sorry, but this is the best I can do for you.' Khadar climbed out the car, bent down and flicked a grubby pellet of paper into Steve's lap. 'That is Quaid's brother.'

Before Steve could respond, Khadar was hobbling away towards *Abled World*. A showroom for wheelchairs.

Fourteen

Steve picked open the pellet of paper.

Hauton Mildestimpft
Clawesdawn Community Psychiatric Unit
The Thiddles
MI23 9MG

An hour later, his satnav had directed him to the southern part of the city. The most affluent suburb of all. The low, crimson sun peeped between spacious and individually built houses.

On a broad, tree-lined street, Steve spotted the small sign—

Clawesdawn

He almost passed it by. The sign was so insignificant and the entry itself was tucked inside an imposing laurel hedge. The concrete drive was just wide enough for one vehicle to pass down and it wove pointlessly to a miserable patch of asphalt on which a few cars were parked as far apart as possible.

Clawesdawn Community Psychiatric Unit was a collection of two-storey, dun-coloured buildings sunk in an air of cold rumination. The rows of metal-framed windows were closed off by blinds. It was secluded from the world by a dank park in which towering beech trees clacked their wooden fingers at the winter sky.

There was no other sound as Steve approached the entrance. It opened into a tiny concourse, where a single moulded plastic chair stood on a rectangle of brown carpet. A notice board hung on the cream wall, without any notices on it, and a set of fire doors faced him, secured by a combination lock. Steve could see no way to call for attention, but when he craned through a wire-glass door panel, a face with oversized spectacles appeared on the other side and stared back.

He waved and silently mouthed, *Hauton Mildestimpft*.

The door opened and a large-bonded woman in a drab floral dress leaned through.

'Pardon?' Her voice was tiny – childlike. The spectacles magnified her eyes, which were jet black and surrounded by pink.

'I would like to see Mr Hauton Mildestimpft.'

'Who?'

'Hauton.'

'*Hauton*?'

'Yes, Hauton. It's important we speak in person. It's about his brother, Quaid.'

'And you are?'

'Detective Steve Smith.'

As he spoke, Steve glanced over one of the woman's broad shoulders at the utility corridor behind her and sniffed the sweltering air that poured out.

'Did you say *detective*?'

'I'll wait here, shall I? He'll want to speak to me in private.'

'In private?'

'Yes.'

'In that case, could you wait here a moment?'

'Okay, I'll wait here.' He felt a trickle of sweat run down his temple.

The woman waddled away down the corridor.

A couple of minutes later a slim middle-aged man, wearing an open-necked nurse's uniform, pushed open one of the doors with both arms – the woman had only needed one. His face had an elfin quality. The nose was upturned and the chin sharp. In contrast to the delicate features, his skin was coarse and seemed soiled.

Steve couldn't help feeling superior to him.

And for that reason, the man's sneering demeanour all the more provocative.

'Yes?' He asked, glancing over Steve's suit with a look of distain.

'Hauton?'

'Yah. That's me.'

'May we speak in confidence?'

'What about?'

'You want to talk here, do you?'

'Why not?'

'I don't want to talk at the door.'

'So?'

'We could come to your home, if you like.'

The tiniest uncertainty appeared in Hauton's brazen front, and was immediately compensated by a jeering bravado. '*We*?'

They were all like this – Porgem the disco dancer and the Joneses themselves. Below their hostility lay the fear you saw in lowly, skulking things.

The bared teeth and round white eyes of a…

'Yes.' Steve smiled. '*We*, as in me and another detective.'

Hauton stuck his pixie nose into the air. 'If it makes it easier to get you over and done with, there's a little interview room. Come'

The unhealthy heat of the building enveloped Steve as he followed Hauton into the corridor. He sniffed at a stink of bleach and faecal matter that could never be rinsed far enough away.

Hadn't he met that smell once in a dream…?

Hadn't it worn a smile?

Stay awake!

Hauton opened an unmarked door and Steve followed him into a small room. A couple of extruded-plastic chairs waited, facing each other.

Hauton dropped into one of the chairs and stretched his legs out as far as they would go.

'So what's up with Quaid?'

Steve sat. He sniffed again, this time at the faint sweat-reek of Hauton's plimsolls.

'There's a lot up with Quaid.'

Hauton rolled his eyes. 'Look, if he's been murdered, just tell me.'

'That wouldn't bother you?'

'Fuck, no.'

'He hasn't been murdered.'

'You sound so sad about that. It's like he's your neighbour.'

'I've spoken to his neighbour. Raj Khadar. He told me about you.'

'What could *he* tell you about *me*? He wasn't here more than a day. His stinky old man got him out with a fancy lawyer.'

'Your brother's a fraudster and criminal, that's what he told me. He plays his dirty tricks to drive people out of their homes.'

'You say so, do you? Arrest him then, if you can. Steve Gasket of the Yard. Ha!'

'I've got evidence.'

'What evidence?'

'He's getting money out of it, I just know it. You too, eh?'

'Money!' Hauton spat the word out. 'You think this is about money? You are blind. What you are going through is beyond your comprehension.'

'Oh sure it is. It's really deep.'

'You look very, very, tired.'

'What did Quaid use on Khadar? The man's sick. Was it drugs from this place?'

Hauton snorted with repressed laughter.

'Drugs? You think we're so crude, don't you, Smith? What we use is mental illness.'

'What?'

He savoured Steve's confusion. 'Yeah, you heard right. I bottle it for them. Vintage stuff I keep stacked in the toilet for time of need. The toilet is our wine cellar, Smith. Home of the very best *Chateau Senility*. Have you been enjoying its bouquet?' He threw back his head and inhaled deeply through his nose.

A fine network of ghost-white scars criss-crossed his neck.

Steve stared at them and an explanation popped into his head. 'You've had your face changed, haven't you?'

Hauton's head snapped down. His eyes were white. Leaning forward, he waved one rat-bone finger in Steve's face.

'Wheeeeessssshhhhhoooooo. Whoooooo's going to fuck yoooo-hooo?'

Steve slapped the scrawny hand away.

Hauton shrank back, glaring even as he cowered. He bared his teeth.

'You can't stop it. The spooks have blown in from the shiny planet and you – you are dead—'

Steve jumped up, his arm drawn back.

Hauton winced, but did not move and when no blow came, he thrust his pointy little chin up at Steve.

'Come on then, if you think you're hard enough.'

Steve forced open his fist and lowered it.

Hauton whooped in triumph and Steve lost control and shoved him. Hauton didn't weigh anything at all and he went flying backwards and rolled over the floor. Whimpering, he crawled into a corner and curled up into a ball. He squealed at Steve from between his bony shins. 'I'll get you. I'll get you when you come here. When you're standing in line for the commode.'

'You threaten me? A maggot like you?'

Hauton grizzled like a whipped brat.

'You better not strike me again. My wife will have you, Smith. She's a big, hook-nosed bitch. That nose got broke fucking over a better man than you'll ever be, and when they send you here she's gonna break yours.'

Steve wrenched at the door handle. Locked.

Hauton hooted mockingly.

Steve tried to turn the twist-latch. It simply would not move.

Hauton began to chant. 'You've got no braaaain, you've got no braaaain! Na, na, na-naaaa, na!'

Steve could actually hear the sucking sound as his mind dislocated. He turned and smashed his fist into Hauton's gleeful mouth.

It was rock hard.

Doink!

Steve's hand exploded. The pain lit the inside of his

head up.

'Argh! Ahhhhh no – *God!*'

He had punched the headboard in his sleep.

Another nightmare.

The nights were crowded with them. Like hilltops in a flood. By now, he had hardly slept in three days.

His lonely cry had left the house more silent than ever. He climbed out of bed and limped around the deserted rooms, bent over like an old man.

He had never felt ill in this way before. And yet he could not pin down any actual physical discomfort – apart from the aching throb in his hand now. In fact, that pain was healthy compared to the *wrongness* that squatted deep within him. He could feel it grinning up at him.

Waiting.

'Oh, Bel!'

He wept so hard he was barely able to draw breath. The heaving sobs shook him like a rag.

The final dissolution had begun.

He was looking down into the toilet bowl. Red, porridge-like stuff filled it to the brim. The fetid odour of rotten flesh was unendurable. The walls around him shook, blurred and swirled out of the shape.

His home was being flushed into the sewers.

And he was going with it.

Fifteen

He was at *Serpinski Gaskets Ltd.*

He was knocking on the boss's door.

'Come!'

Eschops watched him enter, his bristly jowls drooping from his oversized jaws.

'Ah, Mr Smith. What can I do for you?'

'You asked to see me.'

'I did? Fair enough, then. Take a seat.'

Steve sat before the large desk.

Eschops' eyeballs were cracked and the cracks were filled with blood. They scrutinised him with an unwavering stare.

'Are you happy here, Steve?'

'I was just thinking this morning,' Steve said in a voice that sounded remote, 'how much this job means to me. It's the one part of my life that is still real.'

Eschops's brow creased. 'Well that's good. Surprisingly good…and yet, I do wonder whether or not you've entirely settled at *Serpinski*'s?'

'Not settled in? After seven years?'

'You've been a solid performer, Steven, but today's workplace demands and expects one hundred per cent from its employees. If not more.'

'I do my best to give one hundred per cent. And more.' Steve became aware of his throbbing hand, which had swollen. He tried to conceal it behind his other hand, which had grown thinner. 'But recently, I suppose, I have been unwell.'

'Bad stomach? Too many Chinese takeouts, maybe?'

'No, a winter bug.'

'A *head* cold, Steven?'

'Yes, amongst other stuff. But I'm over it now.'

Eschops shifted in his seat with a low grunt. 'Then you're sound in body and… Well, leaving the *mind* aside for the present, let me ask you this: Is your *heart* really in *Serpinski*'s? Your *heart*, Steven?'

Steve found that he was leaning forward, perched on the edge of his seat. Through the haze of his misery, he espied the desolate rocky headland towards which Eschops was steering this conversation.

'My heart? My heart… Yes, of course.' Steve's eyes

grew to points under tears.

'Tell me, Steven, would you be happier somewhere else?'

More than anything, Steve was struck by wonder. The prophecies of Khadar were coming true. Prophecies never came true in real life, did they? But here he was – about to lose both his wife and his job. Then, surely, his house and his life would follow.

'No, I wouldn't be happier anywhere else.'

Eschops grimaced. 'What's the matter with you? Your neck's gone red.'

'Still a bit feverish. It's warm in here.'

'Then you ought not have come in, had you?'

'But I have work to do.'

'Well, that's the right attitude, I'll grant you that. Still, I wonder, what work it is you *are* doing here.'

'Why…everything I'm asked to do, I believe.'

'And who asked you to carry forward *Project X*?' Eschops swivelled his computer monitor around to face Steve. It displayed a list of his current work files. 'See? *Project X*. There, in your directory.'

Long pause.

Steve's narrowed throat squeaked, 'Just brainstorming.'

'*This* is brainstorming, Steven?'

Eschops opened the file and a CAD drawing filled the screen. What Steve had drawn was insanely complex and detailed. Black on white, like an X-ray. A mass of schematic wiring and servo mechanisms. They crisscrossed so densely that most of the detail was blotted out. And yet, as one gazed at it, the confused meshing revealed a…grinning skull.

After a moment of stupefaction, Steve grinned back at it.

'Why, you're nothing but a silly doodle, aren't you?'

Eschops's chair creaked under his restive bulk.

'Steven, you see now why we're worried you might be losing your marbles.'

'We?'

'Alok has remarked on it. He's asked you to join the *Contra-Head-Gasket-Project Team*, but it seems you prefer to gaze off into the distance, or copy and paste a skull.'

'It's just a bit of copying and pasting to clear my head. Copying and pasting doesn't take any time. And at least I'm not gambling on the net.'

'Who's gambling on the net?'

'Not me. And as for fixing the *Raylard-Pin* problem, if I ever I have an idea about how to do it, then I'll be over to the *Contra-Head-Gasket-Project Team* like a shot.'

'Like a shot? So you should be. You should be backing Alok up one hundred per cent. To the hilt. We're team players, aren't we? And in a team we can't all be leaders.'

Steve acknowledged this sentiment with a perfunctory nod. 'Still, it doesn't seem quite right to me. I mean, Alok picking me up on a bit of harmless copying and pasting. Discussing my work methods with you. It's hardly *his* business.'

'Alok spoke as a manager.'

'He's not a manager.'

'No, not yet. But I'm making Alok *Chief Project Manager* next month, because Paul's moving on.'

'Oh. I see.'

'And so you'll have to get used to Alok discussing your work methods. Of course, that doesn't mean you can't come directly to me, if you feel you must.'

Which was Eschops's way of telling him the meeting was over.

On his way back to the design office, Steve met Alok in the corridor.

'Hey, congrats on the promotion.'

Alok seemed to have got taller. The strip lighting blanked out his spectacles, creating the illusion of big white eyes that transfixed him from above.

'Thanks. It's a big step.'

'Massive.'

'But it's a massive responsibility too. And I'm going to have to put in a lot more hours.'

'Well, that's life.'

'Easy for you to say, Steven, you live quite close by, don't you?'

'Twenty minutes, door to door.'

'Me, it's like a two and half hours.'

'You need a closer door.'

Alok tilted over Steve, like he was hinged at the ankles. 'It's not just me who needs a closer door, but Guldip too, you know.'

For some reason, Steve put his hand on top of his head. 'Your wife?'

Alok's glowing white eyes grew even larger. 'Yes. Everything will be most especially hard for her.'

'Most especially hard because…?'

'Most especially hard for her because we're expanding.'

The light in the corridor seemed to dim. Alok's eyes grew brighter.

'Expanding? In the sense of?'

'In the sense of Guldip expecting.'

'Ah! Well we – me and Bel, that is, we're expanding at home too. In the sense of Bel extending…into another home.'

'I don't follow.'

'We're basically separating.'

'Oh. Divorce, you mean?'

'I think so.'

'That means you're selling your house.'

Steve stared into the big white eyes.

'Did I say I'm selling my house?'

'You should be selling your house, I think, because I'm very interested in buying it.'

'Sell the house?' Steve murmured dreamily. 'Sell the... *house*? Sell the house? Of course, *that's* the solution – *sell*... and let someone else take on the curse...'

Alok's eyes merged into a single radiating rectangle. Steve was not able to look away. 'You *are* selling the house?'

'I am.' Steve intoned. 'I am selling the house. Yes. I *must*. I must do it to survive. But still, do I really believe I can?'

'Yes, you definitely should. Guldip and me. And her mom and her dad too – we're *cash* buyers.'

Steve blinked. 'What's that?'

'We can give you cash.'

'For the house?'

'We would want to offer cash so we could move fast with the purchase. I'll be working extra hours soon, very soon, as you know.'

'You want to pay cash for the house?'

Steve moved to one side, so that he could get the glare of reflected neon out of his eyes.

Alok moved to one side to get the glare of reflected neon back in Steve's eyes.

'How much did you pay for your house, Steve?'

'I'd say, 140 k.'

'That much? Did you pay in cash?'

'No.'

'But we, we're cash buyers.'

'*Are* you really buyers, though? You might not like the place.'

'That's true. But lunchtime's coming up and if it's twenty minutes door to door, like you say, we shall have the time to go look now, eh?'

Sixteen

Nineteen minutes later they turned onto Orchard Drive.

The Mothcoats were inert just then. No one at home to torture, was there? The shadowy figures lurked inside the cab of their rusty pick up.

Steve remarked, 'As you can see, they're having some work done next door. It's a bit scruffy just now, but…'

He held his breath as Alok scanned the horrible mess. Despite what Khadar had said, Steve could not bring himself to believe that the chaos and the Mothcoats were illusionary.

'Looks okay. What are they like – the neighbours?'

'Unbeatable!'

'Hmmmm…' Alok studied the exterior of Steve and Belinda's lovelorn home. He sucked his teeth. 'It's older than I expected.'

'Built in 1999.'

'Exactly. And a bit smaller than Mr Eschops's.'

'Come again?'

'Oh, we paid a social call just recently, Guldip and me.'

'Were you looking for something the same size as Eschops's house?'

'I wasn't. But Guldip kept saying afterwards how much she liked his house. By the way, she's out at the moment. In India. But that's no problem.'

And in fact Guldip was going to be present after all.

Alok called her on his phone and her loud, tinny voice dictated instructions while Alok held up the phone so she could look out of it while he traipsed from room to room. Occasionally, he was ordered to essay a rap upon a wall to gauge its solidity.

'So, that's it,' Steve said, as they stepped out into the back garden.

'We like it,' Richard said, raising his voice to be heard over the disembodied Guldip. 'But, like I say, it is a bit older than we had hoped for. So, Steven – how does seventy-thousand sound?'

Steve too had to raise his voice as Guldip's tirade grew noisier.

'*Half* the asking price?'

'Think about it. Take your time. No rush.' Even as he said this, Alok bubbled with impatience. He moved from foot to foot and this made him sway. Looking at him, Steve had the strong impression that a far simpler shape lay behind Alok's face and body. 'Seventy-thousand *cash*.That's a lot of *cash*. In *cash*, that's a lot all at once. A big lump sum – of *cash*.' Steve felt himself swaying in time with Alok. The voice hummed, rising and falling, rising and falling, coaxing and soothing. 'Very well, seventy-five. Final offer. Don't go missing your chance.'

A sparrow hopped up to the patio and as Steve turned, it flew away in alarm. He shook his head. 'You want my house off me for half price? Over my dead body.'

Seventeen

The smack of hard, thin lips woke Steve from an unhappy dream about Belinda floating just beyond his reach.

He rose from his dishevelled bed in the pencil-thin light of dawn and went downstairs.

A hand-delivered letter lay on the doormat.

He read—

Sombre Greetings from Mothcoat and Daughter (Funeral Directors) Ltd.

Dear Sir/Madam

We have the sorrowful duty of informing you that the funeral service for the dearly departed Mr Raj Khadar will take place on Thursday 17th of May at Lower Kornal Crematorium *at 9 o'clock. A wake will be held at the bar of the* Goose on the Green *at 12.30.*

Today was the 17th.

Slowly, like he was walking along the bottom of the sea, Steve left the house and went by foot through the cold, dim streets to *Lower Kornal Crematorium*, which lay on the southern edge of the city, just beyond a well-heeled suburb.

He arrived at five to nine and found numerous cars in the car park glistening from a recent shower. The sky was like one big drift of salt. A few figures were trailing through dank rose beds towards the main building, which had the appearance of an alpine-resort information centre, except for its huge, stone-clad chimney.

He fell in amongst the other mourners. Their lined, ghastly faces glanced at him with wide, lidless eyes and their bodies trembled as they hobbled through the gaping portal.

The interior combined the feel of a modern church and an airport lounge. Most of the seats were taken. Steve sat towards the back, beside an old lady whose palsied limbs vibrated the bench beneath him. Up ahead, the casket was set on a square podium behind a lectern, at which a small, podgy middle-aged man, attired in an immaculate suit of grey, stood and smiled benignly down upon the mourners.

When everyone was seated, he began.

'We come together this day, to celebrate the life of Raj

Khadar. One of two sons, Raj went to university after distinguishing himself at school and earning the soubriquet, *The Loadstar of the Khadar family*. After studying philosophy, law and business, Raj went on to found his own import and export company in North London, relocating to Manchester as both family and business expanded. He had a tremendous work ethic, putting in a seven-day week on a regular basis. He played hard too. An excellent golfer and a gourmet cook in his spare time. And, I might add, more than a mere trifler on the *Casio* keyboard. Furthermore, as a generous contributor to several major charities, we can say without hesitation that Raj was not only the loadstar for the Khadar family, but for all humanity...'

The reader paused and in the breathless silence, Steve thought he could hear a dull thumping noise.

'A life, any life, just like the rainbow variety of Mankind itself, has many hues. Some are light, some are dark. And so it came to pass that Raj's later lustrums were to be streaked through and through by bile-black misfortune.'

Steve tilted his head. Was that a muffled scream for help? Was someone thumping feebly at a door somewhere?

'Hither then, bourn upon the rising tide of the night, came the nitrous angel in his wormy barque. And the angel did visit the house of Raj and swept from the house of Raj everything that Raj had thought to be permanent and indissoluble. By the light of dawn, Raj found himself cast up, alone upon a desolate shore. The most desolate shore of all – the desolate shore of late middle-age. The shore that is desolate indeed – where the wind is loneliness, the sun is reproof, the rain is regret, the rocks are the hearts of loved ones, and the thorns... O Brothers! O Sisters! Let me tell you of the thorns!'

Steve was listening to the hammering and the fait cries. They seemed to be getting more desperate. He turned to the woman beside him and whispered, 'Excuse me, can you—?' He fell silent. With a shock, he saw that her face was drenched by tears.

'For it was at this very time,' the speaker continued, 'O Brothers! O Sisters! It was at this very time that Raj's brother, Rashid, who had failed in education, failed at his job as a bin collector, failed his twentieth driving test, and who had been incarcerated on numerous occasions for the possession of heroin, and who had married a convicted prostitute and who had been fined for punching her in the face, O Brothers! O Sisters! It was at this time, I say – the time of Raj's most dismal disconsolation – that Rashid won the lottery…and, for this reason, he sends his sincerest apologies for not being able to be here today because he's in the Caribbean taking a three-month winter warmer—'

The reader broke off and bowed his head, overcome by emotion. His shoulders shook.

The muffled screaming and hammering became still louder.

The reader threw back his head, his face aglow with beatific light.

'O Brothers! O Sisters! At times like these, we must turn to the words of those who are far wiser than ourselves. Let me read to you, therefore, from this most ancient text,' he opened the huge leather-bound book that lay on the lectern, 'written, my friends, by a man moved and directed by a higher power. A man inspired by the scented breath numinous spirits in order that he might bring solace and comfort to all those who creep and crawl on their bellies in this dark bower, the dusty Earth. In short, he brings good news for every one of us. The text I have before me, of course, is volume twenty-eight of the diaries of Sir Herbert Whinstanley-Cultus-Frotheringhamshire-Melforth-Kinch, Duke and later Duchess of Crambershire. I have turned to the entry that begins—' he read, '*This was writ on the thirty-first of November in this, the fifth year of our good Queen Anne, counsellor, infinite benefactor and cool, healing balm to her ever-loving subjects, at Ulmastandish House of the Ducal Estate of Ulmastandish, while I was sat in the great lavatory after breakfast.*' The reader cleared his throat and paused for effect. 'And this, my friends, is what was written on that day – *BOIL on NECK.*'

The man clapped the great book shut, sending a shudder through the ranked mourners. He scrutinised them severely as the dim hammering and screams of terror continued unabated in what was otherwise a profound silence. A nervous tension mounted in the room, just like one senses in airport departure lounges during a collective daydream about airplanes falling out of the sky like rotten fruit.

'O Lord!'

The mourners started like they'd been electrocuted by the speaker's stentorian bellow.

'...I mean Naga, or Ganesh, or Gnu, perhaps. We commend this, thy child, to your everlasting care. See you in paradise, old friend. Sayonara!'

He slapped a red button on the side of the lectern.

Mellow organ music filled the chapel as the casket began to glide away. The screaming and thumping reached a new level of hysteria. A pair of velvet curtains swished apart and the casket to disappear through them and into the incinerator.

The screams rose to a screech.

Iron doors clanged shut and the screaming stopped dead.

The speaker rolled his eyes to Heaven. 'Ladies and

Gentlemen, let us sing, *My Sweet Lord*, by George Harrison.'

The mourners groaned as they struggled to their feet. But a pair of them at the front sprang up before everyone else.

Even before they turned around and stared straight at him with flat, dead brown eyes, Steve recognised them.

Eighteen

Two hours later.

The toilets in *Serpinksi Gaskets Ltd*.

'Hey Steve, this your new office?'

Steve looked up from his hands, which were submerged in the sink.

It was his new supervisor. A big, thumping fellow who bounded around the place with irrepressible self confidence.

'Alok – I was at a funeral. I'll log in after lunch.'

'Work's not the issue – I'm triple checking that you're still not accepting our offer for your house.'

'That's right – the house. Yes. I do accept your offer.'

'You do?' Alok wasn't surprised, not even for a second. Obviously a little squit like Steve just *had* to accept the offer of *Alok the Great*. 'That's interesting, Steven.'

'Only thing is, the whole transaction has to happen the day after tomorrow.'

'Impossible.'

'You said you wanted to move fast. My house will be empty by twelve o'clock. Get me the cash and you can have the deeds. Then all we need is a legal witness, don't we?'

'No, I cannot do it. I am adamant. But I'll call Guldip

and see what else we can arrange.'

'Don't bother, it's my way or no way.'

Alok stiffened. Even though he was great, there was no mistaking that Steve was going to get very rude if he were contradicted one more time. 'No, no, no, hold your horses, Steven, I already know what Guldip will say.'

'And what is that?'

'To get it all done as fast as that, without us checking the background and stuff, we'll only be able to feel safe risking …forty-thousand.'

'Forty-thousand…cash?'

'Yes.'

Forgetting to dry his hands, Steve headed towards the door.

'I'll start making arrangements at my end. I'll email you the name of my solicitor and she'll act on my instructions. She'll contact you and you can liaise with her.'

'What? You mean—?'

'Yes, for forty-thousand. But it has to be the day after tomorrow, at twelve. Any later and the deal's off. No negotiation is possible. Understand – yes or no?'

'Sure. I mean, yes.'

'Good. Now I have to get going.'

'Steve.'

'Yeah?'

'I've solved the *Unidirectional-Ralyard-Pin* problem.'

Steve rubbed his wet hands on his shirt. 'You're unstoppable, Alok.'

'Thanks.'

'But I wonder, what happens if you meet someone else who's unstoppable? What then?'

'That is never going to happen.'

Steve clenched his swollen hand. Cooling it in water had helped, but the painful throbbing had started up again.

Still, he didn't mind the pain anymore.

He even grinned.

'Of course not, Alok. But anyway, I'd better go hurry up and make myself homeless.'

'Excellent. Keep me informed, eh?'

As Steve passed through reception, he told Mrs Hatlespalle that he'd be on his mobile if Eschops needed him.

He heard her mutter behind his back.

'If he needs *you*?'

He scurried out and drove to Orchard Lane.

This is the last time I'll come back to our home, Bel.

Neither the *Mothcoats* or the Joneses seemed to be around. They had been attending Khadar's funeral and so they must be celebrating the wake in *The Goose on the Green*.

He phoned his solicitor and relayed his instructions for the house to be sold at twelve o'clock, the day after tomorrow. Then he emailed Alok his solicitor's contact details. After that, he arranged for the contents of the house to be collected at one o'clock next day and put into storage. Finally, he began to net-search for rental property. He found a landlord willing to see him in an hour's time.

Once he'd dropped the house keys off at his solicitor's office and copies of the keys at the office of the removal firm, he went to view his new home.

The satnav's soothing female voice directed him to an old suburb of a neighbouring town where late-Victorian redbrick houses stood shoulder to shoulder in what was once, a long, long time ago, an affluent location.

The houses were divided up into flats. Gleaming cars were jam-packed onto front gardens that had been sown with gravel. The street was quiet and the low sun reflected off the dusty windows.

He found number four. The arched, recessed porch was colourfully tiled, though on one side the tiles had been partially smashed away so that a bank of cheap buttons could be mounted onto the brickwork. The dark-green door was peeling.

As instructed, he pressed the lower left-hand button.

Almost immediately, a voice called from behind him, 'Ello, boss.'

'Um?' Steve turned to see a slim man in his early thirties, with a surprisingly thick neck and plump, shining cheeks. 'Mr Eligia?'

'Mr Smith, innit?'

'That's right.'

'Well, I'll show you, then.'

Eligia spoke to him with an unaccountable loftiness – unaccountable till Steve recalled that, as of today, he was a member of the shiftless, floating population of non home owners.

But he was too tired to care much about these class nuances. He followed Eligia up the bare wooden staircase and into the first room on the shadowy landing.

Steve took a quick glance round. The window overlooked an untended back garden, where the shrubs stood tall and winter-winnowed in the low, chill sunshine. A single bed was set under the sash window. A sink, fridge and cooker were lined up against one wall and a gaping wooden wardrobe stood opposite.

Eligia, of course, asked for a higher deposit than he'd asked for over the phone. Steve paid him and signed what he took to be a worthless contract. As soon as Eligia had given him the keys and gone away, he stretched out on the bed and immediately fell asleep.

Nineteen

He awoke with difficulty.

Evening had come on

The sash window above his bed was open. He pulled it down against the bitter-cold darkness and struggled to his feet. The light, when he found the switch, was a bare bulb.

He shuddered, as if the bone-white spectre were already upon him.

So cold. And no sign of a heater in this little palace.

Ah – but you're about to have a brilliant idea, Steven Smith. Yes indeed, the perfect *engineering solution.*

He put the cooker on full blast. Soon, the metal spirals on the hob glowed red. He held his hands over them.

Warmer now.

Even in these bleak surroundings he felt better than he had for months. He had escaped the Joneses. From now on, he would stay on the move, use cash, throw his mobile away, rent a car, become untraceable, go abroad to a country where there weren't any Joneses at all and then… And then… Well, he just knew Bel would join him and they'd start over.

A temporary revival of animal spirits brought on the sensation of hunger.

He pulled his jacket on and went out.

The economic depression had turned off half the street lamps and he beetled through the shadows, past unlit houses and other lifeless edifices.

He arrived at a main thoroughfare where the traffic was bumper to bumper in the groaning darkness. The headlights glared through grainy clouds of exhaust fumes.

A big corporate sign burnished the night. It was a petrol station/grocer combo. Steve circled around the cars that stuffed the station forecourt. They were all monstrous white-bodied machines that were adorned with rows and rows of small lights. The auto fashion of the recession – joyless fairground rides.

Inside the store the stark neon-strip lighting made the goods in their block-colour packaging look hyperreal. A spoilt brat was yelling louder than the muzak and the Han Chinese manager had to raise his voice before Steve could hear him.

'No, you need pay more!'

Steve did indeed pay more.

He went away with a ready meal, tea begs and a carton of milk.

Back at the front door of the house, Steve found the key wouldn't open the lock. He cursed himself for leaving his phone back in his room. Now he couldn't call Eligia.

How shall I survive without a phone?

'Having difficulty?'

A woman appeared beside him, just as he was about to randomly press one of the door bells.

Her face was an almost perfect circle with a big, bent, hooked nose sticking right out the middle of it. Like an owl's beak. But her eyes were the eyes of some other animal. Smaller. More cunning.

'This is the key the landlord gave me, but it doesn't fit.'

The small, round eyes reluctantly left his face, stared at the key as he held it up in the faint light.

'It looks right.' She spoke to him in a slow exaggerated fashion, as if he were slow witted. She held up own key. 'See, it's the same as mine. Let me try.' The door immediately opened for her. 'There you are. You can go first. Go on.'

'Thanks. But isn't it ladies first?'

'Ah, I can hear you've been well trained.'

'It's a matter of common courtesy.'

'But you'll catch your little death of cold if you wait out here any longer.'

Tired of her, Steve began to move.

The woman instantly barged her way in front of him.

He held his tongue and stood back, waiting for her to disappear.

She stopped and turned to him under the fluorescent hallway lamp. Her circular face was almost concave and the fleshy rudder of her nose cast a jagged shadow over the lipless slice of a mouth.

'I'll have to shut the door soon. All the heat's floating out.'

'No, you carry on.' Steve stepped in and carelessly pushed the door shut, making it rattle.

'Temper.'

'What?' Steve snapped.

She was blocking his way.

'Don't have a tantrum, sweetums. Is it past beddy-beddy time?'

'Ugh.'

He shoved pushed past her to get to the stairs.

'Oh, that *is* nice. Very, very nice.'

He glanced back as he kept going. 'Well, it's a nice place, is it?'

'Really? If it's so nice why aren't you happy?'

'You're here.'

'You *what*?' She was close behind. Chasing him. Their footsteps thundered on the hollow staircase and the racket sounded like the house was collapsing. 'Come on, what do you mean? You can't come here and start on me like that.'

They reached the landing.

She shouldered past him and planted herself in front of his door.

Steve snapped. 'Get out of my way.'

'Out *your* way! Who do you think you are?'

'I know who I am. Who the hell are you?'

'Me? I've spent all day caring for people. Dying people.'

'So you're a *nurse*? My God.'

'Sneery, eh? You bastard. I have to wipe the arses of people like you all the time.'

'No you don't.'

'Yes, *just* like you. Think you're better, don't you? Think you're too good for me.'

'I don't think about you at all. Just get out the fucking way.'

'You'll have to think about me soon. You're not so superior you can't lie down and die.'

Steve glared and thrust his arm out to reach the door.

She jumped aside and squawked. 'Oh!'

'I didn't touch you.'

'Oh!'

Steve put his key in the door.

It wouldn't turn.

'God damn.'

The woman yipped triumphantly.

'Need another little helping hand, *Diddums*?'

Steve hunched one shoulder up to block her off and struggled with the lock.

'Come on, let me do it for you.' She began to force herself between him and the door. She was strong. He shook with the strain of keeping her off. She grunted. 'Come on...let me help you...get your...little door open.'

The key remained immobile. It bit into his fingers as he tried to force it. A hot pressure pulsed in his neck.

'You see...it's a little tricky...that's all.' Her sour breath filled his nostrils. Her thin lips were inches from his ear. 'You just have to...be shown once...I did it for...

the boy who lived here…before.'

'No.'

'But it's so easy. Just let me calm you down first…'
Her chubby hand was snaking around his crotch.

'Stop!'

He lashed out behind with his elbow—

Scrunch.

'Yow!' She tottered backwards against the banister.
She wailed like a siren. 'Ow! Ow! My nose! That *really*
hurt. You've hurt me! Do you think you can get away
with that? Are you mad? Are you? Well, *are* you?'

Bodies began to stir in the rooms all around.

Trembling, Steve pulled the key from the lock and
pushed it in again. He strove with all his might to turn it
gently, willing the tumblers to fall.

The woman hollered up the stairs. 'He just punched
me! He's a thug. He's a *mad* thug! We're all in danger.
Don't let it happen to you. For God's sake, help!'

Thudunk! Thudunk! Thundunk!

Big heavy feet were descending from above.

The key turned.

Steve slipped into his room.

'Oi! Don't you think you're getting away— '

He slammed the door on her.

Straightaway, she began rapping on it.

Tup, Tup, Tup…

He stood there, panting and dizzy.

Tup, Tup, Tup, Tup…

He forced himself to move and act like nothing had
happened. He placed the ready meal in the oven and
swilled the few items of cutlery in the steel sink.

Tup, Tup, Tup, Tup, Tup…

He sat on the bare, grubby mattress of the bed to wait.

Tup, Tup, Tup, Tup, Tup, Tup…

On and on. For a full minute. Or two, or three…

Oh, dear God!

He couldn't bear it anymore. He leapt up and—

His phone sang.

'Yah, I'm working pretty damned late,' his solicitor informed him proudly, even though he hadn't commented on how late it was. 'But I'm off now for a well-earned *Chablis* with friends.'

'Right.'

'Yes, well, I wanted you to know that all the arrangements are in place. The Singhs will sign the contract at ten in the morning, after they have deposited the cash into your account—'

'Sorry, did you say ten tomorrow morning?'

'Yes.'

'That's quicker than I asked for.'

'Well, it would be, wouldn't it? They're getting the property at a knockdown price.' Derision thickened her breezy drawl. 'So, until ten tomorrow, then. At that time, I will give you a confirmatory text to say it's all over.'

'Right. Bye —'

'Oh – might I have your forwarding address?'

'Yeah, sure you can. Number Five, Westland Road, North Hill.'

That was Khadar's old address.

You could never be too careful. She might be going off to share that *Chablis* with the Joneses.

He rang off.

Silence.

The fateful rapping at the door had stopped without his noticing it.

I've beaten them!

Twenty

Steve woke from the nightmare and uttered a shuddery moan of horror.

Floating inches above his face was a black-veined ball of pale flesh. The room was filled by a lurid yellow light that dimmed and brightened in time to a slow, deep beat. The throb of a huge heart.

He recoiled spasmodically, rolling off the bed and thudding onto the floor in a flailing heap.

The window was obscured by an immense, bulbous tumour that quivered violently. Something vigorous squirmed within—

Get to the door!

The tumour split apart and a ponderous mass of thick coils slopped out onto the bed.

Steve wailed and scrawled backwards on his hands and heels. The coils writhed convulsively on the bed for a moment and then sprang at him and looped themselves around his naked body with shocking speed. He cried out in disgust. The thing was cold, and so soft he could feel the sharp, narrow ribs beneath its skin, yet it was also tremendously powerful and he could do nothing to stop it gliding swiftly around his chest and belly, drawing ever tighter as it moved.

His right arm was still free.

He punched and clawed the coil as it tried to encircle his neck. His fingers sank into the putty-like flesh. He clawed at the ribs below. These slid up and down to avoid his grasp. A human-sized rib cage was buried in the filthy mass.

He screamed and started to thrash with his free arm. By chance he landed a blow square on the ribs. The coils shuddered with pain, shaking him from side to side like a dry stick.

At the same moment, the extremities of the thing, which he hadn't seen yet, shot up to either side of him.

The coils had a face at each end.

The skin was stretched grotesquely over their deformed skulls, but the faces were just about recognisable as Quaid and Katherine. The eyes were quite dead, as if they were not connected to anything behind, and yet they watched him intently. He whimpered and sobbed. Very slowly, they turned to each other to share an unfathomable gaze.

'Oh you *foul…*'

Quaid's head snapped round.

Click!

His lower jaw dislocated and dropped. The mouth gaped so wide that the rest of his face – the eyes nose and even the cranium – were stretched back and revealed themselves to be nothing more than redundant appendages to the great glistening red gullet.

Steve stared into its depths and saw a man's rib cage deep inside, looking tiny as it nestled over the quaking pink stomach.

He let out a moan as the coils lifted him gently, manoeuvring him around so that Quaid's gigantic maw could envelope his legs. He kicked feebly. The power of the coils drained him of will. He sensed they could crush him in an instant. But they wouldn't. The Joneses wanted him alive, to writhe in unspeakable agony as he drowned in the acid of their gut. His feet momentarily caught the rim of Quaid's mouth and he felt lips to be as hard as solid bone. The jaws clamped down with exquisite delicacy and immobilised his legs. Then they squeezed a little harder and Steve squealed with pain. That's what the Joneses had wanted to hear. Now they grunted. The yellow, throbbing light of their heart beat glowed brighter – each sickening thump made the walls vibrate like a drum. Steve felt a gigantic force begin to suck him down into their gullet. But only by a little. Maybe they would take days to swallow him whole, inch by inch.

Steve's crazed despair found voice as a guttural sob. The beast's rigid jaws seemed to bend up a little.

Quaid was smiling.

Now Katherine, who had lain to one side, slid up and nuzzled him under the chin. Steve lashed out at one of her huge eyes. It squished like thick polythene. The black pupil might as well have been printed on heavy-duty plastic. Katherine drew back slowly, letting him know she was not hurt. And then once again came that disgusting—

Click!

—and Katherine's features flattened and slid away from her bony muzzle as her mouth yawned wide.

A retching sound – shockingly human – was followed by the disgorging of a reddish mess onto Steve's face.

He gagged and shook his head and the thing fell off him onto the floor.

It was part-digested body of a baby. Jellied flesh and sodden skin hung in strips from its tiny skeleton, but the head was still alive and the eyes swivelled in their sockets and looked up at him.

Your son, Steven!

Katherine's face drew close to his, as if to savour his reaction in the finest detail.

He groaned and closed his eyes. 'Go on then, finish it,' he wept.

Their laughter hissed into his ears and he knew they intended to make his agony last for as long as possible.

'No…please help.'

They laughed and hissed louder, but through the noise he suddenly heard—

Chirrup!

—a sparrow calling to him as if a distant shore.

The laughter stopped and a tremor went through the coils of the Joneses.

He opened his eyes.

Katherine's dead face was no longer nuzzling him. She and Quaid were looking at each other in a parody of bemusement.

They had been taken unawares in their leisurely game.

All at once, Katherine's head was darting frantically from side to side, her huge hollow jaws clopping at the air.

Make him die – NOW!

The great muscles of Quaid's throat tensed and Steve was drawn chest-deep down into the squelching gullet.

Too slow! Kill faster!

Steve's eyes blurred with pain as he was lifted from the floor, up and up, till his head almost brushed the ceiling. Then the beast began to shake him, harder and harder so as to snap his neck.

The room revolved, receded.

His back slapped against the floor.

Haaahhhhh

All the air whooshed out of him. His lungs burned and the pain emptied his mind. He clawed at empty space in a blind panic. He couldn't draw breath. The room darkened as an incredible weight crushed him. His ribs creaked and groaned.

Die, Smith! Die! Die! Die...No! No! Not that!

Nooooo!

The weight vanished.

Cool air flooded into him and the light came back.

His arms and legs were unbound. He was free.

Thunk! Thunk! Thunk!

The floor was vibrating.

Quaid and Katherine were thrashing around in a hissing fury. Their leprous white flanks knotted and unknotted as they smacked at the walls and the floor. In its torment, the colossal beast filled the whole room, so that Steve expected to be crushed at any moment. He crawled into a corner and cowered. The coils arched and froze in a final, overwhelming agony and in an eye blink, they shrivelled to what looked like a quaking heap of rotten intestines.

They whipped themselves away under the bed with blinding speed and a second later there was nothing left to show that they had ever existed.

A fist hammered at the door.

'Oi! Any more of this and we'll get you sectioned under the *Mental Health Act of 1984*. You mad bastard, you!'

A flat-footed tread receded down the landing.

It was morning.

The sun burnished the rooftops of the houses opposite and the lilting songs of little birds bubbled up from the garden below.

Steve got to his feet.

He felt peculiar. Light headed.

Was he sick?

He didn't think so. Surely this light headedness was something he used to get all the time, before his skull had filled with cold, sullen clay.

Oh yes, I remember now. The last time I felt like this I was turning into Orchard Drive one sunny evening after work...

And this funny feeling of his – it even had a name.

Blissful happiness.

Belinda!

He reached for his phone. The screen showed that his solicitor had sent him a text. There hadn't been a bird calling from a distant shore. The sparrow's, *Chirrup* was the ring tone he used to signal an incoming message on his phone. He read the text—

Sale concluded at ten.

The time was now three minutes past.

Oh yeah – I sold the house, didn't I?

Thinking about that now – selling the house at far less than half price had been rather rash of him.

Um, that might take some explaining. Still... Never mind!

Why should Bel and him get hung up on petty details like that? They would find a pretty, little cul-de-sac somewhere and buy another house. A brand-new, fresh start was what they needed anyway.

He called her mobile.

She wasn't connected to the service.

'Come on, Bel.'

He tried her parent's landline. He felt more than equal to tackling her mother today. Just as he'd always been before the nervous breakdown. The one he'd finally recovered from.

Jeffery, her father answered. 'Steven, we've been trying to contact you.'

'I wasn't at home. I did call Bel on her phone just now. Any chance I might speak to her?'

'Not at the moment, no.'

'But I've got some urgent news for her.'

'Steven, she lost the baby last night.'

Twenty-One

'Good morning, Mrs Hatlespalle!'

Steve always had a big sunny smile on his face as he sauntered into *Serpinki Gaskets Ltd*.

And the look Mrs Hatlespalle gave him in return made

his efforts to be nice all the more rewarding.

Lately, Mrs Hatlespalle's skin had taken on a buff hue. Not because it had been bathed by the golden sun of a foreign holiday, but because it had been stained the drugs of her cancer treatment.

Stop right there, buddy.

Smiling thinly, Steve had forestalled all further remarks from the grape vine. He did not wish to hear about Mrs Hatlespalle's cancer treatment, thank you *very much.*

Tell you what, I'll give her an extra, extra big sunny smile every morning. That'll cheer her up.

You see, these days Steve accentuated the positive.

And he absolutely refused to deviate from this policy. In his world, *BAD* news was *NO* news. Like his divorce, it was strictly *OFF AIR*, *censored* and *erased* from the history books.

'What?'

'I said, *Good morning, Mrs Hatlespalle!*'

'Mr Eschops wants to see you. He said, *As soon as you roll in.*'

Steve checked his watch.

'Oh, I seemed to have rolled in ten minutes early today. Great!'

As he bounded on into the office, he heard an angry little buzz from Mrs Hatlespalle's waspish heart – that last, dried-up outpost of the Joneses's power.

But he had his answer ready.

Cancer will quieten you soon enough...

'Come in,' Eschops called.

Steve was already in. He had such a spring in his step these days that he found it impossible to stand still and wait once he had knocked on anybody's door.

'Oh.'

'You wanted to see me?'

'I wanted to see you.' Eschops leaned back behind his desk, his heavy brows flexed into a puzzled frown, his jowls more droopy than ever. His mug was going to stick like that one day if he wasn't careful. 'Sit down, Steven.'

Steve was already sitting.

'Ah.'

'Anything wrong?'

'Well – yes.'

'Oh, dear.'

Eschops raised a weary paw.

'No, there's nothing wrong with you, Steven.' His puzzled frown cut a little deeper. 'No, not a thing. Incredible really – the improvement over the past few months. Ever since you got over your nervous breakdown.'

'My nervous breakdown?'

'You know, drawing skulls, creeping around the office like a snake was going to pop up out of every wastebasket.' He smiled genially.

'I don't remember that last bit. But it's true, early this year my personal life sort of hit a wall. Oh, I know it shouldn't be a factor at work, but something like that does take its toll.'

'No doubt, no doubt...' Eschops leaned forward, making his breath wheeze through his nostrils. He searched Steve's face. 'So anyway, what do you think of Alok, then?'

'He's great!'

'No, no.' Eschops rocked his big head – like a sickly bear does. 'Be honest.'

'Okay, he's fine.'

'I like the loyalty. But no, he's not.'

'No?'

'He phoned me at home last night, just after twelve.'

'Hm?'

'Sobbing, he was.'

'Sobbing? What was the emergency?'

'All I got out of him was that he wasn't well enough to come to work.'

'Dodgy Chinese takeaway?'

Eschops's top rattled. His pressure was rising. 'No, Steven. The signs have been there for some time. Don't tell me you didn't notice.'

'Well,' Steve began with the delicate, spooky, tippy-toed caution of a long-legged spider. 'I hate to mention this, but once in the toilets, you know, he was there and I was there and his aim was so off that I virtually had to float like a butterfly to stay out of the…spray. It was *not*, let me emphasize, deliberate. At least I don't think so. Rather, it was his nerves. His hands were trembling like he was throttling a python. A boneless one, I hasten to add. Yes, come to think of it, he had all the signs…loss of nerve, loss of sleep – loss of mind. Just *wrong*, isn't it? I mean, not nice for him.'

'Too many words, Steven. I just want the gist. As a fellow sufferer – once – you'd say he's having a nervous breakdown. Yes or no?'

'I'm not a doctor, but—'

'But he's having a nervous breakdown?'

Steve nodded primly.

'I thought as much. He was blubbering such nonsense. Then he tried to tender his resignation. But I don't let someone go that quickly just because they're going through a sticky patch.'

'Of course not.'

'And you got over it. You're as right as rain now… You are, aren't you?'

'Better, even.'

'That's what I thought. So I said to him, *Don't resign – just yet, Alok. Take time out and rest and see how it goes.'*

'Ah.' Steve weighed this up. 'A rest as apposed to a nightmarish crisis? Um…it might work.'

'I don't understand what you mean. We *can't* rest. The *Contra-Head-Gasket-Project Team* is going all to pot.'

'I had the impression it was already going to pot under Alok.'

Eschops spoke with studied calm. 'But he was ill, wasn't he, Steven?'

'That's right. I of all people ought be more sympathetic.'

Eschops sighed. The weight of the world was upon the poor, weary, five-foot-four grizzly's shoulders.

'That's what I assumed. So, what I would like is that you take up the mantle of team leader. In Alok's absence. Try to keep things moving, eh? Till he's back on his feet.'

Steve looked Eschops in the eye and said, 'But Michel, whether he gets back on his feet or not, I feel I can take this project to completion. Just me. On my own.'

Eschops scowled.

'Oh, you think so, do you?'

'Yes, I do so. Observing from outside, I saw a lot of purposeless activity. Alok was trying to lead from behind. And then he had a habit of taking credit for other people's solutions. Like the problem with the *Unidirectional-Ralyard Pin*. That was *my* solution, Michel. But then he said to me later, probably in the toilet, that he had come up with the solution to the problem all by himself.'

'But didn't he?'

'No, like I say, he didn't. *I* did. The evidence is on the server. I can show you.'

'All right. We'll look. But perhaps the pressure made Alok unwell, so you—'

'Look, I'm giving you my word here. One, I won't have a nervous breakdown and two, that if I lead the team then I shall bring you the goods within the next five weeks.'

'I'm already asking you to become team leader – till Alok gets back.'

'But what I'm saying is, if I put an aluminium prototype of the new design on your desk within five weeks, then I should stay promoted, whether Alok comes back or not.'

Eschops smiled for the first time. He nodded ever so slightly.

'Okay…if I get the new design on my desk before Alok comes back, Steven, I'll seriously think about it.' His smile broadened. '*IF.*'

Twenty-Two

One mellow, sun-filled Saturday afternoon at the very end of summer and Steve lay on the bed in his rented room and let himself be brushed by the curtains as they played in the breeze.

He woke from his tobacco trance, sat up and gazed through the window at the wild garden below – luxuriant and vital because it was untended and ignored by Man.

And yet, despite the Arcadian scenery, he felt sick at heart.

These glorious days were being overshadowed by the ominous possibility that Alok would recover from his mysterious malaise and return to work before the *Steve-Smith Gasket Design* was up and running in cold aluminium.

If that happened, he would be back to square one at *Serpinski Gaskets Ltd*.

And the devil of it was, Steve had found delivering the prototype far harder than he had foreseen. They were nowhere near getting it yet, and as the man had said—

IF I get the new design on my desk before Alok comes back, Steven, you keep the job… IF.

IF…

Well, for reasons too monstrous to dwell on, Steve doubted whether Alok would ever be seen again.

But on the other hand, what if he were wrong?

You see, it was the *not knowing* that was beginning to get to him. He wasn't sleeping on account of it. When you had anxiety gnawing at you night and day like this – who knew to what that led eventually?

To another nervous breakdown, perhaps.

Oh God, I've got *to put my mind at rest.*

An hour later he reached the familiar streets. His heart thumped painfully in his chest. He could not turn into Orchard Drive itself, like he used to in the Golden Age. What torments of remorse and nostalgia would that bring?

He parked round the corner.

He had arrived at the suburban dead hour, disturbed by only the occasional car droning along the main road. He hesitated at the head of the drive and, loaded down by melancholy, walked down and forced himself to look at the house.

Former home of former husband and former wife.

It had a porch now, (the Singh's must have built it) but nothing else had changed. At least, not to look at from the outside. As for the Joneses's house, it was just how Mrs Oliphant had left it. No trace of any home improvements whatsoever.

The illusion that the Joneses had woven into his head had dissolved into nothingness.

That said, an alteration since past times did gradually become apparent to him as he contemplated both houses. They wore a faint air of abandonment. Perhaps the windows didn't sparkle quite as much they should have. And the front lawns were a trifle overgrown.

Steve steeled himself.

Hello Alok! I was just passing old chap. I say, you look great... Um? Really? How dreadful! I know only too well how you feel. No, I think I'll pass on buying the house back. Yes even for half the price you gave me. Still too big for this divorcee. Nah thanks. I think I'll be going now. Ta-ta!

He pressed the doorbell.

Ten seconds.

Thirty.

A full minute.

Deep down he knew no one was going to ever answer this door again. He considered a sortie around the side to the back garden just to make sure.

Ex occupier? Sorry, no ghosts here, please.

And so there was nothing else to do but wander away, take a stroll around the old neighbourhood and finally unburden himself of the past.

One of the familiar streets that he followed led over a bridge that spanned the old disused railway track. The very one that ran behind the house. It had been turned into a public footpath years ago and was mainly used by joggers and dog walkers. Steve and Belinda had never once visited it, even though they would have been able to take a look at their house from there.

But then, why would the blessed want to look at paradise from the outside in?

But a paradise that had been completely ruined — that almost sounded like a sightseer's destination.

He descended to the footpath under the bridge and followed it. When he was in the right spot, he climbed the old embankment and found a gap between the wild briars and the low branches of the hawthorn trees.

After a struggle, he managed to reach the lapboard fence, which he'd put up years before at the bottom of his garden.

He peered over.

What he saw was so odd he couldn't register it at first.

Both couples were outside. The women lay on the ground, sprawled like discarded dolls. Alok's wife, good-old Guldip, lay face down on the patio. Her arms were bent in a way that didn't seem possible. Katherine was stretched out on the lawn. She was on her back. A cloud of flies covered her face. Her mouth was wide open. Who knew what was hatching inside?

The men, meanwhile, were still on their feet and facing each other off across the garden fence. Both were draped in rags. Their dun-coloured flesh was emaciated to the bone. Here and there purple sores glistened as they leaked and dribbled.

They stared at each other, showing no visible emotion as they swayed and wove, undulating like weeds under water. They were fighting with invisible weapons – feinting and dodging as they tirelessly probed for a lethal advantage.

The struggle was taking place in deadly silence.

Steve very nearly cheered them on in their eerie battle, but something told him it would not be prudent to make himself the focus of their attention.

At last, the light dimmed. A cheerful mistle thrush and other little birds commenced their familiar evening songs all around him in the hedge. As ever, they did not care a whit for the gruesome monsters in the garden. But while he himself was fascinated by the monsters, Steve did not care to be alone in the dark with those swaying things.

He slipped away.

Oh yes, he was most certainly followed. His dreams that night were haunted by two dual-headed beasts. But their second heads were dead and putrefying. They were weak.

He batted these nightmares away easily.

First thing next morning, he returned to the scene.

Damn! I missed it!

Both Quaid and Richard lay unmoving on the ground. It seems Quaid's femur had shattered. The jagged end of the bone had thrust itself clear of the grey flesh of his thigh and now it pointed triumphantly up at the sky.

How Steve wished he had heard that rotten—

Crack!

But even so, what strength these creatures had! Even in the unspeakable agony of his death throes, Quiad had *still* brought Alok down.

Exhausted, infected – covered in running sores, they had both died in the night.

Rain was beginning to fall and Steve could already smell a hideous odour. The females were rapidly decomposing.

Soon, their mates would be joining them.

Steve Smith's heart surged with triumph and he gave the nearest hawthorn a high-five.

The spiky branch gouged great bloody lumps from his palm and he trumpeted loud enough to scatter the birds—

'Result!'

RUBBER SOUL

One

Phil (the Hedge Cutter) told Wayne (the Scrap-Metal Entrepreneur) about the big lump of copper in the garden.

'It's on a pillar, because it's a sculpture. I've always wondered whether it was bolted down or not, but as the man's always there I could never check before last week, when he was gone for a hospital appointment. So, it isn't bolted down. It's just a blob of solid copper standing on this low pillar, but with a hole through it, so you can get a proper grip. I reckon it weights well above thirty pounds, but a lad like you will lift it, no trouble, eh?'

'Whose garden is it?'

Phil's gaze drifted around the half-empty bar. The place was grimy and menacing, as bars near train stations are apt to be.

'A good client's, so I feel guilty about him losing his sculpture, like. Except, he's a suspicious bastard and I wouldn't be surprised if he goes and says he won't use me no more. But that won't matter.'

'Why not?'

'I'll be losing his business anyway. Well, how much for the copper, you reckon?'

'A hundred, maybe.'

'A hundred? Us two each?'

'No, Phil. A hundred for the lot. *Fifty* each.'

Phil's mouth collapsed inwards. Most of his front teeth had come out years ago and this was as close to pursing his lips as he could get. 'Don't kid me, boy.'

Wayne sighed. 'Okay. You come with me to *Tracey Stakeholdings* and see how much I get off Ed.'

'Ed Tracey? Well there you are, he's a crook. Why do you deal with him?'

Wayne shook his head at Phil. 'Because he *is* a crook, and he'll melt it down without no papers.'

'This thing don't need no papers. It's a lump of metal rusting in a man's garden. You ain't stripping cable off the railways, or anything serious like that.'

'He most likely thinks his copper's serious.'

'But he's terminally ill, dying like, so he won't be around that long to miss it. And anyway, when he pops off, someone else will have it in a flash. Then *they*'ll get it melted down.'

'And they'll get more for it too, 'cause they'll have papers. Anyway, I'm not doing it.'

'How come? Because he's dying?'

Wayne smiled at the notion. 'Apart from that, I don't like the idea of going into someone's private garden. That is burglary. Stripping cable off the railways isn't like burglary, somehow. Less personal, like.'

'But this ain' burglary neither, boy. It's just trespassing on his garden a bit. And it isn't so personal because he isn't at home this week. He's gone to the Canaries. A winter warmer, he calls it.'

'*That*'s nice.' The only winter warmer Wayne could afford was a two-bar electric fire.

'And he lives on his own, so the house is empty. It's got wide-open access on the left-hand side, so you don't even have to open a gate. And the area's dead by night.

Well heeled, isn't it. Everyone's tucked up by two. And there's a vet's a few doors along, so you can even park off the road.'

'That is a good thing.'

'God above, Wayne, you couldn't make the job easier. Except, just for a hundred it ain't worth it, is it?'

'Well … it *could* be worth more, I think.'

'How much?'

'We won't never know that, will we, unless you tell me where it is.'

Two

53 Dardelle Lane was a large 1970's detached house set in spacious grounds and surrounded by tall, fat hedges that bulged over the pavement. The area was an affluent suburb where everybody's hedges bulged over the pavements. That didn't matter. No one actually walked around here. The locals either sat indoors, or sat in their 4x4s. Everyone else, including Wayne, simply did not belong. That didn't bother Wayne. He was used to passing in and out of places where he did not belong.

The street lamps had been switched off at twelve and now the moon was at the top of the sky and illuminating the house with its merciless stare. Wayne stood at the head of the drive, his breath smoking in the severe cold, and watched the place for some long moment before he advanced to the left side of the house, which Phil told him gave easy access to the rear. The pathway was concealed by total darkness, but he risked scanning the way with his torch, taking just a couple of seconds to check there was nothing to trip over. Then he tip-toed down blind into the back garden, over which the stark moon poured her leprous light. It was expansive, mostly paved, but with a terrace at the far end on which a row of skeletal trees had their heads among the frosty stars.

The copper sat on its pedestal, surrounded by empty space and drifts of leaves. Wayne hurried over. The statue was tear-drop shaped and had a hole just big enough to allow his arm to pass through. He braced himself and the icy air whistled in his nostrils as he raised the copper just enough to test its heft. His grimace changed into a grin of joy. He would get three hundred quid for this, or rather, two-hundred and fifty after he'd given Phil his, ahem, fifty per cent cut…

As he clung lovingly to the blob, he noticed something. Quite what, he could not say. A subtle change of light, or of the density of the air, or even a whisper of leaf that was too faint for the conscious mind. Whatever it was, he twisted round to look over one shoulder.

Just a couple of paces away was the looming, hulking figure of a man. His face was contorted into a fiendish mask that blazed and actually *steamed* in the moonlight. Two neon-white eyes glared at him with pure hatred.

He was holding a baseball bat above his head.

An electric shock of terror lit up the night and Wayne jerked backwards. Not far though – his arm was trapped.

Oh God, I'm going to die!

The man wasn't moving yet. He must have stalked up so very carefully, his utterly resolved on delivering… the death blow.

I'm going to die, I'm going to die!

Wayne struggled and whinnied. He was helpless. The man *still* did not move. His face kept twisting, his glowing white eyes growing larger and larger. Then his mouth gaped, forming a deep black hole. The baseball bat fell from his hands and clattered hollowly on the hard ground as he clawed desperately at his chest. A second later, he sagged, gurgling and hissing. All the living tension went right out of him and he sank to the floor, his limbs dropping randomly and his head going—

Clonk!

—on the frozen slabs.

Wayne's arm came free of the sculpture, just like the nasty thing had let him go, and he leapt forward, frantic to get that baseball bat, then he danced wildly around the body, getting read to make the fucker's head go—

Clonk!

—all round the garden.

By a miracle, of sorts, reason prevailed and he did not deliver a single vengeful stroke.

It's okay, he told himself. *He's dead. Leave off. If he looks like he's been battered the police won't never rest till they got you.*

Wayne was pretty sure the man had suffered a heart attack. He had the clear, childhood recollection of his own father's, *Surprise! Surprise!* death to help with the happy diagnosis.

He slowly lowered the baseball bat.

But then again, was this guy really, truly and *definitely* dead?

In light of the appalling shock he had just received and the mess he would be in if God hadn't intervened on his behalf, Wayne felt sorely aggrieved to think the man might go on to live. He wanted to be certain that divine justice had been served on this murderous son of a bitch. And too, he would like to be able to remove the lump of copper without a pair of cold hands unexpectedly clutching at him from behind. So, he took his torch and held the lens under the man's nose for a few seconds, then he pointed the touch at the sky and switched it on. The light shone bright through unclouded glass.

All clear.

His pounding heart began to slow to its usual even and sullen thud.

He noted now that the corpse was wearing a dressing gown, which immediately suggested that this was the householder, who, having spotted an intruder in his garden, hadn't waited to dress before making a sortie to preserve his pointless sculpture.

So the man had *not* been away on his winter warmer, had he, Philip?.

You toothless old bastard, you ain' getting a penny out of this.

But, as soon as Wayne enfolded the teardrop of copper in his arms, he realised he wouldn't be getting a penny out of this neither. The man was dead in his garden and if the sculpture were missing the two facts would be connected. Sure, a heart attack had caused his demise, the doctors would agree with Wayne, but who had caused the heart attack? Eh? Wayne. And Wayne belonged to the underclass. Everyone knew the courts and what they thought of the underclass. If the cops got hold of him, they would call the man's death a case of *Murder by Heart Attack*. And the fuckers would make the charge stick too. True, the police normally wouldn't have stood a chance in tracing him, because his operations were purely opportunistic, but in this instance there was someone who could inform on him. Somehow, when he remembered Phil's collapsed, flabby mouth, Wayne just knew that mouth would flap without anyone even slapping it.

Goddamn it. I'm going to charge him for the time and petrol I've wasted.

Wayne was hurrying away from the crime scene when noticed the front door was slightly ajar. He came to an abrupt stop. Not because his immediate thought was to go inside and make this visit worthwhile after all, but rather because it struck him then how easily the householder could have shouted at him from an upstairs window and sent him running. Everyone knew most burglars would run, didn't they? But instead, this particular householder had crept out into the freezing night and tip-toed all the way around the house with the fixed purpose of killing him.

He was gagging to for, wasn't he? Wayne thought wonderingly. *He wanted to see me lying there, with my brains on the outside.*

And then, recalling that most of those thugs he knew were currently sitting in prison for far lesser crimes than such cold-blooded murder, he was struck by the certainty that the law would have been far more forgiving towards this solid citizen. Yes, he was absolutely convinced the murderous son of a bitch would have got off scot-free. And yet, if he, Wayne, a mere burglar, were caught, the law would show no mercy.

Stung by injustice of this every bit as much as the most virtuous human-rights barrister, but expecting less by way of remuneration, Wayne slipped into the dark house and gently pushed the door shut.

First he paused, sniffed the warm air and strained his ears for the smallest sound of life. A minute or more passed and he could hear nothing but the, *Geh-lunk, Geh-lunk, Ge-lunk* of a big old clock in the hallway. He put on his flashlight and sending the beam this way and that saw that everything looked like it was worth a packet, including the big, old clock, which was as big as a coffin. In every corner he saw polished sideboards and tables made from rich, swirly wood and on top of these countless silver ornaments, generally in the shape of nude men. The paintings on the walls, when they weren't abstract, also focussed on undressed males. Bunches of them, lolling about together on lawns besides rivers. No pollution or litter or youths shooting up, so like not real. The one picture that really fixed Wayne's attention was – but no, the picture didn't fix his attention after all, but rather the immense frame of solid silver, worked up fantastically into leaves and roses that twined around a sort of shield at the bottom on which was engraved—

Well Met By Moonlight.

By God, though, Wayne's commercial side knew that once the frame was hammered down into a nice cube, he could make spending money on that silver!

Now don't act in haste, guy. Stick to cash. Can't trace cash.

His flashlight beam happened next to fall upon a phone. He stopped, stared and thought, *Oh shit! Did that son of a bitch call the police first?*

The layer of sweat covering Wayne's swaddled body actually went cold.

He pressed redial.

Soon there was a voice, saying that *Centrica Gas Services* were so happy to hear from him, but their office hours were eight to five.

The householder hadn't even called the police first!

Once again, Wayne wondered at the man's dauntless ferocity. It was animal-like. He thought of those white eyes again and shuddered.

Nevertheless, he pressed on and methodically hunted through every draw and cupboard that he came across. Downstairs first. He didn't find a penny. Burglary wasn't natural to him and he had to overcome a certain reluctance to climb the stairs and put himself in a position where he couldn't easily run for it. There was a large, moonlit window on the landing and he paused to look down at the body in the garden.

It could have been me, lying down there, dead.

Dead!

All at once his insides knotted up and his chest felt

tight.

'You *bastard*, you!'

He could see the blob of copper too, standing proud on its pedestal, painfully reminding him that he was set to make a loss on this job.

Unless he got a move and found some money.

Six doors lined the landing and one was open. The master bedroom. Wayne's heart quickened. When he had cash at home, he liked to sleep with it in the same room, so surely … but no, he could uncover nothing.

The second bedroom was unused and the cupboards and draws were empty.

Just can't be easy for once, can it?

He opened the next door. His roving flashlight revealed what appeared to be gym equipment and then…

A naked man, staring straight back at him and with one arm raised as if to throw something!

Wayne ducked. The flashlight slipped from his hand. He let out a cry. The darkness was suddenly full of danger. He grabbed wildly for the flashlight. The beam trembled crazily in his hand and the naked man danced before him, one arm still raised. Wayne kicked out at him.

'Back off! Back off!'

Suddenly, he realised that a struggle was not in fact taking place.

When he managed to hold the flashlight still, he saw that the man wasn't moving. In fact, he was utterly still. Too still to be alive.

Wayne was so spooked, he had to switch the room light on.

Everything was revealed.

He found himself standing in a kitsch dungeon. The naked man was a life-sized rubber doll, chained by one arm to a set of stocks. The other arm was raised, ludicrously, as if to wave, *Hello there!* to the onlooker. The thing was incredibly detailed, down to the genitals. The face even seemed to wear a sardonic smile. Its hair was styled in a fashion that was twenty years out of date and indeed the doll, although of a young man, looked worn and old. Wayne took a step forward and peered into the eyes. So realistic! The more he looked, the more he felt that they were looking back. That, in fact, someone was actually inside the doll. Unable to stop himself, Wayne shuddered and pressed a finger to the doll's chest. The rubber flesh sank sickeningly at his touch. The whole body quivered. It was hollow, like a balloon, weighing nothing.

He gave a start of revulsion and stepped back. Did the doll whisper to him?

Welcome to my filthy world of loneliness and isolation.

He got out of the room, and fast too. Enough was enough. There was nothing here, except…well there were still two doors he hadn't opened yet. You know, his luck had to change *someday*, didn't it?

The first door opened onto the main bathroom, the second onto the householder's home office.

Now this looked more promising.

An oak tallboy stood in one side and a metal filing cabinet in the other, and in between them writing bureau with a snoozing computer on top. Wayne went through the draws and found bundle after bundle of documents, stuff like cheque stubs, receipts and bank statements, all of which indicated that Maximilian Kekoko had an awful lot of money in various bank accounts. However, there wasn't a single actual penny anywhere. At length, he was reduced to searching through the papers piled untidily on one corner of the writing bureau, while listening to himself whine, over and over, 'God, man, this is such a waste of fucking time.'

The whining ceased.

He was reading.

The last will and testament of Maximilian Gerusimus Kekoko

Item One. *That upon my decease, my funeral and interment be carried out by* Selwyn Price and Son (Undertakers) Ltd *of Grimsby, who have been fully appraised of my wishes and have agreed to carry out the arrangements held on record by Bolgrester and Flynn, Solicitors.*

Item Two. *I hereby bequeath my entire estate, excepting the requisite materials necessary for* Selwyn Price and Son (Undertakers) Ltd *to fulfil their obligations, to Christopher Steffensson of Bloven Lane, Surry, SU2 7GB, in the hope that these riches bring him as much relief from unbearable heartache as they have brought to me.*

As Wayne mused over these words, a great bead of sweat ran down to the end of his nose and—

Splock

—landed right in the middle of the will. The ink instantly blurred into an ugly spot.

'Shit!'

He panicked and started whining again, thinking that, just like on the telly programmes, the cops would extract the DNA from the sweat stain using mega-fast DNA machines and then they'd have his address within minutes and then, and then … but hang about—

That's just on the telly. American telly, too. The cops here ain't got enough money to buy a sodding calculator.

Still, he felt he ought to take the will with him and destroy it, just to be on the safe side. How Maximilian's money got divided up was going to be *his* problem.

'You murdering, dirty pervert son of a bitch.'

Having balled the will up and rammed it in his pocket, he hastily restacked the documents on the desk and, as he did so, his hand accidentally knocked the computer mouse.

The screen came to life.

Running across it were the words—

The last will and testament of Maximilian Gerusimus Kekoko...

And so on and so on. Kekoko must have been working on his will just before Wayne had arrived in search of copper.

He clicked the print icon and out came a duplicate will. The signature was just an *MXK*. Now even Wayne could forge that.

He filed the new will away and was about to leave when—

Wait a bit ...! But, I couldn't get away with it ... could I? Well ... why not? It ain't like I'm actually taking anything, is it? They can't call me a thief, because nothing will be missing. There'll be no evidence at all. And it'll up to them whether they believe it or not.

In fact, it would as harmless as buying a lottery ticket.

His heart all aflutter, Wayne sat before the computer and began to add a new paragraph to the will—

Item Three, the sum of 25,000 pounds I do leave to Wayne Wykcliff Mulholland of Flat Five, the Parade, Parcissor Road, Shrewsbury SY8 2PP.

He contemplated the words and couldn't help feeling

they required something more to justify them, because, *Why did Wayne get put in the will?* would be the question on everyone's lips.

Because I fixed his car once? Because I saved him from drowning. Because I offered to donate my kidney? Because I deserve it?

Even *he* couldn't believe that. No, what he needed was something that couldn't be reduced to rubble by two seconds of legal scrutiny. What he needed was something that explained everything without saying anything…

The words came to him, as if by magic. And engraved in silver too.

Well met by moonlight.

An old man's gratitude for a fairly random sexual encounter – now who was going to say that wasn't impossible? Especially when he had a rubber man friend standing in his dungeon.

For that matter, why not add, *Item Four, I do hereby bequeath five thousand pence to my rubber man friend*?

Wayne was on such a roll, he almost did just that. Just for a laugh. But at the last second, he was stricken by a loss of confidence, *What if they paid the rubber doll but not me?*

Who'd be laughing then, eh?

He printed off the new will, signed it *MXK* and placed it where the original had been. His confidence returned. He had never done anything this clever in his life.

So few of us have.

Smiling to himself on his way out, Wayne glanced down into the garden to look at the body one more time.

He froze.

The corpse had moved a couple of feet.

It actually seemed to be twitching.

He yelped at the top of his voice.

That twenty-five thousand pounds – well, he had it all spent already! And now this corpse was pretty well sending the bailiffs around.

Wayne, busting with indignation, bounded down the stairs and out the front door. He hurtled headlong through the darkness into the rear garden and he flung himself onto the body of Maximilian Kekoko. Squatting over the trembling chest, he pinned the man's twitching arms with his knees he clamped one powerful gloved hand over the gaping hole of a mouth, which was noisily sucking life back into itself. He expertly pinched the flayed nostrils with his other hand and the short struggle began.

All the while, Kekoko glared up at him, his moonlit eyes ablaze with undying hatred.

Three

Wayne gave himself a wake-up call next morning with a screech of horror, 'Son of a bitch!'

He jumped out of bed like he was set to run for the hills. Only there weren't any hills to run to, were there? Why didn't he consider that fact last night? What the hell was he about, putting his *name and address* on the will?

It was the sort of stupidity the police prayed for.

If this got out, his total brainlessness would go *Whoop!* in the headlines and viral on the net. Worse, when he was hauled up in court for fraud, the prosecution (always unsympathetic types) would drive home the point that the words he had written in the will implied a casual sexual encounter with the deceased. They might even brand him a male prostitute, and his time in prison would not go well. Not well at all.

The visions he saw crowding his future were so horrible that he even considered getting married to try and establish in advance the true nature of his sexuality.

He had two fair maidens who would say, *Yes! Yes! Yes!*

Mimbissa – care worker.

Nalipha – hair dresser.

Together they probably topped four-hundred pounds. About a sixth of a ton (imperial). Great if they were made of copper, but…

Oh, God!

Anxiety wracked him in tumultuous waves and between the tumultuous waves were flat, oily stretches of suffocating apathy. As the day progress, he couldn't get a thing done. Even eating was a chore. The waiting killed him. The next twenty-four house didn't seem like they would ever get to number twenty four. The night was the worse. The very texture of the dark resembled the material of a police uniform. He expected a rude knock at the door at every moment. Whenever he dozed, he immediately got arrested and arraigned in a dream court.

But then the next day came and went, and so did the next and the next after that. So far as he could tell, they were exactly the same as his hard-bitten days always were. The papers and the rest of the media didn't mention Kekoko's death once, and the police didn't call, or even write. After two weeks, he became bored with the anguish of his private hell, and anyway other stuff came along to divert his thoughts. Like when Nalipha told him she was pregnant. Ha, she was too late! He didn't need to prove he was straight anymore. So he said, *Fuck off and get your fucking paternity test then/ And I ain't paying for that neither!* And she screamed, *No,* you *fuck off, I'm gonna to marry someone else anyway.* That made him laugh all right. So there, he had his old sense of humour back.

And yet, the world is an up-and-down sort of place. No sooner did he *not* get arrested for fraud than a gang of metal entrepreneurs moved into the area he operated in and stripped the metal off anything and everything before he got within a mile of it. These bastards had the corporate mentality and, as a lone trader, he didn't stand a chance. The lead of a church roof in Shifnal Town was stolen in a trice and this was church lead that he had earmarked to get him over the recent lull in his motivation. See, thinking that he was about to be arrested at any minute had really made metal trading seem rather pointless. And now it *was* pointless, on account of the gang. He may well have gone under in the current harsh economic climate if he didn't happen to have a part-time job at an independent garage. This classy outfit was located in a crumbling, mostly vacated industrial estate on the outskirts of town. The only heating they had was an old Alsatian dog you could stroke without getting bitten.

The temperature was down to three below zero and Wayne was outside flushing the oil out of an engine block when Phil the Hedge Cutter's dilapidated Jag came rolling along the concrete apron.

Oh yeah, that big lump of copper...

Amazing – he'd forgotten all about it... The car parked up, the door opened and slovenly, scraping footsteps came closer and closer, but Wayne didn't look up till Phil was standing right in front of him.

'All right, boy?'

'I'm fucking freezing.'

'Yeah?' Phil nodded towards his car. 'The electric box is on the blink.'

'You don't usually come here to get your motor fixed.'

'I thought as I would come see you anyway. I've been out of circulation for a month. Laid up.'

Wayne shook his head, as if to say, *What! Phil the Hedge Cutter laid up? I don't believe it!*

Phil went on.

'I had this new lad, Denford. He's the nephew of Harold – who I don't think you know. Christ though, what a gormless piece of shit. You could just about trust him to feed the mulcher, but, God knows, I wouldn't let him anywhere near the chainsaw. We was chainsawing down these little trees, see, hawthorns they was, on a plot around Derrington and this kid, Denford, all he had to do is help me carry the trunks and throw them on the pickup. You know, that flabby little fucker wrestled me all the way and then he let go too early and before I can tell him, *You're fucking sacked!* a little sucker branch whips round and a thorn stabs me right here. See?'

Phil rolled his sleeve up and revealed a square of bandage taped onto his thick, corded forearm. Running out from under the bandage were inky jagged lines, like black lightening bolts.

'Woh, nasty.'

'Next day, my whole arm swells up and I couldn't move. Fucking helpless. When the doctor seen me, I was rushed to hospital – the day after. The bastard hospital wouldn't take me no earlier. I tell you, I felt like I wanted to die. And I nearly did.'

'I was about to say, you look more fit than usual. You lost some weight.'

'I'm as weak as a kitten, me. That's why I'm here, apart from the electric box. I've got loads of work on and I need a strong lad with, as I've sacked Denford. What about it?'

'What, me?'

Which was *What, me?* as in, *My dear chap, I'm*

worth far more than a fuckwit kid called Denford.

'I mean for proper money, Wayne. Fifty-fifty cut on the earnings. You'll make a packet, and no need to say nothing to the tax, neither. Metal's a waste of time right now, isn't it? You didn't even get that copper.'

'How you know that?'

'Did a job for the neighbour and popped my head over the hedge and I saw the copper was still there. Couple of weeks ago, that was. He's dead you know.'

Wayne flinched.

'Who is?'

'Old Kekoko. Owner of the copper.'

'Not when I went over he wasn't! You said he was abroad, but the fucker wasn't. He was at home … and still alive too, 'cause I saw him through the window, moving about.' Wayne spoke defiantly and examined Phil's ugly mug for any sign of that he was not being believed, but Phil's ugly mug was inscrutable.

'Was he? That's a surprise.'

'It was a surprise all right, Phil.'

'Okay, okay, I didn't know. I went by what he told me. Mind, he was a sneaky, nasty bugger, and all, so maybe, he was trying to catch me out, like.'

'What for? What would he have done if he had caught you out, eh?'

Phil looked baffled. 'I don't know. Phoned the law, I suppose…I don't know.'

'When did he die, exactly?'

'Eh? Oh, weeks ago. You can forget the copper, whoever got it will have melted it down by now.'

'I bet that gang's had it. They're a right bunch of—'

Phil frowned at his watch. 'Hey, look, I better shift – the missus.' He turned abruptly and started back to his car.

Wayne called. 'What about your electric box?'

Phil stopped and turned. 'Oh yeah …But nah, I don't trust them here. Hopeless fucks – except you, Wayne. Think it over today, about giving us a hand, 'cause I need someone by tomorrow.'

He drove off and Wayne finished flushing the block and then did other things that were dirty and only to be done out in the freezing cold.

He was cleaning up when his phone buzzed.

Old Phil's changed his mind. He don't trust me neither.

'Yeah?'

'Hello? Mister Wayne Mulholland?'

This was a different voice from Phil's, or anyone else's in the greyed-out sphere he inhabited. It was a voice that came, somehow, from higher up. From where the sun actually shone.

'Who's calling?'

'My name is Sidney Rose and I work for *Leyland and Sweet, Solicitors*. So anyway, is this Wayne I'm speaking too?'

He decided to risk it. 'Yeah, it is. What's up?'

'I've been asked to contact you with the utmost urgency in relation to a bequest to you made by a Mr Maximilian Kekoko.'

Wayne's mind whirled. 'Who?'

'Maximilian Kekoko. Have you not heard the name before?'

'Oh, *Kekoko* … Max! Yes. He … um.'

'The sum in question is two-hundred and fifty thousands pounds.'

'Two *hundred*?'

'Yes.'

'But—' *That's not what I wrote! You mean twenty-five!*

Wayne went clammy all over. Did he actually say

that last bit?

'Pardon?'

'I said, That's not like – real. I can't believe it.'

'Know what you mean. This is the oddest case I've ever dealt with.'

'Is that right?'

'And I've handled some odd cases.'

This reference to *cases* reminded Wayne that he was talking to a solicitor and, as a rule, he kept conversations with representatives of the law as brief as possible.

'So, you'll be sending me a cheque, then?'

'No. The money's there, but we have to meet up and talk first. It's a prerequisite. And it's got to be today. I'm at the *Golden Lion Hotel* right now. Can you be here within a couple of hours?'

Four

Twenty minutes later, Wayne stood outside the *Golden Lion Hotel*, which had been built long, long ago, when this burg was a kind of country town, rather than a choked up mess surrounded by endless acres of bog-standard housing estates.

He went in. The walls were panelled in dark wood and a big open fire place in one corner had a grate full of glowing coals – so much cosier than two electric bars. A Polish woman at the reception desk told him Sidney Rose was sitting right behind him and he turned to see a square-built young man in a suit sitting in one of the old-fashioned armchairs. All the rest were empty. Rose stood up and shook Wayne's hand. He had the face of a toughie who had gone into sales. His dark hair was slicked back, revealing streaks of blue-white scalp.

'Thanks for coming, Mister Mulholland. Join me for a drink? I've already ordered coffee.' It was that voice again – the voice of someone privately educated and brought up on the better side of whatever town he had come from.

'Sure. Anything'll do. But I still can't believe it. Two-*hundred* and fifty thousand pounds. He really left me that?'

'It all depends.'

'*Depends*? What does that mean?'

'I'll explain. Please, take the weight of your feet.' Rose sat down and Wayne sat opposite. 'Like I said, this is a strange one. Kekoko's solicitor's refused to acknowledge the last will he made.'

'Kekoko's solicitor? That's you.'

'Nope. We represent Christopher Steffensson. You've not heard of him?'

'Um, maybe… Maybe Max mentioned him, but I don't remember what he said.'

Rose smiled. 'No? Strange, because Mr Steffensson must have been an old friend, surely.'

'An old man like that is bound to have lots of old friends.'

'Well Mr Kekoko left this old friend everything owned. Every penny.'

'Except for the two-hundred and fifty, right?'

'Wrong. You see, there's another will. The original will, lodged with his solicitors. No one else knew that another will existed – the will that mentions you, that is. Not before Mr Steffensson happened to look through the files on Kekoko's computer and found it there. The updated version of the will. The will he had written, apparently, the very night that he died. Anyway, Mr Steffensson contacted Kekoko's solicitor for further information about you and he was told in confidence that they had very grave doubts and reservations. Before you ask, I don't know what they were. But anyway, they confirmed that a paper copy of this so-called last will had indeed been found, but since it was felt that there was something... amiss about it, they retained it as evidence. Just in case you, Wayne Mulholland, *Surfaced from the depths*, as they put it.'

'What the hell does that mean?'

Rose shook his head. 'I dunno. I'm just repeating what they told Mr Steffensson.'

'They shouldn't have done that, retained it. That ain't legal, is it?'

'No, they should have destroyed it, I think. Just my opinion. It wasn't notarised, you see. No witnesses. His house was left open for some days before he was found. So, any sort of fly-by-night character might conceivably have popped in and written it. No?'

'No! I don't know. Well, if you say so. Fuck it then, why you talking to me, if this Seffensson guy got the lot?'

'Mr Steffensson wants to honour Kekoko's last wishes. How about that?' In reply, Wayne just stared. Rose nodded. 'Yes, it's a queer one all right. Still, you might get to the bottom of it tonight.'

'How's that?'

'It's a stipulation, Wayne. Mr Steffensson will honour the so-called last will, which he absolutely doesn't have to do, but he'll honour it anyway. However, *only* if, you spend tonight with him.'

'Spend the night?'

Rose leaned back in his armchair and looked around to see where the waitress with the coffee was. He spoke with not fully repressed distaste. 'He gave me to understand he'd like to meet the remarkable young man who's company must have given Max, his old friend, so much *pleasure* towards the end. It is a cruel irony, Wayne, that Mr Steffensson himself is gravely ill. He's given me to understand that he hasn't much longer to live. So, if it's a matter of going out with a smile on your face, I expect a quarter of a million must be a small price to pay.'

As Rose was saying this, the waitress appeared and put the coffee on the table. He had ordered two cups, like he knew the exact time Wayne was going to turn up. Wayne stared at the steam rising from the coffee and saw horrible pictures of embracing male nudes – the sort of pictures that had been everywhere in Kekoko's house. That was bad enough, but he turned positively nauseous when he recalled that odious rubber doll.

Meanwhile, Rose sipped his coffee quickly, as if to rid his mouth of a nasty taste.

Five

They drove South throughout the afternoon and into the evening. At last, Sidney dropped Wayne off on a crescent of large executive houses that sliced into the winter countryside.

'So, I'll collect you in the morning. Have fun.'

A few flakes of snow floated around Wayne while he watched Rose's car depart and then he turned to look around. Not a single light was on anywhere. The street was so bleak that he couldn't believe anyone was alive behind the blank windows around him.

Number five.

He knocked lightly and the door immediately opened, gliding inwards with a faint whine because it was motorised. In the hallway, looking up at him with the fixed gaze of the very, very ill, was a completely bald, heavily bearded man in a wheelchair. He wore a thick, brown dressing gown and his white hands seemed to glow as they rested in his lap. They were wasted almost to the bone.

The man gave him a weak smile.

'Please come in, Mr Mulholland.' His voice was shockingly coarse, like it vibrated off raw gristle.

Wayne nodded and clumped over the threshold with a heavy tread. He looked down at his boots. 'Sidney Rose just dropped me off. He's coming back at nine tomorrow.'

'Yes, I know. You don't have to take your shoes off, the carpet doesn't matter.' He raised and offered one skeletal hand. 'I'm Chris, of course.' Wayne took the hand. It was freezing cold and rough, almost abrasive. 'Thanks for coming.' The hand slipped from his and pressed a button on a remote controller taped to one arm of his wheel chair. The door whined shut. Wayne turned to watch it close and didn't immediately turn back.

Chris cleared his throat. 'I've had the house automated.'

'Oh yeah?'

'The further down the hill I've gone, the more I've automated. I don't have much left to automate.'

Wayne's attention was drawn to the mass of bars that ran up alongside the stair case. The rails of a stairlift. A lot of metal. But he was so preoccupied by the disgusting idea of having some kind of sex with this man that he couldn't even begin to calculate its scrap value. An odour of rot floated in the air. His gorge rose and that was that, he couldn't go through with it. He had a revelation then.

Money couldn't buy him.

Incredible!

'I'll call a taxi.'

'What for?'

Wayne pulled his phone out. 'I ain't doing nothing with you.'

'Wait. I don't understand.' Chris held out his hand

towards him. 'Let me explain.'

'Nah.'

'Listen, please. I know you forged the will. I saw you do it.'

Wayne stopped jabbing his phone. 'You what?'

'Max had cameras hidden all over his house. Running all the time. For security. I watched the recordings.'

Wayne stared into space. He was trying to remember if he had seen anything that looked like a hidden camera back at Kekoko's house. No, he couldn't. But then, he wouldn't have, would he?

What a stupid idiot!

'Bastard, bastard, *bastard!*' He punched the air, just like that was going to make him look any smarter.

Chris flicked a joystick on his wheelchair and smartly reversed halfway down the hall. Wayne was surprised out of his anger. He noticed his mouth had dropped slightly open and he shut it smartly.

'Listen, if you want to go,' Chris said, looking very small and defenceless. 'I'll pay for the taxi. But first you *must* listen. I want you to do something for me. You're just the person I need. And I'm willing to pay. A quarter of a million. I promise. Listen, we'll eat first and then have a drink, then I'll explain about that money.'

Wayne writhed. His scruples were getting in the way of the quarter of a million. And he couldn't buy anything with his scruples, could he? He cried out at his tormentor, 'I can't, I just can't, so stick you money, you dirty homo fuck!'

'Homo?' Chris looked stunned. Wayne cringed then as Chris burst out laughing. 'You thought I wanted *sex* off you? Hilarious!'

'Oh, *piss* off.' Wayne turned to the door.

'No, hold on, I'm not laughing really – it's these drugs. The painkillers. They make everything seem a bit funny. It's not a bad feeling, to be honest.'

'No? Well, have a nice death, then.' Wayne jiggled the latch of the lock and pulled, but the door wouldn't budge. He glared at Chris and took a step forward. 'Open it, or I'll come over and push your—'

'You stop where you are! I've got those recordings in a safe deposit. Try anything and they'll go to the police, I swear.'

'Bullshit. If there were recordings, the cops would have them already.' Wayne went up to Chris and stared down at him. 'Open the fucking door.'

'The video was recorded by the computer, that's were the files were kept and the police didn't check his computer. If they had, you'd been doing life by now, wouldn't you?'

'What you talking about?'

'Max had cameras in the garden too and one recorded you stifling him to death. You're a murderer, and they don't have the evidence…not yet.'

Wayne started breathing hard. 'I'll kill you.'

Chris shook his head. He wasn't going to back away again. 'The recordings are in a safe deposit. I die, they get sent to the cops. Give yourself a break, Wayne. I'm offering good money for a job you can do. Let me order your dinner and then we'll talk about it.'

Six

Wayne was basking in front of the coal fire, swilling pizza debris off his teeth with the best Scotch.

He could get used to this.

Chris had gone to top up on morphine and now he rolled in and parked opposite. The red glow of the coals tinted his shrunken face a lurid red.

'Come on then, what is it you want me to do?'

'I need you to steal something for me. It'll be easy. No one will be at home.'

Wayne sighed. 'Honest, I'm not a burglar. As you saw for yourself.'

'You don't have to break into any building. You're strong and you've got guts, and experience of field work, so to speak. That's perfect for what I need. By the way, I'm really glad you killed Max. I only wish had. He deserved to die, he really did.'

After a moment, Wayne asked, 'Are you telling me you hated him when he left you all that money.'

'I don't care about the money. It's what he *didn't* leave that's the point. His will was his last joke on me.'

'I don't see what's funny about it.'

Chris smiled and revealed long, long teeth sprouting from the black flowerbeds of his gums. 'Funny for him, not me. I was always one of the few who never thought Max was funny. I met him first at London University where I studied architecture. I was easily the most talented student there. That didn't mean I was popular, or unpopular. I was just sort of *there*. No one noticed me, least of all Max. Now Max was a very popular boy. He came from a wealthy, well-connected background and had a way of oozing privilege that attracted many adoring followers. I suppose what they would say is that they found his cutting wit superbly clever. For myself, I took no notice of him, because talent was the only thing I envied and Max didn't have any, as an architect at least. But then, he didn't need any talent. His family were rich.'

'Yeah, they've got it well sown up.'

'That's true, Wayne. So I got a real shock when I found out that privilege and popularity just weren't enough for Max after all. I was in the library one day, working studiously of course and Max himself came up to my desk. I'd never seen him in the library and I thought he must be lost and wanted to ask me where the exit was. *Hi*, he says, *We've not spoken before, but your underground public toilets scheme is quite, quite stunning. Murphy* (the lecturer) *was right to say it dwarfed everybody else's designs.'*

The conversation was suddenly going too fast for Wayne. 'What are you talking about – underground toilets?'

'A project given to us by Murphy, the lecturer. I'm talking about when I was at university.'

'Why underground toilets?'

'It could have been any other scheme. That's not the point. Murphy, who was the lecturer, the teacher, had really praised my work to Max's face. I didn't know yet, but they didn't get on and it was part of some argument, or something. So me, in the library, all I said was, *Did Murphy really say that?* And he said, *Yes. Why so surprised?* And I said I was surprised because, *I'd only happened to scribble it out just before breakfast.'*

'Scribble what out?'

Chris smiled patiently, 'The Public Underground Toilets Scheme, Wayne. But like I say, that's not the point. You see, I'm trying to explain about Max. I told him, I scribbled out this design like I hadn't sweated over it just as a bit of a joke. But Max just hissed right in my face. He said, *Don't get smart with me, you little flunky.* I was left dumbstruck. He leaned over me and said, *My project was the best thing I've ever done. I slaved over it. I slaved over it and Murphy said it was stank.* I began to say something like, *That's only his opinion*, but he cut me off. He said something. Do you know what he said?'

'No.'

'He said, *And I agree with Murphy.* He was twisted up with this horrible malice, like he wanted to kill me. I felt threatened, so I jumped up and faced him. Max just looked confused, like I'd woken him up. He didn't say anything, he just turned and went away. I didn't understand anything about what had gone on, not by a long chalk. Except perhaps, that's when I found out Max really did work hard and that being an architect was really a dream of his, and actually I was burning him up with jealousy.'

All this psychological talk hurt Wayne's head. But he didn't let on. Anything was better than what he had thought he would have to do.

Chris went on, 'The next time I saw him was down the Charing Cross Road, which he pretended to have been a chance encounter. He said, *I'm sorry, Chris, I was rude to you last time we met*. He told me his aunt had died and he admitted he'd been very disappointed by Murphy, but it was for the best. He said he'd have to work harder and perhaps rethink his priorities.'

'He said all that?'

'He also said, *I hope you continue to dazzle, Chris, you really deserve it.*'

'So then, that's why he left you all his money.'

'No, Wayne. He didn't mean what he said, though afterwards he always took pains to congratulate me on everything I did. And the more that Murphy praised me and sneered at Max's work, the more scrupulous Max was about congratulating me. By the way, Murphy was a socialist and hated Max for being privileged.'

'Murphy now, that's the teacher?'

'Right. He was also an alcoholic, actually, and was going downhill fast. Max was already getting his revenge on Murphy, by anonymously sending cases of whisky to Murphy's home. The best whisky. With an unsigned note saying it was from a well wished. So, Max speeded up the death of Murphy's liver no end. Max told me that, by the way, one night, many years later. Anyway, at least Murphy lived long enough to see me, his favourite student, get offered a job by a prestigious London-based architectural firm, *Gloolwult and Associates*. When Max heard that, he sent me a bottle of champagne with a note, *It couldn't have happened to a better guy*. The note came with an invitation to an end-of-course party. Well, *Just this once*, I thought and anyway, everyone else on the course was invited and besides I wanted to wow my girlfriend of the time. Frankly, I was wowed myself when we arrived. Max had hired a ballroom just outside London, with a band and the best catering. Lots of people I didn't recognise were there, all dressed like they were super rich. Then Max was standing beside me and he said, *I'd like you to meet Baroness Ghoomb* and I turned around and there was this giant, seven foot tall maybe, entirely covered in a dark gown with only a slit for the eyes, and even those had lace over them. But behind the lace, occasionally, you just saw something soulless and shiny and black flashing in the light. The Baroness's hands were gloved, which I thought particularly sinister. By the size of her hands you would have supposed she really was a man, except at the same time she had enormously distended buttocks. She was carrying this camcorder, and Max explained that Baroness Ghoomb was making a permanent record of the event. The Baroness said in this hissing, malevolent voice, *Ah, this is the star pupil*. And Max said, *Indulge me, Chris, allow the Baroness to span a portrait photo. Just for me. You don't have to do anything. You can even keep your clothes on*. There was a ripple of low laughter and everyone took a step back, leaving a space around me, and the Baroness got this nasty cheapo plastic camera out from under the folds of her wimple. The thing was really dirty and old, like it was from the 'Sixties, and the

Baroness pointed it at me and hissed, *Say, rubber soul!* I wouldn't do anything of the sort, of course. Anyway, just then, I spotted my girlfriend across the crowded room as she was chatting up the best looking guy at the party and I gave her an ironic smile and a little wave. The camera went, *Click!* and Max and the Baroness instantly melted away into the crowd. I forgot about them, busy just then with being jealous as hell about my girlfriend. Well, my ex girlfriend by then. Later on, however, I got to go home with another woman and she was hotter than my girlfriend.'

That's interesting. Wayne's ears pricked up for the second time that evening, but on looking at Chris, so hideously withered, with tar and morphine for blood, he queried, 'Hot? Really?'

'I didn't always look like this, Wayne. See that picture there on the side table? That's me when I was your age. Go on, take a better look.'

'Nah, you're all right.'

'Look at it, Wayne. I insist. Remind you of anyone? Film star, perhaps? Or...'

Wayne glanced at the photograph indifferently. Took a second take, then peered at it closely for a long time.

'No.' He whispered. 'You *got* to be joking.' He looked at Chris with amazement. That thing in his house. The doll! It's you. The *dirty* bastard. Is that why Max wanted your picture, so he could get that thing made?'

'Now you know.'

'The filthy fucker. When did you find out?'

'When I watched the security-camera recordings on Max's computer. Before then, I never knew that the thing existed. Do you remember meeting it, Wayne? What you felt?'

'Nothing.'

'You were scared. It spooked you.'

'I don't think so.'

'I saw that it did on the recording. But never mind, anyone would feel the same way – meeting it in the dark like that. As for me, as soon as I saw it, I realised what it was. What it *really* was.'

'Well, that's obvious.'

'No, it's not obvious. The eyes – they seemed alive, didn't they?'

'A trick of the light. That's why I got jumpy.'

'You got jumpy because it is alive.'

'How could it be? I touched it… It's just a doll.'

'No, there's more. I can't explain it completely. But you'll understand when I've told you everything. Just remember this for now. Max stole something from me at that party and it's the most important thing in the world.'

Seven

The joke is, Wayne, the morning after the end-of-term party, I woke up feeling like I had everything the world had to offer. I was lying in bed with Madeleine, a beautiful young woman from a rich family and I was about to begin a brilliant career. Better still, I was young and bursting with energy and ideas. See, I'd set my heart on founding a world-class architectural firm and I just knew I could do it.

So, if I had all that, you might ask, what on earth could Max have stolen from me that was more important?

Well, you'll see.

Maddy and I had a good thing for a year or so, but it went only so far. Neither of us was ready to settle down and she liked men in general and there was only one of me. For my part, not even women in general could compete with my ambition. And yet, even while I excelled at work, and even after finding a replacement or two for Maddy, I could never quite escape a feeling that I lacked something.

But what?

A sound night's sleep, perhaps? I slept, yes, but the dreams tortured me. I could never remember what they were. When I woke up, it was like they were hidden behind a wall – just feet away, but unreachable. The only thing I did know was that I always woke up feeling rotten about myself. Degraded. On some days I just couldn't shake off my despondency and then no amount of success at work and none of my lovers could lift my spirits. Over the course of several years, little by little, I began to retreat from the world. I stopped going out. Evening after evening, I'd sit alone in my Soho apartment, wondering why all the joy had been sapped from my life.

And that was exactly what I was doing one night, wondering, while staring at the telly, and suddenly I found myself looking at Max.

He was a guest on one of those panel shows that feature the current crop of with-it comedians. I didn't really watch much TV, but it was inevitable that I should see him eventually. By then, apparently, he was popping up all over as an up-and-coming talent. And the audience just fawned on him, like the students at college used to, whooping at his witticisms. The first words I heard him say on the TV were, *And I said to him, you've already drawn your last breath, buddy.*

The audience roared with laughter. Why? I'd never thought there was anything funny about Max. Least of all now. You see, I hadn't thought about him for years, but at the sight of him, I remembered. That wall I talked about, behind which my dreams were hidden, suddenly came tumbling down, and there behind stood Max. I remembered all my dreams in that instant. And no wonder always I woke up depressed. Every night had been the same. I was standing naked in front of him while he mocked me physically and verbally. Abusing me in every way imaginable. Of course, these were only dreams, but dreams like that, night after night, for two years on end would have destroyed anyone's peace of mind.

As it happened, I had already gone to the doctor about my not sleeping well and he'd been stumped, except to suggest it was a psychological problem. However, I hadn't been able to see what could possibly be wrong. Everything was going so great in my life. Well, now that I had remembered my dreams, nightmares rather, I realised that I suffered from a new and bizarre mental condition. Let's call it *The Max Complex*. But how I had come to develop this disease? The psychoanalyst my doctor recommended didn't help. Her therapy failed. She insisted that now the wall had come down and I could face my dreams, they should disappear. But they did nothing of the sort. They went on, worse than ever. I remembered them clearly every morning, and they were so vivid they could have been real events. As if that wasn't bad enough, Max's career blossomed and he became one of the biggest comedy stars of the time. You couldn't avoid hearing about him, or seeing his face on some screen or poster. My colleagues at work were all great fans and quoted him in the office at least once a day. Now and then, one of my girlfriends would repeat one of his jokes, and I couldn't bear to kiss those lips again.

I lived, burdened with *The Max Complex* for years, just struggling through. However, my pent up anger and resentment could not be contained forever and it eventually came to a head one day when an associate at work, a younger man whom I didn't particularly like anyway, started talking about Max, knowing full well that the subject infuriated me. This time the pert fucker pushed his luck too far and I cracked. I calmly picked up a steaming cup of coffee and was about to dash it into his round, smirking face when I heard him say, *Arrested.*

What? I said, loud enough to turn heads. *Did you say Max Kekoko's been arrested?*

Yes, he little squirt said, backing off a bit. Actually, he was a tall, overweight squirt, but still he backed off. I must have looked like a madman then, dashing across the office, leaving my steaming cup of coffee to fall and grabbing my phone could that I could check the news on my phone.

The police were questioning Max over allegations of child sex abuse. I punched the air and almost cried for joy. That was the most perfect crime he could have ever committed. What other outrage could so comprehensively finish a lightweight entertainer?. For the first time for as long as I could remember, I got a sound night's sleep and woke up next morning feeling absolutely superb. Where the psychoanalyst had failed, the *Metropolitan Police Force* had cured my complex. From someone who avoided learning anything about Max, I followed his progress more avidly than any of his former fans. I discussed the trial in microscopic detail with them at work, even though they didn't care to be reminded of how much they'd loved a filthy abuser of children. Every night, I slept like a baby, as it happened. The only time I dreamed about him again was when he was found guilty and he had a remaining day of freedom before sentencing. That night, I had this dream, different from all the previous ones. I felt him lift me up, like I was light as a feather, and carry me down flight after flight of concrete stairs into some kind of shadowy underground storage facility. He propped me up in a cupboard and then I heard his footsteps as he walked away into the darkness. I felt lonely when I woke up, like I really was locked up in a dark basement, even though I'd actually woken up in my Soho penthouse with a girl beside me.

Max was sentenced to ten years inside. When he was locked up, I felt freer and more thankful than I had since leaving college. True, I had been left with a faint, dull ache of loneliness, which I supposed was a kind of mental wound left behind by *The Max Complex*. However, this nothing like as distressing. And then, being able to sleep was such a blessing. Soon, I had regained my confidence and truly began to live again.

So, I was at this party one evening, some years later, and I saw Maddy across the room. She seemed more beautiful than ever before. And even younger. Captivated, I stared and stared. And then we were talking and I realised that she wasn't Maddy at all. She couldn't be, because Maddy had been my own age, and I was over thirty by then. This was Loraine, who was twenty-five and just happened to resemble Maddy to a degree. Well, at the time when we met, like I say, I had been haunted by this dim but perpetual feeling of loneliness. I put it down to the passage of time. I had always looked a little younger than my age, but enduring *The Max Complex* had aged me. I had changed on the inside as well. I no longer had the ambition to set up an architectural firm of my own. Instead, I wrote a book to publicise my more radical ideas in the hope they would be realised as real-world projects by others. Loraine and I got married. I built a house way out of London, the house in which we're sitting now, and I commuted in once or twice a week as a consultant. I worked mainly at home, which was better anyway, because both our daughters came along within the next couple of years.

My book was called *Enlightened Rooms* and it caused

a bit of stir. You may not have heard of it, I suppose, but still, it has influenced contemporary thinking about architecture. It took me several years to write, years that I enjoyed very much and the reception the book finally received from people whose critical appreciation I actually cared about was a high point in my life. I began to feel that I had explored all the means by which I could ever achieve happiness.

Perhaps this in itself made me wonder, *What next?* I seemed to have said everything I had to say about architecture. Now the only purpose I found I had was to raise a family. Most people seem to see this as their one and only purpose anyway. Me, I couldn't be wholly content with it, and so I was overjoyed, at first, when a whole new set of ideas came to me, apparently from out of the blue. I decided that these ideas would form the basis of another book. Despite my excitement, I was dimly aware from the beginning that these ideas were... disturbing. Not least because they ran utterly counter to the philosophy of architecture that I had propounded in *Enlightened Rooms*. Even the style in which I wrote now was different. Harsher. Full of rancour. Again and again I found myself attacking my earlier ideas. I poured contempt on the notion that rationality and spirituality should be enhanced by the buildings we live in. Rather, my new architectural designs assumed that rationality and spirituality were hopelessly alien to most human beings and therefore buildings should be built to accommodate their opposites – bloody mindedness, hostility, stupidity and sheer wilful ignorance. My new book was to be called, *Pervy Perspectives*.

Anyone in their right mind would assume I must be joking. Was I in my right mind? No, of course not. I couldn't see how ludicrous my work had become, how... creepy. So far as I was concerned, I was giving birth to a new vision of social reality. That was the way I described what I was doing in the introduction. Shameful, hateful nonsense. Even so, I wasn't mad enough to believe anyone would thank me, although I did assumed the critics would acclaim my genius.

The new book became an obsession. I began to sleep badly. My personality altered for the worse. I grew increasingly bitter and antagonistic towards Lorraine and the children and they became reluctant to talk to me at all. Eventually, she could not contain herself any longer. I might never have realised what was happening to me unless Lorraine, during some argument or other, hadn't said, *And you're even talking in your sleep now, do you know that? Last night you kept begging someone to stop. Those were you words. Please, for God's sake MAX, stop!*

That name! Hearing her say it, I dropped onto a chair, too aghast to speak. Lorraine even forgot our argument. She said, *You look really bad. Perhaps I should call a doctor.* And I said, *Don't bother. I don't care if I die.* Then of course, she burst into tears, saying it might be better if I *were* dead, because I'd been so appalling to live with. So there, Max was back in my dreams. I went to my study and read the pages of *Pervy Perspectives* with horror. You see, the wall he had rebuilt while I hadn't been looking had once again been breached. I saw my dreams, just like I had before. But now they were different. He was more evil. More threatening. *Pervy Perspectives* was *his* book. He had been dictating it to me in my sleep, torturing me at night all the more if I didn't write what he wanted during the day. No wonder I had been brimming over with hatred for my life.

But what had caused *The Max Complex* to return?

I checked the net. Sure enough, Kekoko had been released some months before. He had already served his ten-year sentence. How the time had flown! His release had been kept relatively quiet, even so, I must have learned in some way that he'd been freed. Maybe from some online newspaper – a small paragraph that I hadn't consciously noticed, but which had registered on my subconscious.

I was filled by foreboding. I couldn't think what to do. And of course, I couldn't imagine how I should I save my marriage while in the throes of this mental disease.

How about a holiday?

Actually, I'd never thought about our taking a holiday, not before these airline tickets unexpectedly arrived one morning. Tickets for Spain. I checked my emails and I found that I had, in fact, arranged it all. A three-week stay in a villa near an out of-the-way-village on the South Coast. Lorraine was delighted, especially since I'd made the arrangements without telling her, so as to give her surprise. That was just like my old self, she said. But I ought have known better. *I* hadn't made the arrangements. Fool, utter fool that I was, I wouldn't allow myself to face the truth.

The villa was a few miles from the nearest town. Rather isolated. Rather antiquated. I had to wonder why I'd chosen this, of all places.

Things were good for the first few days. I had already destroyed *Pervy Perspectives* and doing that seemed to banished *The Max Complex*. I slept without dreaming...

My wife shook me awake, saying that I'd been having a nightmare. That I'd been screaming, *No, Max, not that!*

I said, *Go check on the girls. See I didn't scare them.*

And I lay there, my heart pounding in the silence, waiting for the inevitable howl of anguish.

Oh yes, I knew it was going to hurt like hell.

She came back, already looking like a ghost. Our

daughters weren't in the room. The tall cupboard had been moved to one side to reveal a concealed entry into a roughly hewn passageway. This led into a ramshackle outbuilding that stood beside the moonlit and deserted road.

The police, the newspapers, the public, everyone did their utmost. We received nothing but sympathy and goodwill. To no avail, of course. The girls had vanished into thin air.

Now, I fully expected the police to note the fact that I had arranged the holiday and that I had rented a villa specifically rigged for an abduction and perfectly located for a quick getaway. But if they thought any of this was suspicious, they never said. Indeed, no one in the press, nor any of the public made the slightest insinuation that I had connived in the crime. And least of all did I get any hint of reproach from Lorraine.

So far as I could tell.

But didn't she reproach me really? I found it impossible to believe not. So I watched her, sifted her every word, listened for the faintest hint in her voice that she was deceiving me. No, not a thing. And yet, I simply could not sustain my faith in her goodness. Or rather, some little, offensive voice, like the buzz of a noisome insect, kept droning around inside my head that she was disguising her hatred for me. That she was determined I would pay for the crime and that she was, in fact, acting as an agent for the police, and the newspapers and even concerned members of the public, who were all fervently hoping to nail me. Lorraine, I was told, was watching me even more closely than I was watching her, watching me with an inexhaustible patience. The voice asked over and over, *How long will you live like this? How long, Chris? After all, you're as guilty as sin.*

I could not endure this appalling mental torture for

long. My despair drained me and the expectation of being exposed and viciously punished progressively drove me out of my mind. My health worsened, and one morning I woke up with an agonising fever. I felt my chest being crushed. I thought I was having a heart attack. I was so wrong. Because to my utter amazement I found there were two immensely powerful arms wrapped around me. They squeezed hard enough to cave my ribs in. I couldn't breathe, or cry out. The pain paralysed me. Then I heard the voice buzzing at my ear and I finally recognised that the voice belonged to Max and that he was actually in bed with me. He whispered coarsely that we had to protect ourselves, because Lorraine had hidden recording equipment in the room and I'd been blabbing in my sleep about my crime. As he spoke, I felt a new agony. Oh, the horror of it! He thrust his huge, spike-covered cock into me and it was so long and hard that the bulbous head was cumming acid straight into my stomach.

I couldn't even scream.

He said, *It's time, you cretin,* and I felt myself being lifted – just like in my dream long ago – as if I weighed nothing. I wasn't able to move in the slightest. Max was kicking my legs up from behind so that I walked just like a goose stepping puppet. Even so, we were fast and stealthy. We were out of the bedroom in seconds. We caught Lorraine as she was just about to go down the stairs, shaking, barely able to stand on account of the drugs the doctor was giving her to numb the grief. Max positioned us behind her, squatted us down, and I was sort of impaled on his lap and he braced himself against the wall and deftly lifted my limp, lifeless foot behind my wife's backside. But the foot that shoved her was his, I swear. And he pushed so very hard that she flew forward beyond the stairs and fell headfirst onto the tiled floor below.

Crack!

The sickening sound woke me. I was still in bed, of course. It had been a hideous nightmare. I got up and went out to use the bathroom, shaking all over. The sound of Lorraine's skull smashing into the tiles kept going, *Crack! Crack! Crack!* in my head and to clear it out and stop my heart banging away in my chest, I went and looked down the stairs, but there she was in reality, crumpled on the hallway floor, with her head smashed in.

You might have expected me to fall to pieces on the spot.

Not a bit of it! I remember thinking at the time, *This is strange*, but I went downstairs, calmly phoned the police and the ambulance, and patiently waited for them. I answered everyone's questions and I accepted their sympathy with a straight face (I mean I didn't burst out into shrieking fits) and I even continued my work at home for the firm, just like I was in complete control.

But I wasn't.

Another will moved my body around, made me talk. I was being operated by someone who was intent on keeping up appearances. Inside, I was destroyed. I didn't care what happened to me. So, when the cops and the doctors had gone, my operator, as I'll call him, took a rest and I simply flopped down on the floor and waited to die.

Unfortunately, I wasn't going to be allowed to die. The next day, and the day after that, I'd find myself being lifted from behind and put through the motions of life. At long, long last, the police began to suspect me of something. The evidence of how my wife had fallen down the stairs was not clear. No matter. I didn't have to say a word. My operator spoke through me, deftly fending off the most awkward questions and putting their minds at rest. My operator was a very convincing talker.

But perhaps there was no operator. No Max. Perhaps

I was insane. Perhaps my dreams were nothing more than dreams, even the one in which I murdered my wife.

I just couldn't be sure. What was a dream or not a dream these days? All the conversations with the police, and everything else that happened afterwards felt like a dream now. What felt real were those times when my hidden operator, as I imagined him to be, quit for the day and I was left to myself. When that happened, I just stayed where he left me, like an object, and did nothing. I didn't move, wash or feed myself. If the operator didn't reactivate me, I would have starved to death. After a time, my operator had me write out a resignation letter, and that was the end of my career in architecture. Naturally, I never wondered for a moment how I should earn money to live. Like I say, I didn't care if I died. Then, for quite a long time, the dreams of being moved around stopped. As if the operator had got tired of working me. This should have been a chance to die of self neglect. However, I wasn't allowed to. My meals were delivered by an arrangement I had never made and I was fed and washed by carers in uniform, all fat young women, just like I was senile. Yes, they must have seen me for what I was, a rotten and empty shell. They wouldn't ask why they had been hired by an outside party to look after me. They even had keys to the front door so they could come and go as they pleased.

Months, maybe a whole year passed and then one night came a slow, *Knock, Knock, Knock* on the front door and suddenly, after so long, I was being operated yet again. I rose and doing my ludicrous puppet goose-step walk, I went outside, where there was a figure waiting for me, seven feet tall and draped in the dark folds of some medieval gown.

Baroness Ghoomb was back.

She never said a word, just raised one gloved hand

and pointed to a big black car. I climbed in. That was the start of the new and final phase of my degradation.

She always came by night, but at irregular intervals. The journeys would take hours. The dark, empty streets might have been on another planet. The place we arrived at would inevitably be some inauspicious institution, a hospice, old folks' home, psychiatric unit, or ward for terminally ill children, all of them built according to the soul-crushing precepts espoused in *Pervy Perspectives*. A style of architecture to be seen wherever the bureaucratic mind hovers like a stink. We would enter by a quiet rear entrance, let in by a collaborator, presumably someone with enough influence to ensure the ritual would not be interrupted. And in my dream, I always knew it was Max who was behind me, using me as a disguise, even threading his cock through mine as he sodomised the mentally retarded, the very old and sick, while Baroness Ghomb hitched her gown to expose her vast, reeking, slime-dripping backside in order to smother the victims while Max once again performed his favourite act of death sex.

Eight

Wayne had been sweating hard as the gloop in his stomach roiled around. Suddenly, he couldn't stand it any longer.

'I've got to be sick!'

'What?' Chris started from his wide-eyed trance. 'Oh, I see. There's a toilet in the hall.'

Wayne went floundering out. He reached the loo just in time and the whisky gushed out of his yawning mouth in a torrent. The munched pizza followed in a second wave of chewed cud.

Farewell, fickle friends.

His relief was enormous. Flushing the vomit away gave him a feeling of having achieved something.

Back in the living room, he sat on the sofa, a little away from the open fire, being loathe to sweat any more. Chris had left the room, but he soon trundled back in, carrying a glass of milky, fizzing liquid.

'There you are. Chuck this down, quick. It's *Alka Seltza* and some *Dimismol,* which stops you feeling sick. It does wonders for me.'

Wayne gulped it down and nodded. 'Better. Thanks.'

'I ought have told you not to keep pouring the whisky down your neck, but to be honest, Wayne, I had my reasons. I wanted to be sure to keep you here.'

'Come again?'

'So that you slept on my proposal. Let me tell you what it is.'

'I'm too tired to think about anything. Tell me in the morning.'

'But I won't be able to.'

Wayne narrowed his bleary eyes, 'Why not?'

'You must think I'm mad. In the morning, you'll slip out the house and disappear forever. You'll probably forget I have the video evidence locked up in the bank.'

'What evidence…? Oh, yeah, the video.' He leaned forward. 'Go on, what?'

'Yes, this thing – you can get it done in a couple of hours. Do it, then you'll be rich.'

'What thing?'

'I want you to dig up Max's grave.'

Wayne searched hard for the sense in this. 'Has he got gold teeth?'

'Gold teeth? I don't know. If he has, you can have them.'

'Come on, what really?' Wayne's next idea, after

gold teeth, was a key to a safe in Max's corpse suit.

'Well … you know about the voodoo doll, don't you?

'Doll?'

'The voodoo doll. You have a doll and you stick pins in it and the victim feels the pain? You've heard of those, haven't you?'

'Nah.'

'This is the same thing. That camera Baroness Ghoomb pointed at me—

Say, Rubber Soul!

——took more than my picture. The camera took something they could put inside the doll. When I saw the video, I recognised you and the room from my dreams. Don't you see? I was *there* with you that night at Max's. I was inside the fetish doll. I've been inside it all along. And Max has been sticking me all these years – but not with pins. No, he fucked the doll, Wayne and in that way he controlled me. But when he went to prison, he put the doll in storage and I was free. That's when the dreams stopped. That's when I had a normal life and I wrote *Enlightened Rooms*. Remember I told you that?'

Wayne was full of disgust. Two uncles had got that brain-rot thing and they, like this bastard here, talked a right load of shit too. 'Yeah, you wrote a book.'

'Then he was released from prison. He was able to do his filthy business again. Only now, he was ten times more vicious. His life was in ruins, so he took it out on me. He made me rent that villa, so his associates could abduct our daughters. He made me kill Lorraine, and then, in the years that followed … all those sordid, sickening dreams – they were real. I can't tell you. He could act out his fantasies in safety through me.'

Wayne thought, *I can't listen to this much longer.* Still, he was curious about what was in the coffin. 'Was Max buried with a priceless antique? Diamonds? Is that why—'

'A year or so ago, he started to die. But he aimed to control me not only in this world, but in the next too. He wanted to stay alive through me. When he did die, I inherited everything of his. He wanted me to have the best care, so that he would be comfortable living through my body. I would never have known any of this if he had destroyed the hard disk of his computer. The correspondence with the clinic was still there for me to read, and the funeral arrangements with *Selwyn Price*. He had an implant, Wayne, to give himself a permanent erection, even in death, so that he could be buried in his coffin while still penetrating the doll. Fucking me in death for all eternity!'

Wayne yawned. 'Sorry. Really tired.'

'Of course you are.' Chris smiled. 'Good. You'll sleep the sleep of the dead. And when I say that, I know what I'm talking about.'

Wayne scowled. Like a lot of people, he instinctively disliked being smiled at. 'What you mean?'

'I still hear him at night. I'm down there, with him. Not in a coffin. Death is a vast palace that's architecturally more banal than the dreariest hospital block. Max is embracing me tightly from behind, of course, but he's not talking to me anymore. He's not making me do anything. He's too busy screaming in everlasting torment. The demons are working on him, Wayne. I can't see them. That's for the best, I expect. But I can hear *Eblis*. That's the sovereign of Hell. I can hear him sigh and whisper through infinitely long and infinitely uninteresting corridors, but even then his voice is louder than thunder. He must be hundreds of feet tall. A titan.'

'Who is that now you talking about?' Wayne blenched. He couldn't really care less. He actively didn't want to know. The question had slipped out by accident.

'Eblis, Wayne, he's sorrowful King of Hell. And he's spoken to me. He said, *Know that come the full moon the doomed soul on your back is allowed to go up to Earth and play his unclean tricks, and know too, that this is the will of the Everlastingly Self-Righteous Light, the homo-creator of the Universe.* Yes, that's exactly what *Eblis* said. By the way, Wayne, is it a full moon tonight?'

'How the fuck would I know?'

'Me, I can't remember. I lose track. Well, I'll knock myself out with extra drugs before I turn in. That should hold him. By the way, Hell is not so bad. I'm not suffering there. Max is. And it's a beautiful thing, really, to hear him paying for his sins. Tremendous. But still, what about when the moon is full? Why has God allowed him to come back, even from the depths of Hell? For that matter, if He is so great, why did He allow Max to exist at all? And then, what about when *I* die? I'm going to die soon, because, as you see, all those diseased bodies have infected me with their putrefaction. So, when I die, I'm afraid that I will have to listen to Max screaming for all eternity. How tedious that will become. Even annihilation would be preferable. So the thing is, Wayne, you have to dig me up. Go to the cemetery and then bring my rubber soul here so I can burn it. Help me find true oblivion. For that, I'll give you every damned thing I own.'

Wayne would have agreed to anything to shut Chris up. 'Okay, I'll do it. But I've *got* to sleep now.' He stood up and the room span around. 'Them videos of me in Max's. Where are they?'

'At the bank, Wayne, nice and safe. Don't worry, you'll get them. Hold on to me.' Chris drove to his side. Wayne gripped the arm of the wheel chair and like that they got to the foot of the stairs. 'Take a seat. One-way ride.'

'Huh.'

Wayne slumped into the stair-lift chair and straightaway he was gliding upwards, the rails of the stair lift clanking while the motor beneath him whined. And then—

Shtumf!

—he fell out of the chair as it came to an abrupt stop at the top of the stairs. He flopped onto the landing. Chris called to him from far, far below. 'What are you doing? Be careful, or you'll break your neck.' He seemed to be laughing.

'I'll fucking well break your neck.' The words came out in one long, slushy slur.

'Straight ahead, son! The guest room is straight ahead. You can't miss it.'

Uh, Guh

Wayne began to climb to his feet, but found himself swaying even while on his knees. He decided he might indeed be in danger of going backwards and breaking his neck. He didn't want to do that, and he started to crawl instead through the semi darkness. His head—

Bonk!

—hit a door,

'Ow!'

—which opened to reveal a room where everything looked like it was carved out of luminous bone. The moon blazed in through the tall windows onto a great oblong block. The bed. It could have been six feet high given the effort with which he clambered onto it. After that, the power to move completely left him. He marvelled at how drunk he must be.

He closed his eyes and perhaps, just perhaps, he was dreaming when he heard the whine of a motor and the clanking of metal rails that resonated from thousands of miles below the earth. All the way up from the very depths of Hell. How he struggled to move! But he couldn't even cry out. And so, he had to watch in silence as the thing appeared and rolled towards him. It stretched out long, crooked hands and they clamped themselves over his gaping, dribbling mouth. How hard and cold they were! Like steel. Within seconds, his chest was boiling with the agonising need to breathe, and his eyes were filled by moonlight as he stared up into the bearded skull that grinned down at him.

FF

One

Darren's brain didn't normally behave like the average dumb-ass driver, but right now it was ranting and screaming "advice" from inside a completely sound-proofed vehicle.

Give me a fucking raise, will you? Come on, come on, come ON!

Jeff shot a glance over his shoulder.

'What's that?'

'Eh?'

'I thought you said something.'

'Nah.'

'Okay, you can shove off now, Darren. I'll finish up here.'

Jeff returned to the task of setting the shop's burglar alarm.

Darren glared at the back of that very bald head and then drifted outside to linger and brood on the busy sidewalk.

Jeff wasn't long following him out, pursued by the tuneless bleeping of the alarm. He frowned to see Darren waiting there, but he had to be quick about locking up before the sirens and flashing lights kicked off.

The bleeping stopped and *Electronic Entertainments (hi-fi – digital – computing) Ltd* was secure for yet another night.

Jeff turned and favoured Darren with a smile.

'So, where you off to now?'

'A friend and me are meeting some young ladies for the evening.'

'Oh yes?'

'At the *Wetherspoons Pub*, on Starling Street.'

'Gosh, is that place still going?'

'Yes, it is.'

'Small, isn't it?'

'No, it's massive. It's got three bars and a stage for bands.'

'They must have extended it.'

'I don't think so. Not in the last few years anyway. You ain't been there for a time, perhaps?'

A shadow crossed Jeff's face.

'Noisy place now, is it?' He glanced at the office workers streaming along the sidewalk, their heels sternly rapping the concrete slabs in their hurry to get home. It was obvious he wanted to get home too.

'I suppose it is pretty loud.'

'Pity, if you want to chat to the ladies.'

Darren grinned. 'We've done our chatting.'

Jeff turned and pulled down the shop's steel shutters. He squatted in order to attach a padlock to the latch at the bottom. When he stood up again, he was a little out of breath.

Darren's brain noted this.

He's like SO out of shape. So OLD, so BALD. How come he's the boss and not me?

'Well, have a nice one, Darren.'

Go on then, ask about your raise.

'Thanks.'

'See you, then.'

'Um – see you.'

God damn! Darren's brain cursed Jeff for exposing Darren as a chicken – yet again. Why was asking for a raise so hard?

You old, bald, mean son of a—

'O Darren!'

He was brought to a juddering halt. 'Yes, Jeff?'

'Could you be here by seven, Monday morning?'

Darren stared.

What? Seven instead of eight-thirty! Forget it!

'You see, we need to do an inventory.'

'Jeff, we did an inventory last week.'

'We did indeed, but I'm not happy about the printer consumables. I want us to know where we are before I negotiate with the new supplier. Okay?'

Darren's heart beat a little faster. He was being asked to put in extra hours. Wasn't this the perfect opportunity to broach the subject of a pay raise?

Go on! Your mortgage repayments are going up, not down!

'Yeah, yeah, that's fine. But I was thinking that—'

'I know it's a drag, but the thing is, Darren, I'm worried about the Saturday staff. Especially our lad, Liam.'

'What? You think he's been lifting?'

'Let's put it this way, if I find any discrepancy this Monday he'll be looking for another job. They're ten a penny these kids. They all think they're God's gift, but you can replace them—' He snapped his fingers. 'Just like that.'

'That's right,' Darren said, focused, despite himself, on Jeff's upraised hand.

'See you Monday, then?'

'Course.'

They went in opposite directions.

Darren headed further into Birmingham City Centre, where the busy crowds were already thinning out, although the cramped roads still seethed with traffic.

Despite his dismal failure to ask Jeff for a raise, Darren soon recovered his self possession. Let Jeff keep his money. At twenty-two, he had an abundance of what Jeff desperately needed but couldn't buy for a billion, billion quids.

Stuff like hair, for instance.

And a long, long future.

And as if that weren't enough, tonight he had a blind date.

Darren felt his chest pleasantly swell when he recalled this interesting fact. Suddenly he was full of a certain lighter-than-air substance – the sprightly molecules of youthful spirits. If you'd used them to fill a balloon, it would soar between the sheer and towering buildings all around. Up and up and up and away into the infinite clear-blue sky.

The pub was about ten minutes walk away. Patrons were already filling the main bar – small knots of suit wearers, smiling and laughing, their ties loosened and their voices loud.

He slipped through the crowd to one of the wooden alcoves and found Marius, a friend he'd known since school, sitting with a couple of girls.

Marius, a stringy, straw-headed, plain-featured man, had always been a little selfish where it came to women and he did not acknowledge Darren immediately. His mouth was working with a mechanical rapidity and the two young women were staring at him, aghast and fascinated. The mouth didn't stop flapping even when Marius was obliged to look up at Darren.

'Hey there,' Darren said, with a hint of irony. He felt

the eyes of the ladies upon him. Appraising themselves of all the good bits.

'Oh, hey.' Marius's shoulders sank slightly as the obligation to introduce everyone fell upon them. 'Linda, Sharon, this is Darren.'

Darren smiled and nodded to the ladies. Linda was dark, Sharon was light.

'Would you like a drink?' He asked.

'Thanks, not yet,' Linda answered without a smile and turned to Sharon.

Marius stood up.

'What you want?'

'Sit down, guy,' Darren said. 'I'll wait till you're all finished.' He joined them at the table, sitting beside Marius. 'I have a limited alcohol intake,' he explained for the ladies' benefit.

'Going to take the pledge?' Sharon asked. As well as being light, she was long-boned and thin.

'Almost have already. Six bottles is my max, innit.'

'What are you going to drink in the club?' Linda asked. 'Orange juice?' For some reason, her tone was accusatory and she glanced meaningfully at Marius.

Darren also looked at Marius. 'Are we going to a club, then?'

'*Oceana*, as usual,' Marius said, with a tentative smile.

Darren frowned. He disliked *Oceana*. Its clientele were even louder and brasher than the music. Still, Marius had arranged this date with his work colleagues and it would be mean spirited to carp.

'Great.'

'What's wrong with *Oceana*?' Linda asked sharply. Somehow, his *great* hadn't sounded great enough.

He shrugged. 'Nothing. I've heard it's a bit druggy, that's all.'

'Don't take no drugs neither then?'

'Yeah, when I was about twelve. Something you grow out of, isn't it?'

'I think I drink too much,' Sharon said, smiling at him. Linda gave her a sideways look. But Sharon kept smiling and added, 'It's good to have a limit. I wish I had one.'

Linda seemed to find this funny.

While she laughed, Darren said to Marius, 'If you had a limit you'd well break it tonight.'

'Hm?'

'Dio Shalcott, innit? He's signed up with *Birmingham City*.'

'DIO SHALCOTT? No shit!'

'Here we go,' Linda hooted. 'Men and football.'

Marius didn't seem to hear her. 'How do you know?'

'Saw it on the television.'

'Ah, of course.' Marius turned to the girls. 'He's got a shop full of them.'

'You have a shop?' Sharon asked.

'I work with an electrical retailer.'

'Linda's after a new android. Aren't you, Linda?'

'Oh, we have plenty of deals.' Darren glanced in Linda's general direction. 'If you get a price somewhere, we can generally beat it.'

'Can you beat anything?' Sharon asked.

Darren smiled. 'Depends. What are you after?'

Linda groaned and rolled her eyes.

Marius said, 'You got yourself a good deal on your television, didn't you? Plus an integrated *Blu-Ray* recorder thrown in. How much did you get your boss to reduce it for?'

'I got a twenty per cent discount.'

'Because you know the boss?' Linda asked, putting an unpleasing emphasis on the word *boss*.

Darren shook his head. 'I don't get no special

treatment. I shopped around first and asked him what he could do to match the other deals. Just like you could too. If I were you, though, I'd say take cash and wave it under his nose. He can't resist cash. Like any little pro.'

Linda simply looked at him.

'And how much did Dio Shalcott cost *Birmingham City*, Darren?' Sharon asked.

'Five million.'

'Wow!'

'You like football, then?'

'Why shouldn't I…like it?' Sharon smiled.

'No reason at all.' Darren smiled back. 'So long as you support *Birmingham City*—'

Linda maintained her derisory tone. 'Is that what you watch on your new television? Football?'

'I actually don't watch a lot of TV.'

'Then why buy one?'

'More or less to pad out my apartment. I moved in last month, and I'm still collecting stuff to make the corners less bare.'

'Where is it?' Sharon asked.

'By the *Electric Clock Quays*. You know, that new apartment block there?'

'They couldn't sell them,' Linda said. 'The building firm went bust in the recession.'

Darren gave Linda a faint, slow smile. 'And that's why I got the place for a snip. Almost half price.'

'Really?' Sharon exclaimed.

Marius meanwhile was looking depressed. He didn't have any bare corners to fill – he still lived at home. Taking a swig from his bottle of beer, he remarked. 'Yeah, Darren's the man.'

Two

Next morning, Darren woke up next to Linda.

He had drunk far more than his upper limit of six bottles. The evil consequences came as no surprise. Disjointed, jarring images from the night before, accompanied by the echoes of blaring voices, bounced around inside his head and made it hurt very much.

Trying to ignore a mounting sense of shame, he looked around the small, dreary room in which he found himself. He was close to the floor, on a futon, or maybe just a mattress. A freestanding clothes rack leaned against one wall. Directly ahead of him, on a low, *MDF* table, a small flat screen TV and a hi-fi mini system held his attention briefly.

Junk.

Intense, early morning sunlight blazed through the gaps of the nylon window blinds.

Linda was breathing deeply. All that Darren could see of her was a shock of dark hair flowing from the top of the eggshell-blue duvet. He turned to survey his clothes, which were scattered over the floor and checked that they were all there. Especially his trousers.

Yup, all present and correct.

Thank f—

And now he had no time to waste. His skull was creaking from internal pressure and his stomach was roiling and getting ready to climb and erupt out of his gullet.

Moving with caution, his gaze ranging restlessly over the second-hand furniture and the grimy, papered walls, he slipped from the bed, pulled on his clothes (his work suit) and opened and closed the door after him.

Linda remained sound asleep.

He was standing now on the landing of a large family

house. But no family lived here any more. And probably never would again. The ambience was familiar from his student days – it was almost a smell – and it told him that each of the rooms was rented out. This was a hive of individuals. No doubt many more than might be imagined.

Through a pressing necessity, Darren used the loo before he left. But doing so didn't feel like an invasion of private facilities. Under the circumstances, he may as well have been using a public toilet.

Outside, he found himself on a street of redbrick houses, typical of the City's older suburbs. Most of these were familiar to him and, sure enough, he didn't have to walk far before he got his bearings. The city centre was half an hour away by foot and after that he would be in his apartment in another ten minutes.

It was six in morning and the streets were still deserted. Without people they looked cleaner and more civilised. The city-centre buildings of concrete and glass towered effortlessly against the limpid sky as if they had been designed for no other purpose than to look fantastic.

The cool air kept his nausea at bay, but the first thing he did when he got home was throw up. Bouts of sickness came and went like a tide of vomit. His throbbing brain seemed to be forcing his eyes out of their sockets. As he suffered, he was struck by how loathsome his body was. Which was like *so* puzzling, because usually he could take it for granted that he was incredibly healthy. Even more puzzling still was that death didn't seem such a bad idea just then. Now that was *really* strange, because, like everyone else under the age of twenty-five, Darren naturally assumed that he was immortal.

The hours of torture passed very, very slowly.

He groaned and endured. But what else could he do?

Only when the morning had passed into the afternoon

did the *Great God Bud* take pity on him. The punishment was commuted to faint queasiness and a dull ache between the ears and he was finally allowed to sleep off the rest of his hangover.

Three

He had been up since seven that evening, feeling well enough to be glad that he hadn't died after all.

Food seemed to be an option again. He nibbled tentatively on toast and in return his stomach gurgled like a baby—

More.

One bacon-and-lettuce sandwich later, he lay languorously on the sofa in order to digest. In his contentment, he was happy merely to stare through the glass doors that opened onto his tiny balcony. Light and colour were draining from the sky. A pale office block on the horizon reflected the last rays of the low sun and seemed to float like an oblong moon full of eyes.

Darren sighed. Not only did he feel at peace in a way that was rare for him on a Saturday night, but the city too was unusually quiet.

The trouble was, he was prone to confusing serenity with boredom. It's a widespread contemporary error.

And so, he switched the TV on.

The screen lit up with two smiling, childlike faces. They belonged to young Tony and Derrick – the public's favourite TV personalities. No lightweight programme was complete without them. This one was a game show.

Seconds later, Darren lost interest and began to channel hop. Two hundred channels to hop onto and yet nothing could hit the spot. Saturday night TV seemed to depict everything you thought about when you had finally given up on real life.

Yeah, he told himself with sour satisfaction, *Watching this garbage is what Jeff does for the weekends*.

Fortunately, he didn't have to watch this garbage himself – he had recorded a late-night thriller.

He called it up from the TV's hard drive.

As he watched, however, flashbacks of the previous evening's antics began to trouble him and he stopped paying attention to the film and drifted away into meditations that were both slightly erotic and slightly sickening.

Chirr-chip, Chirr-chip, Chirr-chip…

The phone.

'Hey there!'

A friend was calling, wondering where he was.

After a long conversation, during which the friend took forever to come to terms with the fact that he wasn't coming out tonight, Darren found the film had finished.

He leaned forward a little and frowned at the screen.

Something was wrong.

The television should have reverted to live broadcast, but instead it was showing the programme that followed last night's film. The programme was *The Sky at Night*, a regular late-night feature about astronomy. Two men, who could have been Jeff's older brothers, were talking about the *Nipomedes*, a shower of meteors that occurred every two hundred and fifty-six years.

I set the recorder wrong.

But he didn't really believe that. To be able to set the time on the TV was the natural inheritance of his generation.

Troubled, Darren pressed the FF button and reached the next programme – the weather report.

'Unfortunately, cloudy skies will mean that we shan't be able to see the *Nipomedes*.'

Damn it! The recording function's fucked.

He fast-forwarded the recording again and a late, late rerun of last Sunday's *Antiques Road Show* popped up. That would have been showing just when he and Linda were falling into bed last night.

Keenly aggrieved, Darren glared at his new kit.

Junk!

Worse junk than Linda's had been, because at least her kit probably worked right.

He pressed the FF button and kept his thumb down. Flickeringly, a whole night's television unreeled on the screen. Soon, the breakfast show was on, with a pear-shaped middle-aged guy planted deep in a bright-pink sofa.

Ugh – just so wrong. This machine is a total screw up.

Yeah, and he'd been the sucker who'd bought it, hadn't he?

Darren was transported back in time and place to the shop *Hi-Fi Solutions*, which stood on the opposite side of the city from *Electronic Entertainments*, where he worked. *Hi-Fi Solutions* was where he had *really* brought his new television and HD recorder. Despite what he'd told everyone last night, his ever-generous boss, Jeff, hadn't offered him even a bit of a discount.

Not that cutting a deal at *Hi-Fi Solutions* was a walk in the park either.

In *Hi-Fi Solutions* he had been disconcerted to find himself talking to a manager who was pretty much a duplicate version of Jeff – right down to his tiny bald head. Not only that, there had been a young assistant scuttling about in the background – a Darren duplicate, if you please – at whom Darren had glanced now and then, wondering whether the lanky dope with the stupid haircut was on the same wage as himself.

Meanwhile, Jeff #2 was claiming, in effect, that the

digital recorder under discussion was on special offer *out of the generosity of his own heart!* Darren knew better. The model had been superseded last week and although it was still a good model it was due to plummet in price any day soon. In light of this information, he made Jeff #2 his own offer.

The same sort of offer he'd already made to Jeff #1 – only to have it foully rejected.

He had held his breath in painful anticipation.

Would Jeff #2 turn out to be an upgrade on Jeff #1?

Would Jeff #2 be aware, unlike Jeff #1, that there was a recession on?

Would Jeff #2 have mortgage repayments to cover, just like any normal person?

Well, *would* he?

YO – RESULT!

However, now, two weeks down the line, Darren was learning a hard and bitter truth – that his triumphant *YO – RESULT!* came with a two-week expiry date. Jeff #2 had turned out to be an even worse bastard than Jeff #1.

Jeff #2 had sold him a pup.

You rotten, swizzling little sh—

As he watched the comical frenzy of the speeded-up television, he gradually left off cursing.

He even began to smile.

Look at all this crap.

That was his brain talking, hinting that perhaps he would be better off without a new television after all. You see, when he got his money back on this dud, he needn't worry about the mortgage repayments for the next two months.

The roof over your head's the priority, old son.

Yes, yes, Darren's brain knew what it was talking about, all right.

But still, might he miss the TV once it was gone?

Well, you've recorded loads of sports stuff over the past two weeks and not watched any of it because you didn't have the time. Isn't that so?

Yes.

And are you inclined to watch any of it now?

Nah.

So the likely conclusion is, you won't miss it when it's gone, eh?

In reply, Darren raised the remote in order to *OFF* the TV.

But he hesitated.

A puzzled frown indented his forehead as he stared into the giddy flow of images on the screen.

He had left the recorder in fast-forward mode, hadn't he?

And yet playback still running.

You know, that actually gave him something to think about.

All that sports stuff I've already recorded should have filled the hard drive up. There shouldn't be any room for all this shit.

And yet, on and on the recording whirred – a mash-up of gaudy images that looked like electric vomit. Not a mere bucketful, but gallons of it.

But that was impossible. The disk could only hold a bucketful.

Curious on a professional level, sort of, Darren fetched the TV's manual from a drawer in the kitchen. The info was there in black and white. This model had only eighteen hours recording capacity.

Jeff #2 hadn't just sold him a defective machine, he'd sold him the wrong model of defective machine. One that happened to have a much larger disk.

That was spooky. A kind of *super-deluxe* raw deal.

Just to be sure, he bent over and checked the decals on

the front of the HD's casing. Strange, these definitely stated the machine had just eighteen hours capacity.. He sat on the floor, wondering how the thing had come to have a bigger hard drive than its factory spec.

But thinking was hard in proximity to the frenetically speeded up slush, and he jabbed the normal-play button.

The recording had reached the late-night rolling news that was screened after three o'clock at night. Darren stared for a moment, knowing something was really wrong, but not understanding it straightaway. The late-night rolling news again? But he had just run through last night's late-night rolling news and got as far as this morning's breakfast show. What night's late news could he be possibly watching now?

The date and time were displayed in the corner of the screen.

Darren leaned forward.

15 th of August, 3.13 AM.

But today was the 14 th and the time was exactly 9.10 PM.

His TV was eighteen hours and three minutes ahead of the rest of the world.

His TV was showing him the future.

Four

Bullshit!

Darren #1's suspicion naturally fell upon Darren #2. That is, someone with like-for-like technological know-how.

On that basis, he reckoned the cunning monkey must have edited the time and date stamp of this news report on a computer and then downloaded it onto the television's hard drive.

Funny, eh?

Hilarious.

Yeah? Well it looked like there would soon be a Darren #3 working in Darren #2's place.

Darren #1 hunkered down and examined the picture on the screen from up close. The practical joker had gone to considerable trouble. The graphics were not the least amateurish. In fact, they looked just like the real thing. As for the news reports themselves – a bomb in Lebanon, a flood in China, a rise in oil prices, unrest on Russia's borders and Arab riots – these could have been copied from last week's news. Or last month's. Or from any time over the past few decades for that matter. Most of the news looked like stock footage to him anyway.

Darren went back to the sofa and put the playback on fast forward again, just to find the end of the recording before he repackaged the thing to take back to the shop. After four minutes or so, he lost patience, and pressed normal play.

The breakfast programme.

The Sunday edition.

Thirty hours into the future.

In other words—

Thirty solid hours of fakery.

The effort put in to creating this silly little joke was hard to credit. Remastering so much footage would have been a huge amount of work, but that was nothing compared to the expense of fitting the machine with a bigger hard drive to accommodate it all.

'It's crazy.'

Got it in one.

He stared at the bland smiling faces of the presenters and understood that Darren #2 was no mere prankster. He was an obsessive nut.

This forced him to consider if it might be so judicious

getting a guy like that the sack. You just could never tell what an obsessive nut might do in revenge.

As he pondered the question of how he would get his refund without incurring the incalculable wrath of a nut, the presenters' faces on screen stopped smiling. They had turned to a serous news item. Till then, Darren had been more focussed on the appearance of the TV picture rather than what was being said, but now his ears pricked up.

'...fans were excited about Dio Shalcott being signed up last week, but few know that the club's biggest sponsor is a born-again...'

Last week?

But Dio had been signed up *this* week.

The editing had been so well executed Darren had almost missed the tiny alteration. In fact, now he wasn't sure he'd actually heard the presenter say *last week.*

Better check that, he thought, and pressed the reverse button on the remote.

Nothing happened.

He pressed the button again, harder, but HD player did not respond.

Evidently, the sequence of events only went in one direction on this machine, just like they did in real life. And just like in real life too, the pause control didn't work either.

Two duff buttons!

That nut really messed this kit up.

Meanwhile the TV presenters prattled on. The Sunday edition of this show had a religious angle and they weren't really talking about Dio Shalcott, or even football as such, but rather about *Birmingham City's* American sponsor, who had become a born-again Christian after his spell in rehab.

But that wasn't the real miracle here.

Rather, it was the effort Darren #2 had put into this

feeble practical joke. Not only had he instated a bigger hard drive, one loaded with hours and hours of old TV footage, but he had gone to the trouble of splicing in a single phrase – *last week* – so seamlessly one scarcely noticed the change. The change was so subtle, so ultimately pointless that one might even call this the work of a *mad* genius.

MAD genius…?

Darren closed his eyes and brought to mind an image of Darren #2's gormless mug.

No, he had to admit that Darren #2 didn't look like it belonged to a mad genius.

'But if Darren #2 didn't do it, then who did?

Well, he'd find out soon, because whoever it was who had buggered around with his HD recorder would surely not be able to resist the exquisite pleasure of yelling, *Hello, sucker!* from the safety of the screen. And that joyful message, no doubt, would be waiting for him at the end of the recording.

Darren pressed FF once again.

The soundtrack squeaked like Minnie Mouse on speed and the screen danced and flickered.

The television was surprising him all over again. It was going a little faster forward every time he press the FF button. The succession of images were becoming more and more and more of a blur. Several days of recording now passed within the space of a few minutes. Never mind, Darren could solve the problem. He had super-fast reactions and he was able to zip through the daytime dross and drop onto the late-night rolling news again and again.

The graphics along the bottom of the screen displayed the date. It jumped to ten, twenty – thirty days from now.

The hard drive seemed to contain a limitless amount of recorded TV.

A hard drive of such huge capacity would be really, really expensive.

So that definitely let Darren #2 off the hook, didn't it? In truth, money was hard to come by for all the Darrens in this world.

Sorry Darren #2. I did you wrong.

The mystery joker was a non-Darren. Someone who was rich. Someone who was powerful.

And yet, this joke was so *dumb*. It didn't make any sense. Who on earth was powerful and dumb at the same time?

Not who, Darren, but – what?

Darren's brain seemed to have the answer.

'What, then? What has the power?'

Television, of course. It's dumb and it's powerful. Furthermore, there's a popular TV show knocking around at the moment that plays stupid tricks like this on innocent members of the public like you. Remember?

Darren did indeed remember. It was called *What's Going On?* and was hosted by the smirking Tony and Derrick. They secretly filmed the public making complete idiots of themselves with the help of expensive special effects.

Darren hated trash like that.

Which only made the abysmal truth all the more sickening.

He was starring in the latest episode!

That's right, television *itself* was playing a joke on him.

And they were filming him right now, weren't they? The HD box would have a camera.

Millions of snickering TV viewers were watching him looking as gormless as Darren #2.

You fucking bastards!

Oops. Had he said that out loud? Or was it just his

brain talking?

Yes. Just act normal, guy!

Darren obeyed. He concentrated all his efforts on appearing as serious and dignified as he had always felt himself to be.

Fuckers, you're invading my privacy, isn't it? I'm going sue the fucking pants off the fucking lot of you... Hang on, what's this he's saying now?

The news anchorman had caught his attention.

'The coroner has passed a verdict of suicide on the actor Billy Reece, who was found dead earlier this week at his Earl's Court flat.'

Darren scowled at the screen.

'What's so funny about that?'

He was asking the crew of *What's Going On?* After all, this was supposed to be a comedy show..

But even as he spoke, he knew with absolute certainty that no television producers in the civilised world would announce the suicide of a well-known actor as a joke.

Would they?

Darren's brain was adamant.

No, no, they wouldn't. Never in a million years.

But if this wasn't a joke…

Then just what is it I'm looking at?

Five

Darren was still glued the television at three o'clock in the morning.

The future was utterly compelling. True, the same sort of events occurred, just as they always had. Floods, droughts, local wars, outrageous revelations about public figures, murders, abuse of the defenceless, crime and civil strife. They all cropped up every year, like they were scripted by a poverty-stricken imagination. He discerned no pattern. Just random repetition.

Speeded up, the economy was the most wildly erratic phenomenon of all. Trade figures, inflation, industrial output, shortages, gluts. They came and went, contradicting within seconds the sage predictions of every expert. And yet the experts were constantly appearing on the news, pontificating and predicting the future with no more success than they'd had the day before.

One consistency Darren *did* begin to notice – and it came as a shock – was how the regular faces aged so quickly. Their hair greyed, their skin sagged, their eyes dimmed. No one seemed immune. Even Tony and Derrick, who yesterday had been as fresh-faced as school kids, looked tainted and seedy.

And because the machine sped forward ever faster at each touch of the FF button, so that a whole FF year could whiz past in forty minutes, the future for Tony and Derrick was looking bleak.

Darren happened to be smiling at Tony and Derrick's bleak future, when, by pure chance, he caught the tail-end of the *National-Lottery Show*.

Only then did the penny drop.

Or rather, the billions of pennies.

The idea was so glaringly obvious that he smacked his palm against his forehead and cursed himself for letting a such a fantastic opportunity slip. If he'd had his wits about him, he could have written down next week's winning lottery numbers and been rich next week.

God damn.

See – he was already five years ahead into TV-Future Land.

He stood up, paced the room and forced himself to think straight. He needed a pen and a notebook, yes. But it was three in the morning. He was tired. So first he needed to freshen up, get some coffee inside him and clear his head.

While the next moronic programme played at normal speed, he took a cool shower.

Away from the television his head did indeed clear. It occurred to him that the machine might break down at any second. In fact, he had already noticed that both the image and sound quality were beginning to deteriorate.

He jumped out the shower and dried only the essentials.

Forgetting about the coffee, he grabbed a notepad and a pen. Then he pretty well tiptoed back to the sofa, as if the slightest vibration might upset the mechanism.

Now he began the delicate operation of speeding up the recording with just a slight tap on the FF button so as to get to the next lottery show before the future went belly up.

His first taps got him nowhere close. The fourth hit a Monday and the fifth the following Sunday, just missing the Saturday draw. The sixth tap miraculously dropped him onto a Saturday afternoon.

There would be another three hours before the lottery show was screened.

Darren agonised over how to proceed. Every time he touched the FF button, the machine went at a faster rate. This much he knew. So, he may well never get this close again. On the other hand, the machine might break down during the next three hours.

This required a careful analysis of relative probabilities.

What do you say, Darren's brain?

Er... Um... Ah...

'Oh, sod it.'

He was exhausted anyway. Better to let the recording run on at normal speed until it reached the next show. If it didn't, it didn't. In the meantime he could catch some zeds.

He turned the volume down, went to the bedroom and set the alarm for six-thirty.

Seconds later he was sound asleep, dreaming about a world where everything and everybody decayed super fast. People rotted away in a couple of years. Then great blocks of iron, wielded from cranes, were used to hammer and crush the filthy corpses into the ground. And there, below the surface, in darkness and dirt, their broken bodies merged and…

Mercifully, the bleep of the alarm clock jerked him awake.

Holy fuck, that was BAD.

But he couldn't lie around dwelling on crazy dreams. He had a mega fortune to earn – now!

He staggered to the living room, feeling hot and rancid. His head was throbbing again like he was having a flashback to his hangover. The television was screening the tail end of a new game show called *Ma and Pa*, hosted by Jimmy and Algy, the upcoming talent set to replace those cranky old timers, Tony and Derrick.

But Tony and Derrick were still hanging in there. They were on next, hosting the lottery show.

No time to get an aspirin.

Despite his pounding headache, Darren turned up the volume. He needed to HEAR and SEE those numbers.

Belt and braces.

Here they come!

Darren wrote the digits down twice normal size and then he held the piece of paper right up alongside the screen to make absolutely quadruple certain he had got them right.

12, 3, 32, 9, 5, 1, 26

'Yo, I'm the man! …God – my head!'

His brain was definitely requesting that he calm down now—

Relax, guy! There'll be plenty of time to shout, Yo! We're rich. *No need to sweat it anymore. In the meantime, some aspirin,* PLEASE.

On taking a couple of aspirin tablets, Darren noticed he was developing an appetite. And yet, having pinged a ready meal in the microwave, he did nothing more than pick at it. He kept feeling too hot – and then too cold. His throat was dry and painful. Clearly, a dose of flu was on the way. What he should do was go to bed and sleep.

Yes, some restorative slumber was the order of the night.

However…

While he wasn't looking, an even greater imperative crept up and took hold of him. And it came as little bit of a surprise too.

You see, having won the lottery once, Darren found that he was very much minded to win it again. And even after that, who knew whether he would be satisfied or not?

Probably not.

In fact, he had a notion that he wanted to keep wining the lottery till either him or the television flaked out.

I must be the greediest person ever in history.

And noting with interest this startling new revelation about himself, he settled down in the sofa and tapped the FF button.

The weather report.

A fresh-faced guy in a suit was saying with an extra-smooth delivery, 'We shall find plenty of fog rolling in from the East this evening…'

Darren hooted in derision. This dude couldn't predict the weather for the day after tomorrow and here he is, predicting the weather five years from now!

No, guy, Darren's brain patiently explained. *You're tired and not thinking straight. He's predicting what will happen next day in* his *time. Us – we got to wait five years to see whether or not he's right about the fog rolling in from the East—*

Five years!

Only now did the stupendous quantity of time that he must wait to become rich finally hit him.

Christ! Like a proper eternity, innit?

He slouched back and groaned, lamenting once again that he'd been so very slow on the uptake. His mega riches were currently unavailable.

But Darren wasn't stupid. He quelled his impatience with happy thoughts about what he would do when his mega riches were available.

The possibilities would be vast.

Like…

Like…?

Well, for a start, he could buy Jeff out. And Jeff #2 for that matter. Then he'd sack Darren #2. Yeah, that would be sweet.

Seconds later he was laughing at himself.

What was he thinking about? He'd be a multimillionaire! Why would he waste his time buying up piffling little electrical stores just to get even with some sap who still had to work for a living? Nah – that wasn't happening, because he was going to be too insanely busy doing the really exciting stuff.

Stuff like…?

Well wasn't there a film script under his bed, which he'd been playing around with for the past few years?

Yup, there was.

Well there you are then. He could produce that, couldn't he?

Direct it too, if he so chose.

Except, every now and again, over the past few years, his brain had sort of whispered to him, *You know that film script under your bed? Honest, guy, it sucks.*

Never mind! If he was super rich, he could set up a film company and produce and direct other people's film scripts. Scripts that didn't suck.

How about that?

Yeah, that'd be cool, I suppose…

Okay, he could set up a music recording company instead.

Except…all those rappers were just a bunch of hopeless wankers, weren't they?.

Well, do you want to know what I'd do…?

Darren paused to listen to his brain and, as usual, he had to agree it had the best idea.

What he should so, was grow his very own multinational corporation, it said. Something like Branson had with *Virgin.*

Yeah! I could rival Virgin. *Drive it into the ground. Kick* Apple*'s butt. Crush* Sony! *Those guys, Branson, Trump – I could dwarf those suckers.*

All at once he couldn't sit still.

He went out onto his tiny balcony.

It was getting light.

Already?

The first breath of dawn passed over his hot, glowing skin. He eagerly filled his lungs. Sunday morning now. The city was quieter than ever. His headache had subsided, but he felt shivery and his bones ached. Retreating from the cool air, he decided to treat himself to a medicinal chicken *Cup-a-Soup.* A champion in the war on colds.

Meanwhile, his mind kept racing away above the speed limit, even while he stirred his *Cup-a-Soup.*

In the future he would have already won the lottery,

wouldn't he? So it wouldn't be long before his mega corporation started hitting the news. He could actually preview himself being really, really rich and successful.

Now *that* seemed to him to be a programme that was actually worth watching.

Nursing his cup of soup, he settled back on the sofa and put his forefinger to the FF button.

Six

Not only was the sound deteriorating, the colours on the screen were dimming too, becoming less vivid. Darren didn't care. News of his mega corporation wouldn't require a sharp picture. He also noticed that although the game shows, cookery programmes and undemanding documentaries were the same as ever in the future, somehow the hosts were less shrill and the contestants more restrained than in our day. Sombre even. Well, he didn't care about that either. When they announced that he had made his first billion, or zillion even, he'd be happy to provide all the shouting and yelling himself.

By the way, he had decided to call his corporation *eDynasty*.

He was also rather hoping to bag another lottery win. However, the speed of replay was so fast by now that no degree of finger dexterity could deliberately land him onto a lottery show. He had to rely on chance alone. And chance, just like the lottery itself, was not kind.

Less pleasing still, the appearance and rise of *eDynasty* was not as swift as he might have hoped. Time was marching on faster than ever. Still, if no one was talking about *eDynasty*, no one was talking about *Virgin*, or *Sony*, or *Apple*, either. Nor Branson or Trump.

What had happened to them?

Well everything comes and goes. Change happens.

In fact, as Darren looked into the future, he had begun to notice that change had a surprisingly dynamic and malevolent character. How very quickly the familiar faces aged and dropped out of sight! And those that replaced them rapidly aged in their turn. Soon, they too would be replaced.

...in darkness and dirt, their broken bodies merged and...

'Ugh! That nasty dream.'

It must have been the hangover. Or the effect of watching all this television...

That's right – he had been watching it for almost ten solid hours by now. No wonder he was sick of the future. It was scarcely different from the past. The faces were new, sure, but the personalities were the same. And so were the fixations of the commentators.

The poor are getting poorer and that isn't right,
and
I blame the politicians for everything,
and
Too many people are dying too early,
and
Too many people are living too long.

Meanwhile, a bomb blast was a bomb blast was a bomb blast...

After all this, who could blame Darren for feeling the need of a little diversion?

Perhaps a bite to eat and a stroll outside...?

Just then, TV landed on a football match and he was glued to the screen.

What a relief to watch something he actually enjoyed!

True, the match was close to the end of the first half and he didn't support either teams, *Albion* and *Gillingham*, nor did he even recognise any of the players.

But still, the standard of the game was high and, having signed up as a temporary *Albion* supporter because their players displayed admirable passing skills, he was disgusted by a *Gillingham* player getting away with a blatant foul. Worse still, the player who committed the foul went on to score, putting *Gillingham* ahead just as half-time was called.

He was all agog to hear what the pundits would say about this turn of events.

As usual there was a panel of three, including the anchorman.

The first to speak – an old, bloated, ill-looking guy – began by complaining that surely the referee needed his head examined and *Albion* might even be robbed of a well-deserved victory, et cetera, et cetera.

And this is what Darren thought—

Yeah, yeah, yeah, you're dead right, old man. But Lord almighty, what you on TV for? You look like you're fucking well ready to die.

And then Darren stopped thinking.

He leaned forward, staring with disbelief.

He actually clutched himself in horror.

The fat old guy was – Dio Shalcott!

The once lush black hair was quite white, the honey-coloured skin had turned a kind of buff yellow and was scored deep with black lines. Dio's face had been morphed into something like an oversized and shapeless leather bag. Worst of all were his eyes. They were all cloudy and seemed to have sunk into his skull. And they had this haunted look about them, like they knew they were going to keep sinking and sinking till they vanished into never-ending darkness.

Darren was having a really bad feeling about seeing Dio like this. But why? True, he was an ace player. But he wasn't central to the team. And sure, it was sad to see a strapping A1-fit lad reduced to a badly deteriorated husk. Of course it was. Still, as La Rochefoucauld said once (and Darren's brain agreed):

We are all strong enough to endure other people's misfortunes.

How very, very true!

So, how come then he wasn't shrugging off Dio's misfortune like La Rochefoucauld undoubtedly would have? After all, he himself wasn't all crumpled, buggered up and dilapidated like Dio, was he?

'No, not yet, young man. You've still plenty of years to go—'

Oh fucking hell!

Darren had just remembered something truly terrifying.

He was actually two years *older* than Dio Shalcott!

Those icy chills running up and down his spine…there was a reason for them.

He was seeing the future, all right.

His future.

Oh dear God, look at his eyes!

Their haunted look, their knowledge of imminent personal annihilation, stayed with Darren, even as the match resumed.

His heart was numb as he watched the players race back and forth. Once upon a time, like a whole full minute ago, the notion that he could have run out on the pitch himself and sort of kept up with them (with a bit of training) wasn't altogether ludicrous.

But—

The next time I see this match, I'll be too old to walk, let alone run around like these guys. I'll look just as bad as Dio.

But was that the end of the horror?

You wish!

That icy chill moved from his spine and wrapped itself around his heart…

…*no!*…

…because when this match came to be played…

…*no, no, please, not that*…

…he might not even still be alive to watch it.

Seven

Darren was out on the balcony, warming himself in the sunshine.

The city looked so beautiful. In the distance, the concrete and glass towers were luminescent against a dark blue sky. Down below, amongst the old bridges, wharfs and tow paths of the ancient canals, couples strolled hand in hand and the occasional jogger flitted by. A holiday barge, painted all over with pictures of flowers, was moored by a lock.

Out there, life bloomed contentedly, as if it would last forever. Meanwhile, in the room behind him, the television squawked, blared and yapped – the idiot messenger of ultimate oblivion.

The sunshine gently kissing his skin did not reach the coldness inside him.

What was the point of anything?

The dream of owning a mega corporation…? He felt his cheeks tingle with shame at the very recollection of *eDynasty*. The sound of the stupid moniker was full of hollow mockery. Why hadn't anyone in the history of the world ever seen the truth – that money was meaningless without youth and health? He didn't want to be rich. What he wanted was everything to stay the same. Just that. Nothing else. Simple. To be twenty-two forever and working for Jeff in *Electric Entertainments* for all eternity.

That would be true happiness.

Incredible. He'd never suspected for one moment till today that he had been living in paradise.

But alas, no longer.

The intimation of his own mortality had ruined everything.

From now on, there would never be an unsullied moment of joy.

All at once, Darren was fed up to the back teeth of being alone. It was eight o'clock on a sunny Sunday morning. He had to get away from the television and somehow cancel out its soul-destroying message.

He hurried indoors, dressed quickly and snatched up the remote control so as to OFF the TV.

He hesitated for just one second.

A woman's husky, sexy tones were issuing from the TV speaker.

And then it was too late.

You see, she was saying, 'Fine lines? Wrinkles? What next? Only perfection! – with *Oreale's Only Perfection*. Our antiaging, multieugenic skin-rejuvenation-creme system will give you the skin you *honestly* deserve...'

Darren's brain saw the potential straight away.

Of course! They'll cure old age eventually, won't they?

The rejuvenating effect of this realisation was dramatic. He felt all of twenty-two again. And the magic ingredient was...hope.

Offered by *Oreale*'s multieugenic creme system.

Of course, the multieugenic creme system hadn't been able to hold back time for poor old Dio Shalcott. True. However, unlike Dio, and everybody else in the universe, what Darren had in his possession was the technology to see into the future. *Far* into the future, to a time when *Oreale* weren't bullshitting anymore and had truly developed a creme for immortality.

How would that help him, living so far back in the past?

Well, once the fuss had died down, the ingredients would become common knowledge, wouldn't they? So, if he searched long and hard enough, these ingredients would appear in some documentary and then he could make the stuff for himself.

Now.

When he needed it.

And then…

He could be twenty-two for ever!

Brimming with breathless eagerness, Darren prepared to dig himself in for as long as it took to glean the secret of immortality.

He went to the kitchen to brew coffee.

While he waited for the kettle to boil, it occurred to him that if he had made himself immortal, the last thing he'd ever want to do was drawn attention to himself by setting up a mega corporation. People would notice that he never aged. They'd get jealous. They'd hunt him down.

So *that's* why *eDynasty* had never appeared in the news!

His spirits soared higher still.

In fact, he even underwent a moment of philosophical enlightenment in which he understood that the root of all human sadness is the awareness of mortality.

Uh, maybe I oughtta write that down.

Stop! He didn't have time to write books on the human condition. He was a mission to change it – for himself.

He got prepared. With a large writing pad and three

pens ready, Darren planted himself on the sofa, picked up the remote control and pressed FF.

Eight

The future had undergone a sinister change.

Something had happened.

Of course, Dio Shalcott, Tony and Derrick – even their fresh-faced young rivals, Jimmy and Algy – had all turned to dust long ago. Death ruled supreme. Yes, Darren knew that already. Still, at least the TV programmes had remained recognisable, even if the faces hadn't. The same, good old formats persisted. As frothy as ever. Thank heavens a gardening programme was still a gardening programme and a quiz show a quiz show.

However, the speed of fast forward had not stopped increasing and now the merest touch of the FF button would zoom him along by decades.

So it was that Darren missed the exact point that marked the sinister *mental shift* behind what appeared on the screen. He was as bored as ever one minute and then the next, after an idle stab at the FF button, he found himself staring at… Well, actually it *did* appear to be the usual cookery show after all, owing to the fact they had filmed it in a steel-lined kitchen. But then, nothing was happening. That wasn't normal television in Darren's book. Something always had to be happening. On this show, however, nothing happened except two women, dressed in what looked like hospital gowns, with their hair set in peculiar, asymmetrical styles, held between them an enormous, twitching eel-like creature for ten whole minutes and didn't move a muscle or make a sound. They just stood there. Their expressions were utterly vacant. It was eerie. The longer he waited, the more disconcerted he got, so that he was given an unpleasant start when a chef waddled into view. He was fat, moustachioed man, dressed in blue checks and whites and waving a wickedly long steel knife. The women came alive, gabbled some words too quickly for Darren to understand, then fell silent and gazed at the chef fixedly as he began to sing. The tune was like nothing Darren had ever heard and it made the hairs on the back of his neck stand up.

And the words?
Big good for yumyum,
Head bigbig goodgood,
Yo!
But leave eyeballs to Aunty Spider.
Yo!
Gloguthum!
The English language had been changing.

Darren watched, waiting for the next development. But the chef continued to sing his nonsense and the women stared and grinned in what could have been sheer, mindless terror. They remained as motionless as possible, as if their lives depended on it. After twenty minutes, Darren couldn't bear to see or hear any more.

He jabbed FF again – and again.

As he plunged ever deeper into the future, activity of any sort on the screen became ever more protracted and cheerless. In home-improvement programmes, for instance, the hosts did not *use* their tools, they *talked* to them, in elegiac tones and incomprehensible language, accompanied by music from a Theremin and trombone. The quiz masters didn't ask questions, they declaimed like demagogues to glum-faced audiences wearing party hats. In sports the games would stop randomly – a huddle of players would form, reporters would dash onto the pitch and a solemn debate lasting ten, twenty, thirty minutes would ensue.

When it came to the news, the items exclusively covered interminable meetings of the political elite that took place in airport lounges, deserted apart from the occasional cleaner.

Abruptly, some two centuries into the future, the game shows, the gardening and cookery features, the sport programmes and even the news – everything that made any sense at all – utterly vanished from the screen.

Now there was only one programme left on TV.

The outdoors.

Hour after hour, day after day, week after week…year after year – nothing but long static shots of various streets.

The locations would change, but not according to any method that he could see. A view from a roof might occupy the screen for months. The close up of a drain might last an afternoon. Or the other way round. The camera was positioned at random. Once, for a whole summer, it faced a brick wall from six inches away.

Views of entire streets would crop up now and then. The majority were empty. But those in the city centre would feature at least a scattering of pedestrians. Very occasionally, the camera would capture busy crowds.

The faces of the people never showed any emotion as they went about their business. The manner in which they moved hinted at a certain restlessness. A persistent anxiety to get somewhere else. The craze of previous decades for interminable discussion and soliloquy had died out. No one paused to exchange views, express concern or regret.

In fact, no one spoke at all.

The cameras ran continuously. They filmed as many scenes by night as by day. If ever the sky was in shot by night, it was revealed to be a horrible hectic red and bright enough to fully illuminate the rooftops and tower blocks. He could often see large, ominous looking birds flapped silently between the chimneys. These animals – or any other living creatures apart from people – were never to be seen by day.

One night, the sky was ablaze with great swirls of ghostly light, which Darren recognised as the Aurora Borealis.

The buildings didn't change. Nor did the design of the cars. But then, cars too abruptly disappeared. And so did bicycles and any other sort of vehicular travel. Everyone walked.

Complete silence had descended upon the world.

It took time, but Darren eventually realised that he no longer saw children. The number of people seemed to decline a little, though not dramatically. In fact, the churning crowds in the cities actually grew denser.

The shops, when he caught a view of them, all bore wholly unfamiliar names by now. They sold clothes and shoes. Nothing else. The fashions never changed.

Altogether, the scenes on TV became so monotonous and so very little happened in them that Darren fell into fast forwarding the recording with regular, almost automatic depressions of his thumb.

Not surprisingly, when something finally did happen, he only caught a bare glimpse of it. His thumb had pressed the FF button again before he could stop it.

What he had seen, or thought he had seen, was a curious greyish-white figure. It had moved so much quicker than everyone else, flickering amongst the crowd as it nimbly wove between the much larger and slower pedestrians.

Darren could not say why, but the sight of the thing and the way it moved instantly made his flesh creep.

The next scene, to which he'd fast-forwarded too quickly, was a dribbling overflow pipe.

He was staring at it now. Watching water dribble away under a dry, grey sky.

Revolted, he forced himself up onto his aching legs and stood indecisively in front of the television.

Must the futile search for immortality go on?

The door to the balcony, which he had left open, revealed a sunlit city that was more alive on a single Sunday afternoon than the whole of the future would ever be.

Irked and bored, discomforted by the first stage of flu, Darren wondered at his earlier enthusiasm for immortality. For a start, it was evident there wouldn't be a documentary about the secret of life. Why would they bother making it? In the future, the audience would be content to watch a dribbling overflow pipe. Even if he did cheat death, that would be the only thing he would have to look forward to.

No, he hadn't lost out so badly. He still had his winning lottery numbers. In five years he could collect his millions and live while life was still sweet to the taste. He shouldn't waste his youth on mirages. He should enjoy himself. Yes, that's what he should do.

Actually, that is what he *did* do.

He knew this for certain now, because his corporation eDynasty had never materialised and obviously this was because he hadn't wasted precious time slaving for a meaningless legacy.

He had wised up.

Good for you, Darren.

Glad to have pleased his brain, he went to the bathroom and took some *Paracetamol* to knock his fever back and washed the taste way with a swig of orange juice. There – he felt better already.

He took his coat from the cupboard.

On his way to the door, he picked up the remote to turn the television off.

For good.

On the screen, the overflow pipe was still dribbling. What would the audience be thinking as they watched this programme? He pictured countless faces, staring inanely for centuries to come.

But really, could *that* be the future?

Nothing else…?

What about the wonders of the next age? The space ships? The teletransporters? The artificial life forms? The self-replicating machines?

Where were they?

The inheritors of the Earth had achieved nothing. Nothing at all.

The waste of it!

Darren shouted at the barren screen, 'You boring bastards. You don't deserve life.'

He pressed his thumb down on the FF button and kept it there. He sent the hard disk spinning ever faster.

It began to whine in mounting agony. Darren smiled to himself. He wanted to run this machine into the ground, together with its dismal inhabitants. He wanted to see the future dead. And then, he would do his best to forget that he had ever glimpsed it. The future at most would be a fading memory.

The whine of the spinning disk got louder. It sounded like a dive-bombing plane, plummeting to destruction. The stink of melting plastic and ozone rose to his nostrils. Part of the casing collapsed and smouldered.

And *still* the bitch wouldn't quit.

Ten minutes passed.

The noise was drilling Darren's brain. Decades, centuries tumbled away, as insubstantial as litter in the wind. Generations perished faster than houseflies. The disk was screeching, tearing into the fabric of eternity. The unearthly din made Darren's heart pound. It wasn't going to stop till it had driven him mad.

He jerked his thumb off the FF button and the screen filled with a…street scene.

'You've got to be joking!'

He flopped onto the sofa to stare at the TV in utter disgust.

By the hue of the light, he reckoned they were broadcasting on a late afternoon. The camera was pointed across an empty road towards a shop. Occasional pedestrians, no different from those that had lived hundreds of years before, walked past. Their faces were so slack there could no longer be a connection to the brain behind.

Darren couldn't help laughing.

He addressed the television in the most courteous of tones.

'See what you gone and done now, old chap? You've outstayed your welcome, that's what. So, it looks very much like I will have to kick the shit out of you.'

He rose to his feet and took a preparatory step towards the screen and…froze.

'Jeeze!'

That greyish-white figure he had glimpsed earlier had just stepped out of the shop.

It moved so fast that its legs flickered in a blur, like those of a cockroach. It was halfway across the road in a blink of an eye, where it stopped and became absolutely still. Darren couldn't see that it even breathed. A second later, it turned and retreated back into the shop with the speed and precision of an insect. This happened over and over again. Twenty times or more.

Darren shuddered and felt his skin crawl. Surely he

was looking at some kind of humanoid bug.

Look out.

The thing had left the shop but didn't even pause – it was coming straight at him. Darren flinched. The figure passed within inches of the camera and was gone. It happened so quickly Darren caught only a glimpse of the creature close up. He saw it didn't wear clothes and that its body was cruder than that of a shop dummy. Its face was drawn on. A wobbly line for a mouth and two blobs for eyes. Over the eyes were jagged dashes to represent the brows. In other words, a child's drawing of a face – except Darren was left with a distinct impression of mocking sarcasm in the features. The squiggly lines artlessly suggested a knowing smirk. It wasn't child's drawing.

Staring at the screen, Darren waited for the thing to reappear. The repugnance he had felt at seeing it turned into an outright horror at the thought of ever meeting it in the flesh. He thanked his lucky stars that he never would. Whatever the thing was, he sensed it wasn't a wonder of the age to come. It wasn't a robot, or anything human beings had manufactured. Rather, it possessed *otherness* – a soulless malignancy that put him in mind of a... disease.

He needed to get out, escape into the sunshine and shake this morbidity off.

But eventually he would have to come back, wouldn't he?

And the television would be waiting, infected with the grey bug. He was already feverish with the flu and dazed by lack of sleep. The grey bug might finish him off.

'Well then, before I go, I gotta purify the television, ain't I?'

That's right, sterilise the future.

And so he started fast-forwarding again. But this time

he drove it at a steady pace, so that the hard drive didn't whine too loudly. He had calmed down. He was determined to sit this programme out. When the last camera failed, he could breathe easy again, happy in the knowledge that this horrible, horrible world had come to an end.

Out of curiosity, he let up every now and then to take a glance at what was happening down on the streets.

Nothing much, of course.

That said, another change seemed to be taking place. The number of people were visibly thinning out.

And the grey-white figure was no longer alone.

Two appeared in one shot. Later four. Then eight... sixteen...soon too many to count.

They were identical to each other. The sameness suggested that they sprang from a single squirming nest – that they were an infestation. Even the way they walked creeped Darren out. Only their thin legs moved, no other parts of their body. And they were so nimble. About two thirds of an average person's height and much faster, they sped through the crowd effortlessly. The more he saw of them, the greater his revulsion. It was the instinctive abhorrence roused by vermin. He sensed they had no weight at all. Somehow that unsettled him most of all. And he just knew that he would find their touch, and even their proximity, unbearable. Again, like with insects. And yet, the remaining humans did not seem to find their presence the least bit odd or repulsive.

Darren did not linger over these uncanny scenes. He kept his goal in sight.

He wanted to see the screen go blank.

And when he did, he could happily drop this heap of junk into the trash can.

He pressed FF.

Half an hour went by. An hour.

Still the machine whirred on.

Darren was amazed at how much of the present the future was taking up.

Another hour passed and he had started to give up hope when, all at once, the machine let out a rough, grating noise.

At long last! The death rattle!

The noise became more laboured , hitched, grew faint. Stopped.

This was it – the end.

FF no longer worked.

The frenetic dance of images had been replaced a steady picture. A motionless last frame. And this showed…

Another street scene.

'God damn!'

Darren almost threw the remote through the screen.

But really, what was there to get annoyed about anymore?

Nothing moved. The white spooks and the last of the humans – they were all gone. Someone had left the camera running, that's all.

Darren contemplated the dead world.

Three, five, maybe ten thousand years had laid a leaden patina on the street. Innumerable showers had washed away all the colours. Everything was grey from the sky down.

'That's that, then.'

Darren shook his head at his own folly. He had frittered away hours and hours of his life to reach this grotesque anticlimax.

Hold on.

Darren's brain had spotted something before Darren had.

'Eh? Is that…? No, it can't be.' He leaned forward.

'Oh God. No!'

He had just recognised the building across the way.

It was his own apartment block.

Centuries of erosion had stripped it down to the underlying poured concrete. The place where he (used) to live looked like the most decayed and ancient object he had ever seen.

The minutes passed. Only his heartbeat broke the silence. A mounting dread chilled the air.

Something was about to happen.

But nothing can happen now. This is the end…

A great balloon of white bobbed up and peer at him with dead eyes.

Or rather, mere black blobs.

He cried out like he'd taken an electric shock.

The awful dead face in the screen seemed to scrutinise him and then, a moment later, the camera panned back revealed the face belonged to one of those maggot-white creatures that had infected the world thousands of years ago, when humans still existed. It motioned with its fingerless hand, using that quick, flicking action with which they always moved.

It was beckoning him on.

And as it turned and walked away, the camera duly followed.

Darren found the last-ever TV show to be riveting stuff. As a viewer, he simply could not tear himself away. He seemed to be floating behind the humanoid insect. They crossed the street together and passed through the dark, gaping doors of his apartment block. The tiled concourse was veiled in dust. The metal doors of the lifts were rusted away into jagged blades. Today's host took the audience by way of the stairwell. The concrete treads crumbled under weightless footfalls. The silent millenniums had rotted even concrete.

The two-legged cockroach walked more slowly, as if to build the tension.

Surely this thing was not capable of such deliberate action. No more than any other insect.

And yet, as they reached Darren's floor, the filthy bug's head bobbed vilely on its narrow shoulders, just like it was snickering at the wicked joke they were about to play.

Now they were following the corridor outside. They stopped outside his front door.

Once again, the bug turned to the camera. The hint of a smirk around its false mouth was more pronounced than ever.

The thing knocked just once on the door and it collapsed into a heap of powder.

They entered.

Darren's apartment was a dull, mouldering chamber in the most banal of hells. The shattered windows were open to the grey, hot, lifeless skies. The world was utterly silent. And yet, as if a big band somewhere was playing a triumphant fanfare, the host stood to one side and, with a courtly flourish, presented the winner of today's show.

Crumpled on the sofa was a shrivelled mummy. The empty eye sockets stared at the blank TV screen and one bony hand still clutched the remote control.

Once again, Darren pressed the FF button.

www.ingramcontent.com/pod-product-compliance
Lightning Source LLC
Chambersburg PA
CBHW030541190726
48283CB00006B/1968